'**What has Count Pentransky to do with anything?**'

Cassie's unease grew. The last place she had expected to hear word of the Count was here, in Anton Sommer's office.

'Let me enlighten you, my dear Fräulein Haydon.' The sarcasm in the doctor's voice was cutting. 'When a command from Count Pentransky himself arrives on my desk, instructing me to take you into my employment, then I have to do as I am told. That is the *only* reason why you are here!'

Dear Reader

We have Pauline Bentley back with a vengeance! REBEL HARVEST looks at the ramifications of the 1715 Jacobite uprising, which lead to paranoia in all sections of the kingdom. Just how can the heroine rescue her young brother from his folly without being noticed by the hero? Elizabeth Lowther takes us to Austria in 1904, where the heroine's efforts to be professional in her job are thwarted by the villain—will the hero believe her reputation has been wrongly maligned? BREATH OF SCANDAL has the answer. . .

The Editor

Elizabeth Lowther taught for a while, but began to write when suffering a bout of jaundice. She has since published a variety of things, but historical novels are her favourites. Sensibly she married a man who could correct her spelling, and now lives in Devon with him, and that obligatory writer's companion, a black cat.

Recent titles by the same author:

LOVE'S PAROLE
THE RANSOMED BRIDE

BREATH OF SCANDAL

Elizabeth Lowther

*First published in Great Britain 1992
by Mills & Boon Limited*

© Elizabeth Lowther 1992

*Australian copyright 1992
Philippine copyright 1993
This edition 1993*

ISBN 0 263 77990 4

*Masquerade is a trademark published by
Mills & Boon Limited, Eton House,
18–24 Paradise Road, Richmond, Surrey, TW9 1SR.*

*Set in 10 on 10½ pt Linotron Times
04-9301-85296*

*Typeset in Great Britain by Centracet, Cambridge
Made and printed in Great Britain*

CHAPTER ONE

1904

As THE train began to slow down, the last vestige of
Cassie's travel weariness disappeared. With a growing
excitement she pressed her face against the window.
All the way from Salzburg she had watched the sun
setting on mountains capped with snow. Beyond the
lights of the approaching town she was glad she could
still see those mountains. Now they were pale spectres
against the night sky, the embodiment of everything
she had imagined. She was here in Austria at last!

The train puffed into the station and a voice called,
'Bad Adler! Bad Adler! Passengers for Bad Adler alight
here!'

Cassie did not need a second bidding. Grasping her
portmanteau, she leapt down on to the low platform,
to be caught up briefly in a surge of bodies as her fellow
travellers made for the exit. Nimbly side-stepping to
avoid being swept along, she waited in the shelter of a
pillar until most people had departed and the station
had begun to clear. Then, in the flickering light of the
oil lamps, she looked round for Dr Sommer.

'My dear Miss Haydon, I will meet you personally,'
he had written. 'I could do no less for a lady who will
travel so far and has been so highly recommended by
my good friend, Dr Mossman.'

Cassie suspected that this was a signal honour. She
was sure that the director of a flourishing spa like Bad
Adler did not normally greet humble employees when
they arrived. She wondered what Dr Sommer looked
like. He would be dignified, as befitted a man in his
responsible position, she decided, and was probably in
his sixties like their mutual friend, Dr Mossman.

There was a definite lack of dignified elderly gentlemen waiting at the station. In fact, only one man was waiting there at all and, though he was certainly distinguished-looking, not to say almost handsome, he appeared to be in his early thirties, far too young for Dr Sommer. Incongruously he was in full evening dress, and this immediately put Cassie on her guard.

Although she looked considerably less than her twenty-two years, she was far from being an innocent. She knew it was not unknown for bored 'gentlemen' to frequent railway stations to see what the train had brought. She had some experience of such men, on the look-out for gullible female companionship. More than once she had had to rebuff their unwelcome attentions, sometimes forcibly with a stout hat-pin. To her chagrin she seemed to attract such types; it was the price she had to pay for being independent.

The man was now gazing speculatively in her direction, as if to confirm her suspicions. Immediately Cassie put her hand up to her head, to ensure that her hat-pin was in place, then retired behind the pillar.

If he thinks I'm fair game, he is sadly mistaken, she told herself.

'Your luggage, *fräulein*.' A porter came along, trundling her box on a barrow. 'Would you like me to get you a cab?'

'No, thank you, I'm being met,' Cassie replied in German.

Noting her reflection in the waiting-room window, she made to adjust her hat, ramming home the ornamental pin. She had had such hopes of that hat. It was plain and unadorned, and, combined with her new, severely tailored blue two-piece and a high-necked blouse, she had been convinced it would make her look capable and efficient. One glance in the murky glass was enough to tell her she had failed abysmally. Its wide brim and simple lines merely made her look like a schoolgirl playing truant, as usual. She suspected that this waif-like air accounted for her unwanted

appeal to the opposite sex. Now, to make matters
worse, pale strands of her hair, which was never amenable to even the most rigorous of pinning, were beginning to work loose. When he eventually arrived Dr
Sommer was going to get a totally wrong impression of
her.

There was considerable activity at the end of the
platform. It seemed as if all the station employees,
from the station-master down, were congregated there.
The reason was easy to deduce. The last carriage was a
private one, its gleaming green paintwork quite distinctive from the neat red and cream livery of the railway
company. It was embellished with a huge, ornate coat
of arms. Cassie wondered vaguely who the aristocratic
passenger who travelled in such style might be, but then
her attention strayed. She was far too concerned with
looking out for Dr Sommer.

The good doctor was late. Had he forgotten about
her? Cassie began to wonder what she would do if he
did not arrive at all. She had no idea where she was to
lodge.

As she looked about, her gaze alighted on the man
in evening dress, who still loitered by the exit. No,
'loiter' was an inappropriate word to describe the erect
way he paced up and down, occasionally slapping his
white evening gloves against his thigh. He was the
picture of impatience. As his eyes met Cassie's he
paused in his restless pacing, then he took a step
towards her. This was enough for Cassie. The last thing
she wanted was for Dr Sommer to arrive and find her
fending off an over-attentive roué. She ducked round
the corner to make her escape and immediately can-
noned into an oncoming body. The body was plump,
and bore with it an over-bearing scent that reminded
Cassie forcibly of funeral lilies, but the arms that
pinioned her were like iron.

'Hello, what have I caught?' asked a slurred voice.

For a moment Cassie was pressed too tightly against
the protruding stomach to see much of her captor. She

was conscious of metal uniform buttons pressing into her flesh, and of a reek of alcohol which fought unpleasantly with the funeral lilies cologne. The grip that held her lessened a little, as a hand took sharp hold of her chin and tilted her head back.

'Nice! Very nice indeed! I've caught myself a very tasty little bird.' The words were slightly incoherent, but the lechery behind them was all too evident.

Cassie glared up at the man. But for a few defects, he might have been considered good-looking in an insipid, blond sort of way. Apart from the fact that he was overweight, his features were marred by the indecisive mouth lurking beneath his fair moustache, a chin that was threatening to multiply, and pale blue eyes that held one of the most licentious gleams Cassie had ever seen. The realisation that he was drunk and breathing brandy fumes all over her did nothing to increase his allure.

'Let me go!' she demanded, none too clearly, for his fingers were digging into her jaw.

He seemed to have understood her, for he replied, 'Let you go? But I've only just caught you.'

Nevertheless, he did remove his grip on her face.

'Let me go, I say!' Cassie protested again. She tried to struggle and kick at him with her feet.

His response was to lift her off the ground and tighten the hold on her waist so severely that she winced with pain, fearing for her ribs. He was no more than medium height, yet he towered above her, an advantage that he was clearly willing to exploit to the full.

Cassie answered by struggling even harder, to no avail. Oh, how she wished she could get at her hat-pin! But her arms were still crushed impotently against her body. It seemed incredible that no one had seen her predicament.

'Will no one help me?' she cried aloud. 'I thought Austria was a civilised country, not a place where respectable females were accosted in public!'

If anyone heard her cry for help they did not respond.

Certainly none of the group of men, some of whom
were in military uniform like her captor, who lounged
beside the private carriage. They merely looked on with
bored indifference. One of the porters, perhaps? But
they scurried by, trundling barrows piled high with
expensive luggage. From the way they all deliberately
kept their eyes averted, she guessed she would get no
help from them. True, the station-master did come
hurrying up, an expression of concern on his face, but
when he was still some distance away one of the
military-looking men stepped forward in a threatening
manner, and intercepted him. In desperation she
looked around for the man in evening dress, but he had
disappeared. There was no one left to come to her aid.

In the midst of her fury and growing nervousness,
two facts were becoming apparent to Cassie. Firstly, if
she were ever to escape it was going to be by her own
efforts. Secondly, the more she continued struggling
the more excited her captor became. Already his pale
blue eyes were gleaming with an expression she recognised as lust, and she feared the increased rate of his
breathing had nothing to do with his attempts to hold
her prisoner.

If there was one creature Cassie despised it was a
woman who used her wiles to get what she wanted. In
her opinion intelligence and ability were the only
weapons any self-respecting female should employ.
However, common sense told her that on this occasion
intelligence and ability were not going to be much use
so, in the absence of her trusty hat-pin, her woman's
wiles it would have to be! At once she ceased to
struggle, hanging limp and supine as a rag doll in her
captor's grasp.

'Sir, you are frightening me. If you are a gentleman,
please let me go,' she said in a little voice that held the
suspicion of a sob. Then she looked up, her huge eyes,
as blue as harebells, dominating her features. For good
measure she caught her lower lip with small white
teeth, as if to prevent it from trembling. The effect, as

she knew very well, was of a woebegone waif, a
creature of pathos to touch any man's heart. At any
rate, it worked on her captor enough for him to set her
on the ground again and to slacken his hold slightly.

'You mustn't be frightened! I was only playing,' he
said, in a winsome little-boy voice that went ill with the
lecherous glint that still shone in his eyes.

'Well, you're too rough.' In other circumstances
Cassie would have been disgusted at the coyness of her
own tone, but when needs must. . .

'Did silly old Bobo frighten his little bird, then? His
little English bird, to judge from the accent. He didn't
mean to. Bobo likes pretty little English birds.'

Cassie decided that this conversation was getting
rather sickening. If only she could think of some other
means of escape.

'A gentleman would say he was sorry, then put me in
a fiaker and let me drive away,' she said persuasively.
If Dr Sommer came now it was just too bad. She could
deal with him later. At the moment her present predicament was all she could handle.

'Of course I am a gentleman!' Bobo sounded quite
haughty. 'More than that, some of the noblest blood in
the whole Austrian Empire flows through my veins. I
can claim sixteen quarterings to my coat of arms, which
entitles me to serve our beloved Emperor Franz Josef
himself. That is why I wear the uniform of an officer in
the Imperial Hussars. I am no less a person than Count
Ludwig Pentransky!'

The statement would have been more impressive if it
had not been interrupted by a decidedly inebriated
hiccup.

Cassie did not dare abandon her charade now.

'You are a count?' she breathed, her eyes opening
even wider. 'A real live count?'

'Indeed I am.' He sounded pleased at her incredulity.
'And to make up for frightening you and to show what
a true gentleman I am, I am going to do more than

send you off in some hired cab. No, I shall transport you in my own carriage.'

'I don't want to be any bother. A fiaker would do,' said Cassie hastily.

'It's no bother. See, my servant has already put your luggage in with mine.'

True enough, her modest box was being pushed out of the station on a barrow piled high with trunks that were emblazoned with the same crest as the private railway carriage.

'Won't it cause all sorts of fuss, getting my box from among your fine luggage?' she asked.

'No fuss at all. My servants will unload them together when we get there.'

'When we get there?' Her voice became a strangled gasp.

'Yes, I've decided you are coming with me. You can keep me company at my hunting-lodge in the mountains.'

If ever Cassie's brain needed to work at top speed it was now! Somehow she had to get away from this man, yet instinct told her that to protest would be fatal. She would have to try some other ploy.

'How exciting! A real count with a real hunting-lodge! I can't believe this is happening. It would be such fun if only. . .' And here she delicately smothered a huge yawn with a gloved hand. 'If only I wasn't so tired. I've been travelling for simply ages, and I'm so afraid I'd be all sleepy and boring, which would be frightfully rude, after you've been kind enough to invite me to be your guest. If only I could stay somewhere here in town for tonight and have a good rest.'

'You can rest all you want at my hunting-lodge. It's only an hour away.'

'Another hour's drive! But I've travelled so far already! I'm absolutely exhausted, truly I am. I can't go any further! I just can't!' To add weight to her story she pressed her hand dramatically to her forehead and

swayed most convincingly. Surprisingly, the Count
believed her.

'Poor little English bird. You really are tired. Very
well, you shall stay here in Bad Adler for tonight, and
tomorrow I shall come to fetch you. Then what fun
we'll have together!'

Cassie had serious doubts about this last statement,
but she was not foolish enough to contradict him. Her
relief was tempered with doubts, however. She still had
not got rid of him, and her luggage had disappeared
completely. It was too much to hope that Pentransky
would bow to her wishes and put her in a cab. Instead
she was obliged to accompany him in his carriage.

As they bowled away from the station she saw the
man in evening dress once more. He had paused at the
kerb, waiting to cross the road. They clattered past
him, and for a brief moment his eyes met hers. He
recognised her instantly, she could tell, and even in the
light of the street gas-lamps there was no mistaking his
expression. It showed utter contempt. Cassie withdrew
sharply, a little taken aback by such undisguised disgust. When she looked again there was no sign of the
stranger; they had left him far behind.

The idea that the Count might carry her off to his
hunting-lodge after all settled uncomfortably in her
mind. It caused her to pay even greater heed than usual
to the landmarks on their route, just in case she might
be forced to leap out and flee throught the darkened
streets of Bad Adler.

Her worst fears were not realised. When the carriage
drew to a halt it was outside the Hotel zur Post. Apart
from its size the hotel appeared to be modest enough,
plain and neat. Once Cassie climbed the steps and
passed through the arched doorway, however, she
found the interior to be very different. The entrance
hall was one of the most richly decorated places she
had ever seen. Her immediate reaction was that the
Hotel zur Post was far, far beyond her modest purse,
even for one night.

As they entered, a small neat man, whose ingratiating manner shrieked 'Manager', rushed to greet them. Pentransky swept him aside literally—the poor man staggered and nearly fell—and turned his attention to his servant, who was waiting for them.

'Is everything arranged?' demanded Pentransky.

'Yes, Excellency.' The servant bowed. 'The best suite has been reserved for the English *fräulein*. I have seen to it myself. By your leave, Excellency, I think you will find it satisfactory.'

How the servant had managed to reach the hotel so far ahead of them and have time to make arrangements Cassie had no idea. Pentransky seemed neither surprised nor appreciative of his man's efforts.

'It had better be satisfactory or you'll be looking for a new situation,' he snapped. 'Lead the way! Don't dither, you fool! The young lady is tired. The bills are to come to me, mind. I hope you made that clear?'

'Yes, Excellency.'

The Count had made no attempt to lower his voice during this exchange, and all round the foyer newspapers were lowered and heads turned to see what was going on. Cassie felt her face grow crimson, but it was no use trying to escape. Pentransky's hold on her arm had not lessened once.

As they began to ascend the staircase, the main door of the hotel opened, and in walked the man in the evening dress. He could not help but see her and Pentransky, and the sight brought him to a halt. Cassie turned away, her head raised defiantly and hurried upwards with the Count. She had no intention of being an object of scorn twice in one night.

The suite reserved for her was not as opulent as the foyer, but it was a close-run thing. It consisted of a bedroom, sitting-room and bathroom, all so extravagantly furnished that Cassie reviewed her ideas about the cost. She fancied the price of one night here would more than empty her purse, it would consume the emergency money she had sewn in her stays as well.

Pentransky had said the bill was to go to him, and she certainly was not going to argue. But then she had no intention of staying at the Hotel zur Post for one moment longer than was necessary. One blessing was the sight of her box, standing, out of place and shabby, in the middle of the Persian carpet.

'It will do, I suppose,' said the Count grudgingly, looking about him.

'Thank you, Your Excellency.' The servant bowed. 'I have taken the liberty of ordering some supper to be sent up for the *fräulein*.'

'Very well, that will be all.' Pentransky dismissed the man and turned to Cassie. At long last he let go of her arm, leaving it undoubtedly black and blue. She had not bargained on being left alone with him—so it was comforting to know that, with her arms now free, she could reach her hat-pin. However, fate was on her side, for on this occasion it was Pentransky who swayed ominously. The alcohol he had consumed on the train journey, not to mention the large flask of brandy he had drunk in the carriage, were beginning to have their effect. He put out a hand to steady himself. Promptly Cassie caught hold of it and steered him towards the door.

'You poor dear,' she cooed, 'you're nearly as tired as I am.'

'You're right. . .suddenly, very tired. . .'

As she had expected, the servant was waiting outside. He caught hold of his rapidly subsiding master and, with a deftness borne of long practice, hoisted him into a more or less upright position. Then he began to bear him away. Such was Pentransky's state that he resisted only once, long enough to turn round and wave.

'Bye-bye. . .till. . .morrow. . .' he slurred, then he was dragged away.

The moment he had gone Cassie slammed the door and turned the key. Thankfully it was a true Austrian door—solid wood and inches thick–and she leaned against it weakly, annoyed at herself because she was

shaking, yet unable to stop. She would have considered
Pentransky as nothing more than a fool if, beneath his
buffoonery, she had not noted the viciousness and a lot
else besides. He had gone now, though, and she had to
make her escape as swiftly as possible. A sudden sharp
knock on the other side of the door made her heart
leap with alarm.

'Who is it?' she demanded, forcing her voice not to
quiver.

'The floor waiter, *fräulein*. Supper was ordered for
you.'

Letting her breath go in a long sigh of relief, she
undid the lock. A bored-looking waiter entered, bearing a silver tray covered with an immaculate white
cloth. Putting the tray on the table, he would have
departed, but as he reached the door Cassie cried,
'Wait a minute!'

'*Fräulein?*' he said, in a lacklustre voice.

'I want to leave this hotel without being seen. Is that
possible?'

'Why, yes, *fräulein*, if you went by the delivery door.
No one uses it at this time of night.'

'Good. Then would you take my box down, if you
please? Oh, and could you have a cab waiting at this
delivery door for me?'

'Yes, *fräulein*. . . Certainly. Your pardon, *fräulein*,
but you want to leave, you say?'

'Yes, with as few people knowing as possible.'

'But, *fräulein*, what of Count Pentransky? I understand he's paying for this suite. What will he say?'

'Rather a lot, I imagine, which is why I have no
intention of staying to listen. Are you willing to help
me?'

'Certainly, *fräulein*.' There was no trace of boredom
about the waiter now, only enthusiasm. 'You wait here
while I go and get a cab. Be sure to lock the door after
me. Oh, and I'll give three short knocks when I get
back, so you'll know it's me.'

Cassie was sure she was too tense to eat, but the

smell of fresh bread and fragrant coffee emanating from
beneath the white napkin prompted her stomach to
think otherwise. By the time the waiter returned she
had made considerable inroads into the poppy-seed
rolls, the smoked cheese, and the slices of ham which
she had found on the plate. Hastily draining a cup of
coffee, she was ready to make her escape. First, though,
she dropped a few kronen on to the silver tray.

'There's no need to do that,' remarked her new
friend   as   he   shouldered   her   box.   'Count
Pentransky——'

'I ate the supper, so I pay,' she said firmly.

'Yes, perhaps you are wise.' The waiter nodded
approvingly. 'Now follow me, *fräulein*. The way should
be clear.'

The corridors and back stairs were deserted and their
departure from the suite was uneventful. The delivery
door opened on to a narrow alley at the end of which
waited a horse-drawn cab.

'Where to, *fräulein*?' asked the cabbie, as she got in.
That was a point! Where was she going?

'Can you recommend some decent, cheap lodgings?'
she asked the waiter.

'Frau Meyer, at six Elizabethplatz. Tell her Franz
sent you,' he replied promptly. As Cassie attempted to
reward him for his help he pushed the money away.
'No, thank you, *fräulein*. You've provided me with
more excitement tonight than I usually get in a week.
Besides, I might see you again; Frau Meyer is a special
friend of mine.'

For a second time that evening Cassie found herself
hurtling through the darkened streets of Bad Adler.
Number six Elizabethplatz proved to be an apartment
in a tall, plain building, and if Frau Meyer was annoyed
at being disturbed at such a late hour she did not show
it. Instead she seemed delighted to have a lodger for
the night, however unexpected.

Now that she was safe, a sudden overwhelming
exhaustion swept over Cassie, making her incapable of

taking in any of the details of her new accommodation save that it was very clean and the bed looked comfortable. The bed lived up to its promise. Within seconds of crawling under the vast goose-feather quilt she was fast asleep.

The unaccustomed sound of children's voices woke her next morning. Cassie was tempted to snuggle back into the cosy warmth of the bed, until she took a bleary-eyed look at her fob watch. She was going to have to seek out Dr Sommer immediately, to sort out the muddle of her arrival. If she were to begin her new career today she could not be late. She was in such a hurry that she scarcely did justice to the substantial breakfast of fancy breads and cold meat provided by Frau Meyer.

'You did much travelling yesterday, *fräulein*, and now you are dashing off again. You must eat to keep up your strength,' her kindly hostess admonished her.

'I've already eaten enough for two strong men,' protested Cassie, laughing. 'But now I really must be off; I have an appointment with the director of the spa.'

'You have an appointment with Dr Sommer?' Frau Meyer's pretty face split into a huge smile. 'He is a wonderful man! I have known him all my life. We come from the same village, you know. His father is the doctor there. Yes, you won't find a kinder, more delightful fellow than Anton Sommer.'

'I'm glad to hear it, since I am to work for him. His office is in the Kurhaus, I believe. Can you tell me how to get there?'

Frau Meyer's directions were clear and explicit.

'And don't worry about your luggage, *fräulein*. You can leave it here for now,' she added.

'Thank you, I'd appreciate that. In fact I may need to stay longer, if it is convenient. I don't know what arrangements for accommodation the doctor has made for me.'

'I would be happy to have you, *fräulein*. I'm not

likely to let the room to anyone else this early in the
season.'

Cassie set off, confident that at least she was assured
a bed for the night. The route from Elizabethplatz to
the Kurhaus was simple—all she had to do was cross
the ornate iron bridge over the river, then continue
along the main street. It was a sore temptation to
linger, for Bad Adler in daylight proved to be delightful. The river rushed by dramatically, still in full flood
from the melted mountain snows. Along its banks were
fine old houses, their coloured walls glowing mellow
apricot, peach and amber in the spring sun.

Despite the diversions she reached the Kurhaus after
a quarter of an hour's brisk walk. It was set in attractive
gardens, and although the season had not yet begun
and the hour was early there were a number of horse-
drawn carriages waiting. The spa was evidently open
for business, so it was likely she would catch Dr
Sommer in his office. First, though, she had to find it in
this vast, imposing building. She began by searching
among the potted palms of the main hall until she found
an attendant. At hearing her request, this muscular
female led her along countless corridors and up numerous flights of stairs, finally leaving her in a small room
furnished with elegant but uncomfortable-looking
chairs and an aspidistra on a brass stand.

Not knowing what to do next she waited. . .and
waited. . .and waited. Just as she was considering aban-
doning the aspidistra in favour of more amenable
company the door opened and a woman swept in,
though 'woman' was not a very apt description. God-
dess might have been more appropriate, for she was
cast in the mould of a classical beauty. With her fine
features, her Junoesque figure, her regal bearing, she
might have been a Greek statue carved in marble—and
she exuded just as much warmth!

'*Ja*?' she demanded, with an iciness few mountain
glaciers could rival.

Cassie rose and pulled herself to her full height.

Unfortunately this only brought her eyes on a level with the magnificent bosom, but she refused to be intimidated.

'I wish to see Dr Sommer,' she said.

'Dr Sommer is not available. I am Frau Arlberg, his assistant. What is your business?'

'My business is with Dr Sommer,' Cassie replied calmly.

Frau Arlberg's grey eyes grew a touch more wintry, as she retorted, 'I deal with the hiring of domestics, and we are not taking on any more.'

Cassie had never been one to reject a challenge.

'I'm glad to hear it,' she said. 'It means you must be free for other duties. Perhaps you would be kind enough to go and tell Dr Sommer that Miss Haydon is here.'

Fury swept over Frau Arlberg's handsome features.

'Miss Haydon, you say?'

'Yes. Miss Cassandra Haydon from England. He is expecting me.'

'Indeed!' replied Frau Arlberg haughtily, but she left the room. She was back in a matter of minutes.

'Come this way!' she commanded, and swept off in a rustle of black taffeta, leaving Cassie to follow behind like a small dinghy in the wake of a full-rigged schooner. At the end of the corridor she stopped abruptly, flung open a door and announced, 'Miss Haydon! From England!'

Cassie stepped into the room.

'Good morn——' she began, but got no further. 'No,' she said in a stunned voice. 'No, I want to see Dr Sommer!'

The man behind the desk rose to greet her. Tall and elegant, broad-shouldered and dignified, he was everything the director of a spa like Bad Adler should be. He was wearing an immaculately cut grey morning suit instead of evening dress; otherwise, everything about him was uncomfortably recognisable from the night before. The fact that he was as surprised to see her as she was to see him did not lessen the disapproval on his face.

She guessed what he was going to say before he opened his mouth.

'I am Dr Sommer!' he said.

'How can you be? You're too young!' She knew he was speaking the truth, but part of her did not want to accept the fact.

Clear hazel eyes looked at her coldly out of a lean face—too lean and hawk-like, perhaps, to be conventionally handsome.

'What has my age to do with anything?' he asked in a voice that was ominously quiet.

'Because Dr Mossman said he had known you for thirty years.'

'That is correct. I have known him from my childhood.'

'Then why did he not say so? I expected someone his age. That was why I failed to realise who you were.'

'I was at the station for a considerable time, so long that I was late for my dinner appointment. Surely you must have known I was the person waiting for you, yet you deliberately avoided me. Why?' Dr Sommer's tone betrayed that he was not a man accustomed to being left standing about.

'Because I thought. . .' Cassie stopped. She could scarcely say it was because she had thought he was a libertine, there to pick up a girl for the night. 'Your pardon, *Herr Doktor*, but you did nothing to identify yourself.'

'I confess that I, too, was expecting a much older person. I was convinced someone so young could not be the lady I was to meet. From Dr Mossman's description I anticipated someone middle-aged, mature, respectable.' He gave the last word an uncomfortable emphasis. 'I'm afraid I have been somewhat misled. No doubt you have excellent qualities, Miss Haydon, otherwise my friend would never have suggested you to fill the post here at Bad Adler, but I have to inform you that you are simply not suitable. I am afraid I must withdraw my offer of employment.'

'Withdraw. . .? But you assured me the job was mine! I have got it in writing!' Frantically Cassie scrabbled in her bag for the letter. She could not find it so she went on more calmly, 'You are angry because there was a mix-up at the station last night. I can explain all that——'

'My dear Miss Haydon, explanations are unnecessary. And when you do find the letter I wrote to you I think you will find that it includes the term "if you prove suitable", and you, *fräulein*, do not!'

'Oh, come!' Cassie protested. 'How can you say that? You have known me scarcely two minutes. That's not long enough for you to decide whether I am suitable or not.'

'It is quite long enough for me. I am sorry that you have travelled so far to no purpose. Naturally, your expenses will be reimbursed, including lodgings in Bad Adler for a few days in order to recover from your arduous journey. I hope you enjoy your stay in our beautiful town, but I regret there is no post for you here. Go back to England. If you see Frau Arlberg on your way out, she will attend to your finances.' His bow was abrupt and dismissive.

'I think we should discuss this,' said Cassie.

He paused in the act of sitting down.

'There is nothing to discuss,' he replied firmly. 'You will not do.'

'But reconsider——'

'Miss Haydon, I am in the habit of coming to decisions swiftly. When I do, I never reconsider!' An increasing note of anger was creeping into his tone.

'That must be very trying for those obliged to work with you! On this occasion I must ask you to make an exception. I quite understand, you see. I am perfectly aware that I do look rather young—it is a great drawback, and I find it a considerable inconvenience, for people think I am incompetent, which is not at all the case. But I do assure you that I am twenty-two, nearly twenty-three——'

'Miss Haydon, your age is immaterial! You simply will not do!'

'And my qualifications are sound,' Cassie continued, as if he had not spoken. 'As you must be aware, I am fluent in German, and I also speak French, as well as my native English. I am extremely experienced in home nursing, having cared for my mother for two years until her death. I have also worked at an English spa——'

'I have no intention of employing you! Why will you not accept the fact?' Dr Sommer's voice was rising steadily.

'I worked at Bath, which is considerably larger than Bad Adler, if I may say so.' Cassie's words flowed undiminished. 'I was mainly involved with administration. I am conversant with bookkeeping, typing, shorthand. . .' Then she remembered his mention of a dinner appointment and their near encounter at the hotel. It made her colour rise with mortification, but she went on steadfastly, 'Also, I appreciate that you might be under some misapprehension concerning my companion last night. The explanation is simple——'

'Will you get out?' Dr Sommer's voice was a full-blown roar now. 'Go away! I do not want to hear your explanations! Take your expenses and be——'

At that point the door opened and Frau Arlberg rushed in.

'Is something wrong, *Herr Doktor?*' she asked in alarm. 'I heard shouting.'

'I am not surprised.' Dr Sommer was controlling his fury with difficulty. 'I have been endeavouring to tell this young person that I have no intention of employing her, and she has had the temerity to question my decision.'

'You questioned the *Herr Doktor's* decision?' Frau Arlberg stared at Cassie with shocked awe. Clearly it was an occurrence way beyond her comprehension.

Seemingly it was not the done thing to argue with the elegant Dr Sommer. Well, Cassie had other ideas.

'Indeed I did,' she replied. 'I have been given no reason why I have been turned down in this cavalier fashion and——'

'You have been turned down because you are not the right person for the post!' Dr Sommer's voice had risen to an angry roar once again. 'Frau Arlberg, please remove this female. Pay her expenses. Do what you like, but get her out of my sight!'

'You have made the *Herr Doktor* lose his temper. It is unheard of! Come!' Pausing only to cast a bewildered glance in the doctor's direction, Frau Arlberg put an imperious hand in the small of Cassie's back, urging her towards the door.

However, Cassie had not finished. She ducked under the woman's arm, and returned to face Dr Sommer, who was now sitting at his desk, distractedly running his fingers through his dark hair, which until that moment had been immaculately groomed.

Drawing herself to her full height, diminutive though it was, she said calmly, '*Herr Doktor*, no matter what you say, I was promised a post at this spa. Now you have broken your word. Such is not the action of a gentleman, and I admit to being disappointed. I expected better conduct from a friend of Dr Mossman. As for my expenses, you may give them to the poor or do what else you please with them, for I have no intention of accepting them, or returning to England. Since I am in Bad Adler, I intend to stay. I am sure I will soon find a far more amenable employer than would have been my lot here at the Kurhaus!'

So saying, she turned on her heel and stalked out past Frau Arlberg. As she did so, one of her hairpins fell to the floor with an audible 'ping', and a silky strand of pale blonde hair tumbled down her back. Otherwise her exit was indignation and dignity personified.

CHAPTER TWO

CASSIE's dignified demeanour did not last much beyond the door of Dr Sommer's office. It was replaced by a smouldering fury. Of all of the insufferable, pompous, conceited, intractable, obstinate. . .

Her stride lengthened along with her list of insults as she walked away from the Kurhaus. She was so angry that she took no notice of where she was going. By the time she had run out of uncomplimentary descriptions of Anton Sommer she found herself on an esplanade running along by the river. It was such a pleasant place to walk, with the rushing water at one side and beds of spring flowers at the other, that her temper gradually subsided.

She took a deep breath of cool, clear air, and began to stroll at a more leisurely pace, taking stock of her situation as she did so. She still considered Dr Sommer to be despicable. He had lured her to Austria with the promise of a post, then rejected her out of hand for no reason. Belatedly, she did wonder if her tendency to argue might have had something to do with it. She had to question everything, that was the trouble. She could never accept a situation without putting forward her own opinion—usually volubly. Now this trait of hers had seemingly lost her what had promised to be a lucrative and interesting job.

But Dr Sommer was not the only employer in Bad Adler. In a spa town there were bound to be plenty of invalids needing nurse-companions, or children requiring English lessons. She would soon find something else.

Upon one thing she was determined; she was not going back to England. If she did, she would probably have to live with her brother and sister-in-law. In fact, she had more or less promised to do so if 'this foreign nonsense', as Maud had called it, did not turn out well. It was not that she was not fond of John and his wife, it was simply that Maud, who was conventional right through to her corset-bones, would try to regulate her life, her behaviour, her ideas. Already she could hear Maud's plaintive cry of 'Cassie, such a thing is simply not done!' following her for the rest of her days. . .

No, she could not bear that. She would remain in Bad Adler, and stand on her own two feet, and bother Maud! And bother Dr Sommer too! she decided. Cassie purchased a copy of the local newspaper and a map of the town then headed back to Elizabethplatz, to inform Frau Meyer that she would be needing the room for a night or two more.

When she reached the apartment she found Franz, the waiter, there, seated at the table with a glass of wine. He looked very much at home.

'Ah, *fräulein*, I said I might see you again,' he smiled, rising to greet her. 'I've just been telling Trudi—Frau Meyer—of your departure from the hotel last evening.'

'You were wise to get away from that awful Count Pentransky, Fräulein Haydon.' Trudi Meyer nodded her head approvingly.

'Well, it was either that or risk finishing up at his hunting-lodge,' replied Cassie. 'I don't think I thanked you properly, Franz. I would never have managed to escape without your help.'

'There is no need for thanks, *fräulein*. It's been pretty quiet at work; I was glad of the excitement, and doubly glad to help someone outwit that rogue.'

'I gather that his reputation is well known. After my brief encounter with him I can't say I'm surprised.' Cassie sank into the chair that was offered her, but declined a glass of wine. 'I presume he turned up at the hotel this morning? He didn't make things difficult for you, I hope?'

'Fortunately I was off duty by then.' Franz grinned

briefly at the thought. 'I was told about it, though. I
gather he was in a real fury.'

'He can't cause anyone real harm, can he?' Cassie
asked anxiously.

'He can do that, right enough, I'm afraid.' Franz's
face grew grave. 'His family owns a fair slice of the
town, and he's the sort who's only too ready to use his
power and influence to get what he wants.'

'Or to pay off old scores,' put in Frau Meyer. 'Which
is why we are anxious about you, Fräulein Haydon. He
is a vicious man when crossed. He'll get his own back,
given half a chance, so beware, we beg of you.'

'I don't think you need worry about me too much,'
said Cassie, touched by their genuine concern. 'But I
promise to watch out for him.'

'Good.' Frau Meyer looked relieved. 'Now let us talk
of more cheerful things. Was your meeting with Dr
Sommer successful?'

'No, it was not,' said Cassie bluntly. 'He refused to
give me the job he'd promised me. And to tell the truth
I am quite glad. Working for such an irascible, cross-
grained man would not suit me.'

'Irascible? Cross-grained?' Trudi Meyer looked
astonished. 'Are you sure it was Dr Sommer you saw?
Dr Anton Sommer?'

'It was certainly a Dr Anton Sommer. You aren't
suggesting that there might be two of them, are you?
Heaven forbid! The man I saw was tall and dark and in
his thirties. He bore a definite resemblance to an ill-
tempered hawk.'

'There is only one Anton Sommer that I know of. I
grew up with him, and he was always such a pleasant
fellow then. Very energetic, always busy with something, but I don't ever recall him losing his temper. He
was a very unruffled sort when I knew him,' replied
Frau Meyer, quite dismayed by this change in her old
friend. 'Of course, I haven't seen him to talk to
recently.'

'Then he must have deteriorated in the meantime,' said Cassie.

Frau Meyer gave a sigh. 'Perhaps. People do change. And he was the youngest director of the spa ever appointed, you know. Brilliant though he is, so much responsibility must have affected him.'

'And what of you, *fräulein*?' asked Franz. 'Will you go back to England now?'

'No.' Cassie was very firm on that point. 'I'll simply find myself another job here.'

In the privacy of her room Cassie began to scrutinise the 'situations vacant' column of the local paper. Methodically she made a list, setting down the jobs in order of suitability and preference. Then she located the addresses on the map she had bought. By the time she had finished she had a good working knowledge of the layout of Bad Adler, and an encouraging list of potential employers. She also had a problem. Without exception, the advertisers required one thing—references! Cassie's references were exemplary. They were also, at that moment, in the keeping of Dr Sommer. She had sent them to him when she applied for the post at the spa. That morning she had been so intent upon making a dignified exit that she had forgotten to ask for their return. It was no use. She knew she had no chance of finding employment without them. She would have to go back to the Kurhaus and see Anton Sommer once more!

It was not an interview she anticipated with any pleasure. Frau Arlberg's hostile glare, when she arrived at the Kurhaus for a second time, suggested that the feeling was mutual.

'I wish to speak to Dr Sommer,' said Cassie. She could almost see the other woman gathering herself together to put forward objections, so she went on swiftly, 'Frau Arlberg, it would save us both a lot of time if you didn't go through the routine of trying to prevent me. I need to speak to him on a matter of some urgency, and I will keep returning until I do. I will only

take up two minutes of his time. Therefore, kindly save
your breath and find out if he is free.'

Frau Arlberg gave a strangled gasp. Then she emitted
what sounded suspiciously like a snort and stalked
away. She was back almost at once.

'Come!' she said imperiously, and strode quickly
away again, leaving Cassie to follow as best she could.

Dr Sommer rose as Cassie entered the room. Today
he was again in morning dress. Perhaps such formality
was normal for his post, perhaps he wore it because he
knew it suited him. Cassie preferred the latter explanation. She suspected he might be something of a
dandy. Certainly the perfect cut of his dark grey frock-
coat did suggest it, not to mention the precisely tied silk
cravat which he had anchored with a pearl pin, and the
red carnation in his buttonhole. No doubt the female
clients of the spa ran after him in droves—he had the
assured air of a man who knew he was attractive to
women.

'*Gruss Gott, Fräulein Haydon.* How can I help you?'
His greeting was polite, but his expression was wary.

'In our interview this morning I forgot one thing—'

'I assure you I've no intention of reconsidering you
for employment,' he interrupted.

'And I've no intention of accepting it if you did,' she
retorted. 'I only came because I forgot my references.
You still have them, I hope?'

'References? Ah yes, of course.' He seemed almost
relieved. 'Please sit down. I will get them for you
immediately.' He went to a cupboard, extracted a large
packet, and sat down at his desk. All of his movements
were swift and precise, with no hint of hesitation. He
had gone unerringly to the right shelf, the right packet,
and the right envelope—Cassie could recognise her
own handwriting on the outside. He was efficient, she
had to admit, and that was something she admired. His
efficiency did not run to giving her the references,
however. Instead he sat holding them in his hand.

'I am glad you came back. It gives me another

opportunity to persuade you to return home. I am still willing to pay your expenses.'

'No, thank you.'

'You mentioned the death of your mother. Is it perhaps that you no longer have a home in England? If such is the case I do feel an obligation——'

'Maybe you should have considered my situation before you refused me the post so unfairly,' Cassie broke in sharply. 'But don't worry. Your charity is unnecessary. I prefer to make my own way in the world.' Then she relented. Clearly he was not completely without conscience. 'Such a course of action is my own choice, I am not obliged to do so. Although neither of my parents is living, my elder brother and his wife would be more than happy to give me a home with them.'

'You would work in a foreign country, alone and friendless, rather than have the security and protection of your family?' He sounded disapproving.

'Have you any idea how boring security and protection can be for a female?' demanded Cassie. 'I've no wish to spend my life embroidering antimacassars until some man can be induced to marry me. I intend to use what intelligence and ability I possess to the full.'

'I suspect you are what the English newspapers call a New Woman, wanting votes and careers and independence. I confess I find the old order quite charming; I would not want to change it.' He spoke with decision, as though there was no more to be said on the subject.

Cassie had other ideas.

'No, you wouldn't! You're a male,' she retorted. 'It's New Men we need, not New Women, for it is the selfish, outdated attitudes of your sex that makes life impossible for any female with brains.'

He looked taken aback at her forceful comments. Cassie surmised that few people—certainly few women—ever answered back to Dr Sommer.

'Nevertheless, I am surprised at your brother, giving

his permission for you to travel so far alone. Though no doubt you gave the poor man no peace until he did.'

'Such a course of action was not necessary. My brother knows perfectly well that I am competent and can take care of myself. Besides, arguing with him is no use, he never listens. It's far better to wait until the next explosion and tackle him then.'

'The next explosion?' Dark brows rose questioningly.

'Yes, they are a frequent occurrence at home. He is an inventor, you see, at present working on the production of an indestructible electric light bulb. Unfortunately, his still tend to destruct forcibly on a regular basis. When one does it's the best time to tackle him about anything controversial.'

'You catch the unfortunate man at his most vulnerable?' demanded Dr Sommer, even more disapprovingly. 'A somewhat unsporting course of action, surely?'

'You say that only because I'm a woman. If I were a man you would praise me for my initiative.'

'We Austrians are noted for our conservatism. I would not have thought our country a particularly good place in which to exercise such initiative.' The superiority in his voice irritated her.

'You forget. I had the inducement of the post you advertised,' she said sweetly. '"A position of responsibility and initiative," those were the very words. I know them off by heart. When Dr Mossman showed it to me I felt it was exactly what I was looking for. "To be in charge of the comfort and welfare of all English guests patronising the renowned Austrian spa of Bad Adler." There, I'm word-perfect.'

'Surely you could find a similar outlet for your abilities in other spas—Vichy, for example, Marienbad, even Spa itself?'

'It is no use trying to encourage me to move to some other country. All my life I've wanted to come to Austria. Now I'm here, I'm staying.'

'I wonder what we've done to deserve such an

honour.' He did not sound as though he considered it a compliment to his fatherland.

'Your country provided me with my paternal grandmother, who came from Vienna. She told me so much about her native land that from my childhood I have been determined to come here.'

'Your grandmother was Austrian? She schooled you well in our language,' he admitted grudgingly.

'It was the only way we could communicate. In forty years of living in England she never spoke one word of English.'

'Some people do find foreign languages difficult.' He felt obliged to stand up for his fellow-countrywoman.

'She understood it perfectly. She simply refused to speak it. Sheer obstinacy.'

'Ah,' said Dr Sommer.

'That was a very significant "Ah", Herr Doctor. If you mean to imply that I am like her in character, then you are correct so, you see, my initiative, about which you were so scathing, has its roots here in Austria.'

'Ah,' said Dr Sommer again. This time it had a more indecisive tone to it. He was lost for words, Cassie noted with satisfaction.

The doctor had not yet relinquished her references. She gave a polite cough and gazed pointedly in their direction. Dr Sommer looked down at the envelope and seemed a little surprised to find it still in his grasp.

'Your documents, Fräulein Haydon,' he said, handing them over as though they burnt his fingers. 'I wish you good day.'

He rose to bid her farewell politely enough, and he bowed politely enough, but by the time she had reached the door he was already sitting down engrossed in the papers on his desk. Cassie decided that he was the most unpleasant man she had ever met, with the notable exception of Count Pentransky. If they were typical specimens of Austrian manhood her heart went out to all Austrian women.

As she left the Kurhaus she felt inordinately tired,

the after-effects, no doubt, of recent events and her long journey. For a while she gazed in the windows of Bad Adler's undeniably smart shops, but even this proved too exhausting, so she made her way back to Elizabethplatz. A welcoming smell of wood-smoke and coffee greeted her when she entered the apartment, and at once she began to relax. It was astonishing how much at home she felt here already.

Next morning she awoke invigorated and full of optimism. Today she was to go in search of employment. Even if she had not been in such good spirits the enormous breakfast provided by Frau Meyer would have put new heart in her. Eventually she could eat no more and she set off.

At the end of the day she was obliged to return to Elizabethplatz and confess that she had been unsuccessful. Not that she was discouraged! She had scarcely made any inroads into her list yet. By the second and third day she was obliged to cross off an uncomfortable number of potential posts, but still she was optimistic. These were only the situations where she had applied in person; many of the advertisements required application by letter only. When the postman arrived on the next few mornings he brought with him an encouraging number of replies to her enquiries. Without exception the would-be employers were interested and suggested interviews. It was only at this stage that they turned Cassie down.

'I can't understand it. Some of them were decidedly offhand, not to say rude,' she complained when she returned to the apartment.

Franz was there, ostensibly to mend a broken window-catch, but in reality he was tucking into a dish of Trudi Meyer's pancakes filled with cream and raisins.

'Don't take it to heart, *fräulein*,' he said, wiping his mouth with a large handkerchief. 'There's no accounting for some folks and the way they behave. Look, I've brought the local newspaper. Why not see if there's anything new in this week?'

Thanking him, Cassie took the paper and turned to the 'situations vacant' column. There were three new entries, all of them very promising. But it was not these fresh additions to her list that caused Cassie to exclaim, it was the other items on the page.

'I applied for that one. . .and that one. . .and this one—they told me the posts were definitely taken!' She ran her finger down the newsprint column.

'Maybe they were telling the truth,' said Frau Meyer, looking over her shoulder. 'Perhaps they paid to have the advert in for two or three weeks. Some people do.'

'You could be right.' Cassie gave a grin. 'And let's be honest, my looks are against me. It's happened time and time again. Something about me makes people think I'm untrustworthy or incompetent.'

'You just look very young, *fräulein*,' Franz consoled her. 'It's nothing another twenty or thirty years won't cure.' And they all laughed.

Cassie felt less like laughing when another week went by, and another, and another, without her finding employment. It was not that there was a lack of vacancies. The columns in the paper seemed to grow sooner than diminish as the season progressed, and she followed up every opportunity. The results were depressingly similar.

'We regret that you are unsuitable, *fräulein*.' How often had she heard those words? They gave Dr Sommer an unlooked-for distinction. He had been the first to use them when rejecting Cassie for a job. But, oh, how many imitators he had by the time she had been in Bad Adler a month!

Sometimes she saw Anton Sommer as she went about the town. He was invariably with a beautiful woman— one of the unmentioned benefits of being a spa director, no doubt. He usually did acknowledge her—just! But Cassie was growing reluctant to acknowledge him in return. More and more she was beginning to see him as the architect of her present trouble. If only he had kept to his word. . . The truth was that she was growing

seriously worried. She had never dreamt it would take
so long to find work, and her modest resources were
rapidly growing more and more slender. Even the
stitches retaining the emergency fund in her stays had
had to be unpicked. So far she had been able to pay
Trudi regularly for her room, but she would not be able
to continue for much longer.

'You're not to worry about the rent,' Trudi had told
her more than once. 'You can pay me when you are
able. It's not your fault you can't get work. It's not your
fault!' There was always a strange intensity in her voice
when she said it, and she would exchange a look with
Franz that was at once concerned and knowing.

What do they know that I don't? wondered Cassie,
then dismissed the thought as mere foolishness. She
much preferred to concentrate upon blaming Anton
Sommer for all her troubles.

One day she was walking down Bad Adler's main
street, feeling rather depressed. She had just had an
interview for a position in a dress shop—a situation
rather below her original ambitions, but she was growing desperate. Things had not gone well. The shop's
proprietress, who could have given many a duchess
lessons in haughtiness, had looked down her long nose
at Cassie and said, 'You are not the sort of female I
wish to employ.'

She had said it in a disparaging manner, as if to imply
that something was lacking in either Cassie's character
or her morals. Cassie was at a loss to know why the
woman had taken such an attitude. It was both annoy-
ing and perplexing.

Bad Adler was very busy. It was astonishing how
many people had crowded into the spa town in the last
few weeks to take the waters, to benefit from the
variety of healing saline baths on offer but, most of all,
to enjoy the social life. The cream not only of Austria
but of the whole of Europe was here.

Cassie gazed wide-eyed at the smart fashions. Not
even during her sojourn in Bath had she seen such

elegance. Watching the colourful cavalcade absorbed her completely, driving away her concerns, putting a fresh lightness into her step as she turned down the alley, which was a short cut to Elizabethplatz.

She was quite unprepared for the hand that grasped her elbow like an iron vice.

A cloud of sickly perfume enveloped her and an all too familiar voice said, 'There, I've caught my little English bird again. I knew I would.'

'Count Pentransky!' she said with annoyance, then belatedly more winsome, 'Why, Count, fancy meeting you here!'

The face now glaring at her was flushed with anger, not inebriation, and the pale blue eyes gleamed with malice instead of alcohol. Cassie decided that Pentransky sober was not much of an improvement on Pentransky drunk.

'Did you think you could run away from me? That was very foolish of you.' The grip on her arm tightened viciously.

'Run away? Now how did you get such a silly idea?' Cassie forced herself not to wince. Instead she gazed up at him through her lashes, hoping desperately that her innocent-little-girl act would work again.

'You left the hotel. I didn't like that. People who make a fool of me always regret it.'

The blatant menace in his words made Cassie go cold inside. Franz and Trudi had warned her to beware of the Count; it was foolish of her not to have been more on her guard. It was going to take some very quick thinking to escape from him a second time.

'It was naughty of me, wasn't it?' She lowered her lashes demurely to fan her cheeks. 'You must think me absolutely dreadful. I don't blame you at all being cross with me.'

Pentransky was evidently expecting a more terrified reaction; her air of girlish repentance disconcerted him.

'Why did you do it? That's what I want to know,' he demanded, his tone becoming more petulant.

Cassie's brain worked at double speed. She had to think up an explanation which would appease him. In addition she felt extremely vulnerable here alone with him in the alley. She would be far safer back on the main street, among the crowds. The strong fragrance of coffee wafted out of a window, giving her inspiration.

'I can explain, honestly I can. . . Must we stand in this smelly old alley? Can't we go somewhere where we can talk?' she pleaded.

Pentransky paused only for a second.

'Very well,' he said, strengthening his grip on her elbow, and he pushed her towards the street.

Cassie took in a deep breath, partly with pain—she had only just lost the last lot of bruises on that arm—and partly from relief. So far things were going her way.

As she had hoped, he steered her in through the gleaming doors of the Café Tauber. The Café Tauber was *the* meeting place in Bad Adler, the fashionable rendezvous for the consumption of coffee, cakes, and scandal—not necessarily in that order. Was it her imagination or was there a brief, pregnant lull in the hum of conversation as they entered? Conscious of inquisitive eyes marking their progress, Cassie allowed herself to be guided to a table, and sat down.

If she had hoped to throw caution to the wind and make a quick dash for the door she was doomed to disappointment. Herr Tauber, the founder of the café, had furnished his establishment with round tables so small as to be scarcely adequate for their function, and compounded the difficulties by cramming as many of them as possible into the room. It was worth such discomfort for the privilege of consuming the best-made coffee in all Austria and cakes whose quality and variety had become a legend.

Fifty years later the layout of the café had remained unaltered, and Cassie fumed because of it. Not that she let one whit of her frustration show her face. Instead she simpered and dimpled and tried to ignore the host of ears that were strained in the direction of their table, trying to hear what was being said. The waitress brought them tiny silver trays bearing coffee and glasses of water, and large wedges of chocolate cake drenched in kirsch.

When she had gone Pentransky leaned across the table, pushing his face close to Cassie's, and demanded, 'Well, why did you run away?'

Cassie made a great play of crumbling her cake into tiny pieces with her fork.

'You'll be angry when I tell you,' she said coyly.

'No I won't', retorted Pentransky irritably.

'Yes, you will, but you must promise not to shout at me. I don't like being shouted at.'

'I promise I won't shout,' agreed the Count, even louder.

'Very well, I'll tell you,' she said, in a soft breathy whisper. 'It was after you'd left me in that lovely hotel. I began to have second thoughts. I suddenly saw it wouldn't be at all proper for me to go to your hunting-lodge with you. Well, it wouldn't, would it? I should have realised it sooner, only I was so excited, what with meeting you—a real live count—and your being so kind and inviting me to your lodge and everything. And . . .and I began to wonder if you might be having second thoughts too. You're such a great gentleman and so kind. . .well, maybe you'd issued the invitation on the spur of the moment and then regretted it. . . And I didn't know what to do. I was so afraid of doing something that was not respectable, and the last thing I wanted was to compromise you so. . . . I ran away. . .' Her voice tailed off to nothing, and she remained staring down at her chocolate crumbs.

Whether it was her portrayal of a timid innocent which caught Pentransky's imagination or the unaccustomed picture of himself as the compromised party she could not tell. All she knew was that her ploy had worked. Count Pentransky was transformed into Bobo again.

'Poor little English bird. Was she frightened, then?'
he said, in a baby voice so repulsive that it almost—but
not quite—put Cassie off her cake. 'She mustn't be
frightened. Bobo's here to look after her.' He leaned
forwards and none too gently clasped her hands, cake
fork and all, in his.

A battery of lorgnettes, pince-nez and unadorned
eyes swivelled in their direction, taking in every
detail—compensation for not being able to hear
Cassie's half of the conversation.

'Oh, you're so nice!' She beamed up into
Pentransky's face, silently deciding that she had never
seen a sillier expression.

'I looked for you, you know,' said the Count. 'I
looked for you everywhere, then I traced you to the
Kurhaus. I'd have found you long before this if I hadn't
been obliged to go back to Vienna. The Emperor
needed me,' he added importantly. 'I've only just got
back.'

'How did you know I'd been to the Kurhaus?' she
demanded, almost surprised out of her role.

'It was easy. When I heard of a little English *fräulein*
having a shouting match with that dry stick, Sommer, I
guessed it was you. I did laugh. You made him lose his
temper, so they say.'

'He was rather cross,' admitted Cassie. 'I'm so
embarrassed. I've no idea how the story got out.'

'It couldn't help becoming common knowledge. This
place is a hotbed of gossip. A juicy titbit like that was
bound to spread. Your disagreement was over Sommer
going back on his word, I hear. To do with a position
at the Kurhaus.'

'Something like that,' she agreed, disturbed by the
accuracy of his information.

'So you made Sommer get into a tantrum, eh?' An
unpleasant leer lit his face as he savoured the idea.
'That man needs putting in his place! It's something I
intend to do permanently one of these days.'

Cassie felt a moment's concern for Dr Sommer. She

had no reason to like him, but she was sorry for anyone who earned Pentransky's enmity. Then she reconsidered. Pentransky! Sommer! As far as she could see, honours were just about even in the disagreeability stakes. They were welcome to each other!

'I can't understand why you wanted to work for a lump like Sommer,' the Count remarked.

'It seemed such an adventure, coming to Austria. And I thought it sounded such fun, working at a spa.'

'Well, you've no need to work at all. Bobo will look after you.' He was back using his repulsive voice again.

'Oh, I couldn't let you do that.' Cassie hoped her alarm did not show.

'Why not? I want to do it. I'll buy you lots and lots of pretty things.'

'You are such a kind gentleman. It seems dreadful to refuse you, but would you be terribly cross if I said no, thank you? You see, I think it would be tremendous fun earning money all by myself. I've really set my heart on it.' She braced herself for his arguments. None came.

'You little English birds! So independent! Very well, I won't spoil your fun. I'll let you spread your wings. It'll make it all the more enjoyable when I come to clip them.'

There was such an underlying menace in his last remark that Cassie felt her stomach contract painfully. Although her smile never faltered she pushed aside the remains of the chocolate cake. Her appetite was gone.

Pentransky ordered another confection, a mountainous concoction of sweet pastry and cream. Cassie declined to join him, barely concealing her shudder at the thought of more food.

'So, you aren't working at the Kurhaus, are you?' he remarked, with his mouth full and a frosting of icing sugar clinging to his moustache. 'Didn't that louse, Sommer, give you a job after all?'

'No——' began Cassie, then stopped, for at that moment Dr Sommer himself entered.

She had to admit he made an impressive entrance. As ever, he was formally dressed, yet he wore his frock-coat with a casual elegance few men could equal. It was something to do with his easy movements and his athletic stride. He was not alone. A fashionably dressed woman, clad in spotted organza and with an overblown flower of a hat, clung possessively to his arm. While his companion concentrated upon gathering her delicate skirts into the inadequate space allotted to clients at the Café Tauber, Dr Sommer gazed round, nodding to an acquaintance here, acknowledging a familiar face there.

It was only a matter of time before his eyes alighted upon Cassie and Pentransky. His dark brows rose in disdain at the sight of them. Really, he had remarkably expressive eyebrows! One gesture, and there was no doubting his opinion! At that moment his opinion was pretty low. His bow to Cassie was so slight that it was probably missed by most of the habitués of the Café Tauber. However, no one failed to notice the hostile looks that passed between the two men, and a buzz of excitement flitted among the coffee-cups.

Cassie saw that, whether by accident or design, when Anton Sommer sat down he had his back to them. She was glad. Things were tricky enough without having his censorious eyes on her. Pentransky was reaching the end of his pastry; she would have to move now if she was to make her escape. It did occur to her to appeal to Dr Sommer for help. Disagreeable as he was, she guessed he was not the sort to stand idly by if a female was in trouble. Unfortunately, she could picture all too clearly the expression on his face after he had delivered her from the Count's clutches. Nothing, she decided, would induce her to be on the receiving end of such smug superiority! She would be her own salvation!

'If you will excuse me. . .' She rose.

'Where are you going?' Pentransky demanded.

'Well—er—um. . .' She made fluttery inarticulate noises, as if acutely embarrassed.

'Oh, I see! Very well, don't be long. I'll wait here!'

The Count turned his attention back to his plate and began scraping up the last of the cream with an energy that in a less aristocratic person might have been considered bad form.

Thankfully Cassie collected up her purse and hurried away to the ladies' room. She had not been to the Café Tauber before—her recent need for economy had cut out such luxuries—but, as she had anticipated, this very necessary convenience proved to be a small outbuilding down an outside passage. Her hopes that there might be a back door were soon dashed, but the wash-room had been provided with a window. It was fairly high and she had to climb on a rickety wash-stand to reach it, but reach it she did! Within minutes she had climbed out, dropping to the ground rather painfully. Still, what was a bruise or two if it meant she had evaded the Count?

She found herself in an alley between high buildings, which in turn led into another alley. Immediately she recognised it as the short cut she had taken earlier, when she had encountered Pentransky. This time she made sure he was not lurking in the shadows. Only when she was certain that there was no suspicion of a protruding stomach or any whiff of sickly lily cologne did she hurry out, reaching the safety of Elizabethplatz at a very unladylike trot.

For the next few days Cassie had to admit to being decidedly nervous whenever she left the apartment. After having heard of her adventure, Trudi pleaded with her to stay indoors.

'Just keep out of sight for a while. He'll soon get bored and go after someone else,' she begged.

The idea was tempting, but Cassie could not do it. One look at the few coins left in her purse was enough to drive her out in search of work once more. Her sights were considerably lower now than when she started. Her finances were in such a state that she was seriously worried, and was quite prepared to take

anything. It made no difference. Time and time she was
turned down.

'What do employers want in this town?' she
demanded angrily. 'I wish I could find out. I'm beginning to feel as if I'm a marked woman or have grown
an extra head or something. . .' She paused, having
intercepted a look that had passed between Trudi and
Franz. It was a look she had seen before—at once
knowing and concerned. 'Very well, you two! You both
know why I can't get a job! You've known all the while!
It's high time I was let into the secret!'

'There's no secret. . . It's nothing really. . . Only
silly gossip!' Trudi flushed, unable to meet her eyes.

'Tell me, just the same,' Cassie insisted.

'Perhaps we'd better.' Franz gave Trudi's hand a
comforting squeeze. 'We kept quiet because we thought
it would all die down, but seemingly it hasn't. The thing
is. . .well, you must know by now what a place this is
for gossip. The slightest breath of scandal and it's blown
from one end of Bad Adler to the other faster than
lightning. Nine times out of ten there's no truth in it, as
in your case, but it makes no difference.'

'What do you mean, "*in my case*"?'

'When you arrived at Bad Adler, that very first
evening, you were seen leaving the station with Count
Pentransky,' explained Trudi gently. 'By morning the
whole place knew he had taken you to the Hotel zur
Post, and from that moment everyone decided. . .you
and he were. . .' She stopped, unable to say what
everyone had decided.

'Are you trying to tell me that people think I'm
Pentransky's kept woman? His mistress?' Cassie was
incredulous.

Franz nodded. 'It's what's being said,' he confirmed.

'Of all of the ridiculous things! There must be dozens
of people in the town who know I'm no such thing!'

'We've tried telling people. Whenever it's mentioned
we deny it. Much good it does!' Franz gave a hopeless
shrug. 'Your name has been associated with the Count's

and, as people say, "Mud sticks". Besides, the folks in this place aren't interested in the truth, not when there's a nice bit of scandal to be chewed over instead.'

'But it's so unfair!' Cassie protested. 'It's not even as though I could stand the man! I think he's repulsive! And are you saying that no one will employ me because they think I'm a loose woman? I never realised Bad Adler set such a high moral tone.'

'It's not just a matter of good name,' said Trudi. 'It's because you are associated with Pentransky. That awful creature has the most terrible reputation, and not just for being a lecher. We've warned you already about him, he can be terribly vindictive. Cross him in the slightest way and he can make life very uncomfortable.'

'Oh,' said Cassie quietly. 'I see. And I shouldn't think being seen in the Café Tauber with that fat pig improved my case much, either. No wonder I've been having such trouble finding work! I suppose one half of the population won't employ me because they think I'm immoral and the rest won't employ me because they're afraid of Pentransky.'

'That's about it,' agreed Franz.

'What will you do now?' asked Trudi.

'There is only one thing I can do,' Cassie said gloomily. 'Write to my brother while I can still afford the postage, and ask him to send me my fare home.'

It was the unfairness of her situation that gnawed at Cassie. She had failed through no fault of her own. If it had been her incompetence or inability to manage, she could have borne that, but to have to return home so ignominiously because of stupid, untruthful scandal cut her to the quick.

Dutifully she wrote the letter to John, but before she could post it another letter arrived, one with a Bad Adler postmark. As soon as she opened it she recognised the writing—so strong, competent and energetic.

At her yell of surprise Trudi came running. 'What's wrong?' she demanded. 'Have you had bad news?'

Cassie could hardly speak for astonishment.

'It's from Dr Sommer,' she gasped at last. 'He's requesting me to call upon him at my earliest convenience. He's offering me a job!'

CHAPTER THREE

CASSIE dressed with particular care for her interview with Dr Sommer. She was forced to acknowledge that she had misjudged the man. True, he should have given her the job in the first place, but that was now in the past. Quite why he had decided to offer her the post after all there was no knowing. She guessed it might be because he had received no other suitable application. The important thing was that he had ignored the slur on her reputation. He had the generosity to see it for what it was—malicious gossip without foundation. A knot of anxiety had been her constant companion during these recent weeks. Now it had been dispelled by the hope of employment. For that alone she was prepared to let bygones be bygones, as far as the doctor was concerned.

'Will I do?' she asked Trudi, gazing into the mirror.

'You look beautiful,' was the heartfelt reply. 'Once you start working at the Kurhaus you're going to have to fight off the gentlemen in droves.'

For all her wardrobe was so small, she felt her outfit was very satisfactory. The cream, wrap-round flannel skirt trimmed with matching braid and the toning tussore-silk blouse looked summery yet at the same time businesslike. She was thankful that the vogue for bustles had finally faded. It was not a fashion flattering to one of her short stature; it made her look cut off at the knees. There was nothing wrong with the proportions of her silhouette now, though. The simple uncluttered lines emphasised her slender figure and seemed to give her extra height. Her one touch of frivolity was her hat, a Leghorn straw adorned with cream and peach flowers.

The road to the Kurhaus had never seemed more

pleasant, the band playing in the gardens more tuneful,
nor the flowers blooming in the early summer sunshine
more beautiful.

Frau Arlberg must have been looking out for her, for
she pounced as soon as Cassie entered the pump-room.

'Come!' she said, imperious as ever. 'The *Herr
Doktor* cannot be kept waiting, he is a busy man.'

Cassie was in too good a mood to be put down by the
other woman's manner. Instead, she climbed the now
familiar stairs to Dr Sommer's office with a light step
and a light heart. Frau Arlberg looked as though she
would have liked to delay Cassie's entry into the office,
but her instructions must have been to show the English
fräulein in without delay, for she flung open the door
and stood aside to let her enter. Somehow she managed
to express disapproval in every classical line of her
being.

'Ah, Fräulein Haydon. It was good of you to come in
response to my letter.'

Dr Sommer greeted Cassie politely and offered her a
chair. However, he did not look particularly pleased to
see her. In fact he appeared more hawk-like than
ever—proud, and upright, and almost disdainful.

Cassie's good mood would not let her be discouraged.
His offhand manner she put down to the fact that he
was probably feeling ill at ease. Not an emotion very
familiar to a self-assured man like Anton Sommer, no
doubt; he would have to disguise his awkwardness with
a veneer of hauteur. She had already suspected he was
a man of conscience, and she surmised that this conscience had been troubling him recently. He must have
known she was having difficulty finding employment—
after her recent enlightenment she was convinced that
every detail of her life was common knowledge
throughout Bad Adler—and her plight must have
troubled him. What other reason could there be for
such a complete change of heart?

'I understand you have a post to offer me,' she said,
when she had sat down.

She regarded him steadily. Just as she had had to reconsider her judgement on his character, so she was obliged to reconsider her opinion on his looks. He was far more handsome than she had at first admitted. His eyes, clear and hazel, were his best feature, yet the strong curve of his nose added to his attraction sooner than detracted. His complexion was lightly tanned, giving him the air of a man who spent much time out of doors, which was unexpected in someone who was bound to his office for much of the time.

If the doctor was conscious of the growing appreciation in her gaze, he gave no sign.

'Yes,' he said, in reply to her question. 'The post is the one for which you originally applied. I am sure you remember the details. As I recall, you have an excellent memory. The position requires you to deal with and assist all English visitors to this spa, to ensure that their stay here is as pleasant and free from trouble as possible. Will you accept?'

That was it! No preamble! No apology for the inconvenience she had suffered! No explanation for the sudden change of mind! She had to fight down a rising indignation.

Then he said, 'It will be at double the salary offered to you in my letter,' and her indignation melted.

'Double?' His first offer had seemed pretty generous! She wondered if this was his way of compensating her for the trouble he had caused her.

'Yes,' he continued, 'there will be rather more to your duties than I've mentioned so far. I want you also to act in an advisory capacity. It was in my letter.'

'Yes, I remember, but you did not give any details. Who do you want me to advise and on what?'

'"Advisory capacity" was perhaps not a good choice of phrase.' He rose, and began walking slowly about the room, as if the exercise helped him to marshal his thoughts. 'Fräulein Haydon, I have ambitions for Bad Adler,' he said suddenly. 'As a spa it does well, but it could do better. It is not in the same class as Baden

Baden, for example, or Carlsbad. Mainly our visitors
come from within the Austrian Empire—Austria,
Hungary, Bohemia, or else from across the German
border. We need to expand, Fräulein Haydon, and
become more international. That is why I intend to
make a deliberate effort to encourage English visitors
to come here. You may well ask "Why the English,
instead of the French or Italians or some other nationality?" And I can tell you in two words—King Edward!
Your king is known throughout Europe as a leader of
fashion, as a sportsman and as a *bon viveur*. If we could
only attract him to visit Bad Adler it would at once
become a centre of fashionable society, not just for
England but all Europe!'

Cassie swallowed hard.

'It is only fair to tell you I have no connections in
high society, and I certainly don't know anyone who
has any direct association with royalty,' she said.

'Never for one moment did I suspect you had!' There
was a disparaging edge to his voice. If he were trying to
make amends he was going about it in an odd way.
'Nor do I expect all this to come about overnight. Any
changes to Bad Adler must be gradual and in impec-
cable taste. It would benefit no one to encourage one
group of visitors only to discourage another. No, my
plan is to provide all those things which would make
English people feel at home here, without altering Bad
Adler too radically. Once Bad Adler becomes well
known in England, then we will set about trying to
attract your royal family. In the meantime we must
begin the ground work. That is your responsibility. Will
you take the post?'

'Yes!' said Cassie without hesitation, not simply
because she needed work. This was a job after her own
heart. It needed imagination and initiative. Above all it
was interesting and a challenge—two things she could
never resist.

'Good!' Dr Sommer certainly did not sound either
pleased or relieved that she had accepted. 'Would it be

convenient if Frau Arlberg showed you round the
Kurhaus now? It is essential that you get to know its
geography as soon as possible and, of course, all the
facilities that we offer here.'

'I have no further engagements today,' replied
Cassie. 'When do you want me to start work?'

'The sooner the better. Already we've had too many
delays. Any more and the season will be over. Can you
begin tomorrow?'

He was not wasting any time. If he were seeking to
disconcert her by being so prompt she would show him
she was up to anything required of her.

'Yes,' she said promptly.

'Good. I'll ring for Frau Arlberg.' He rose, seeming
eager to be rid of her.

Cassie remained seated.

'There are one or two more details I would like to
know,' she said.

Dr Sommer sat down again.

'And they are?' he asked, with ill-concealed
impatience.

'Firstly, to whom am I responsible?'

'In everyday matters, to Frau Arlberg. Where anything connected with our drive to attract English visitors
to the spa is concerned you must consult me.' He made
to rise again, but still Cassie remained seated.

'And finances?' she said. 'I can see a certain amount
of expenditure will be required if I am to function
efficiently. How will they be governed?'

'You will be given a small working fund for everyday
expenses. It will be overseen by Frau Arlberg. Any
larger outlay must be approved by me. Now, Fräulein
Haydon, if you are sure that is all?'

It was not! There were many other things Cassie
wanted to discuss, this business of Frau Arlberg looking
over her shoulder and querying the outlay of every
krone, for one thing. She could see a dozen snags in
that arrangement. She opened her mouth to say so,
then changed her mind. Already her queries had caused

a frown of irritation to settle between the doctor's expressive dark eyebrows.

Really, does no one ever question his decisions? she wondered. Or is it only women who must accept his word as law?

No doubt she would find out soon enough. She rose, and saw the doctor's expression of irritation change to something near relief. He certainly did not seem a very willing employer where she was concerned. In fairness, however, before she was swept away in the glacial wake of Frau Arlberg there was something she had to say.

'Dr Sommer,' she said, 'we began our association on the wrong foot, through one reason and another. I simply want you to know how much I appreciate your generosity in forgetting past misunderstandings and giving me this second chance. It shows true kindness of spirit, also, to ignore the malicious stories which I know are circulating about me. I see now why our mutual friend, Dr Mossman, held you in such high esteem, and——'

'Fräulein Haydon!' Dr Sommer cut in abruptly. 'You seem to be under some misapprehension. Before you say any more I must make it clear that I have no wish to give you a post at the Kurhaus. I have accepted you here under the strongest protest.'

Cassie stared at him.

'I don't understand. You say you don't want me here? Yet you offered me the situation.'

'Correction! I was obliged to offer you the situation. There is a difference.'

'If there is I'm afraid I fail to see it.' She was totally bewildered.

'Oh, come, Fräulein Haydon! Reserve such appealing innocence for your admirers—it does not fool me. You know very well why you are here, and at whose instigation.'

'I do not! And I never will if you don't stop talking in riddles,' she snapped, beginning to lose her temper.

'Are you trying to persuade me that you don't know Count Pentransky is behind all this?'

'Pentransky?' Her anger withered, swept away by a growing unease. The last place she had expected to hear word of the Count was here, in Anton Sommer's office. 'What has Count Pentransky to do with anything?' she demanded.

'So you don't know? He's such a good friend of yours and you haven't guessed?' The sarcasm in the doctor's voice was cutting. 'Then let me enlighten you, my dear Fräulein Haydon. Even I have people in authority over me, and when I receive an order from one of these exalted beings I must obey, no matter how much I disapprove. So when a command from Count Pentransky himself arrives on my desk, instructing me to take a certain English *fräulein* into my employment, then I have no choice but to do as I'm told. The alternative is for me to pack my bags and find other employment for myself. That, Fräulein Haydon, is the only reason why you are here, and no other!'

Cassie was stunned into silence.

'Count Pentransky!' she said when she could speak again. 'I don't understand! Why must you obey his orders?'

'Because, as the largest landowner in this area, he is a major shareholder of the spa, not to mention being far and away the most influential member of the board of governors. Believe me, in Bad Adler, when Count Pentransky speaks you ignore him at your peril.'

'But why should the Count go to such lengths on my behalf?'

'You ought to be able to answer that better than anyone else, *fräulein*. I only know that he was here the other day questioning Frau Arlberg most particularly as to your whereabouts.'

'Frau Arlberg, eh? I am sure she couldn't wait to come running to you with that juicy titbit.'

'I will thank you not to be impertinent about the good *frau*!' His eyes glittered angrily. 'She was absolutely right to report the conversation to me. She informed me that Count Pentransky was exceedingly disappointed not to find you here.'

'I am sure she did!' Cassie said heavily.

She had only met the woman three times, yet there had been no mistaking the animosity in the air on each occasion. How Frau Arlberg must have gloated at this chance to show her in a bad light. Cassie could also now hazard a pretty good guess how the Count came to be so well-informed about her interview with Dr Sommer. She took a long, slow breath, trying to summon her thoughts into some sort of order.

'Dr Sommer, I swear to you I had no knowledge of this. I want nothing to do with Pentransky. I dislike the man intensely. If I could find some way of dissuading him from pursuing me, I would.'

'I congratulate you on your methods. Yes, accompanying the Count to the best hotel in town, taking coffee with him at the Café Tauber. . . These are extremely novel ways of rebuffing him.'

'For heaven's sake use your intelligence, man!' Cassie retorted. 'You know Pentransky's reputation. Have you no notion what would happen to any female who openly spurned him? He's the sort who relishes unwilling victims. The only way to outwit him is with cunning—then hope someone else catches his attention pretty quickly.'

The appeal to his intelligence had not gone down well with Dr Sommer. The lines of his face stiffened, as if carved from amber stone.

'In that case I commend you on your strategy,' he said coldly. 'I can only go by the evidence of my own eyes: whenever I have seen you in Pentransky's company you have always looked particularly content.'

'How can you say that?' she cried. 'Didn't I try to fight him off at the railway station? Didn't I call for help? Not that it did any good. You and all the other so-called men preferred to ignore me!'

'I know nothing of any struggle or cries for help!' He

spoke with an icy fury. 'The first time I saw you with
Pentransky you were riding in his carriage. Are you
telling me he carried you in bodily?'

'No, but——'

'Exactly! In my opinion he is one of the most
despicable creatures on this earth. But I realise that
men of his sort, repugnant as they are, have appeal for
a certain type of woman. Perhaps it is the attraction of
wealth and rank——'

'Now you go too far!' Cassie fairly spluttered with
rage. Then she realised that getting into a temper would
serve no purpose. Swallowing her anger, she forced
herself to speak calmly. 'I tell you again, *Herr Doktor*,
I am not in any way associated with Count Pentransky!
I never have been and, God willing, I never will be!'

'If you say so, Fräulein Haydon, then I must believe
you.'

But he did not! She could tell so from his eyes.

'And if you think I'd accept any post procured for
me by that repulsive character then. . .'

'Yes?' He waited expectantly, almost hopefully.

'. . .then you would be absolutely correct!' she
retorted. 'Especially when it is a situation that should
have been mine in the first place!'

She had been within a breath of throwing the job
back in his face. Only that glint of hope in his
expression had stopped her. She would come to the
Kurhaus after all, just to spite him! There were other
considerations too, of course, such as not having to
return to England and live with John and Maud, but
she would relish them later. At this moment she was
happy simply to annoy Dr Sommer. In a final defiant
gesture she called, 'You can come in now, Frau
Arlberg. It must be very uncomfortable having your ear
so near to the keyhole!'

The door opened immediately and Frau Arlberg
entered, as close to looking disconcerted as chiselled
marble could.

'Do you wish me to remove Fräulein Haydon now,

Herr Doktor?' she asked, her grey eyes like slivers of steel.

'Yes, please. Immediately!' Dr Sommer's voice still shook with suppressed fury.

In the doorway Cassie paused.

'I presume the double salary was another of Pentransky's notions? Well, that is his idea, not mine. I will work for the salary you originally offered me, not one krone more! And if you are hoping for the satisfaction of being able to criticise my work, *Herr Doktor*, then you are doomed to disappointment. I intend to be good at my job! Not that it matters, of course,' she added as an afterthought. 'It's not as though you could dismiss me, is it? Count Pentransky would not approve!'

'Get out!' bellowed Dr Sommer, his temper snapping. 'Get out and don't come back!'

'Not until tomorrow,' said Cassie sweetly, then she closed the door behind her. She had aggravated him enough for one day.

Frau Arlberg was regarding her with horrified disbelief.

'How dare you speak to the *Herr Doktor* so disrespectfully!' she breathed in an outraged tone.

'Frau Arlberg, Dr Sommer is a man like any other, not some deity from Mount Olympus. I treated him without respect because in my eyes he has not earned any. I give respect only where it is due, not as a social obligation.'

'Hmm! We'll see about that! Come!'

Cassie followed after Frau Arlberg. Something in the other woman's voice told her she had another fight on her hands! They reached the ground floor and came to a halt before an enormous double door of polished oak.

'We will begin with the baths!' stated Frau Arlberg, grasping the gleaming brass door-handles as if intent upon doing them injury. She gave a push and swept through. Cassie barely had time to leap after her before the heavy doors swung to again.

Down marble stairs they went, to enter a strange subterranean place, all clinical white tiles and gleaming brass pipes. The atmosphere was different too, more damp and humid. Condensation dripped down on them from the roof, and Cassie's hair, so fiercely pinned into submission that morning, began to subside in little wisps.

'As you know, the saline waters of Bad Adler are famous for their therapeutic properties.' Frau Arlberg was moving along the dim corridor at a great rate. 'In this room we have the descending douche treatment, where the healing water descends on the patient from above. In here we have the ascending douche treatment, where the waters ascend to the patient from below. . . '

The tall classical figure strode on, flinging open doors, first at one side, then the other. The rooms so revealed were identical—small, damp-floored and gloomy. They differed only in the position of the water outlets or in the size and shape of the baths which were supposed to give benefit to the suffering. Cassie saw them all—sitz-baths, brine-baths, foot-baths, baths where the water bubbled alarmingly, baths where it lay turgid and mysterious.

The damp and the heat were beginning to take their toll. She was already aware of an inelegantly soggy patch between her shoulder-blades, and, as for her hairpins, they were dropping to the floor as if drawn by some giant magnet.

It was as well that the morning treatment sessions had ended, otherwise the way Frau Arlberg was charging along opening doors was bound to result in an embarrassing moment sooner or later. As it was they encountered one room which was occupied. Cassie feared they had strayed into a morgue, and that the figure stretched on the slab was a corpse, for it was bound tightly in white sheeting.

'*Fräulein*, would you be kind enough to tell me the time?' asked the 'corpse'.

Cassie started in alarm. Then she saw that the face peering at her from the mummified wrappings was red, perspiring and very much alive.

Frau Arlberg had already moved on to pastures new, so it was left to Cassie to reply.

'It's twelve o'clock,' she said, consulting her fob watch.

'It can't be!' wailed the 'corpse'. 'It must be later than that!' In the distance the town clock struck noon, and the corpse gave another wail. 'I've only been here half an hour! It seems like ages!'

'How long are you supposed to remain here?' Cassie asked, noting with interest that the sheets covering the corpse were wringing wet and beginning to steam.

'Four hours!' came the depressed response. 'Four miserable hours! I've never been so uncomfortable in my life. I can't even move a finger.'

Certain obvious questions about the consequences of being immobile for so long immediately sprang to Cassie's mind, but delicacy forbade her from voicing them. Instead, she took a relatively dry towel from a rail, and wiped the trickles of perspiration from the corpse's face.

'Thank you, *fräulein*,' said the poor soul gratefully.

Less than grateful was Frau Arlberg's voice booming from the doorway. 'Fräulein Haydon, you must never interfere with a patient's treatment!'

Cassie gave the patient a sympathetic grin, then hurried out.

'What sort of treatment was that?' she demanded. 'It seems more like some sort of Chinese torture.'

'It is a means of curing gout,' stated Frau Arlberg. Then she added, 'Admittedly it is a controversial treatment. Dr Bauer, who is one of the spa's senior physicians, believes in it implicitly. However, Dr Sommer is not convinced of its effectiveness.' From her tone there was no doubt that Dr Sommer's opinion had to be right.

The guided tour, which Cassie felt was beginning to resemble a cavalry charge, continued.

'The dressing-rooms,' boomed Frau Arlberg, her words echoing round the gloomy chamber. 'Gentlemen to the right, ladies to the left, and fraternising is *not* permitted.'

'No,' said Cassie. 'I don't suppose it would be.'

'And here we are at the grand bath.' Frau Arlberg spoke as though they had reached some sort of Elysium. She flung open the doors.

Cassie had to admit that, after their recent excursion through the sombre nether regions, the room into which they emerged might indeed seem like the place of ideal happiness. It was of marble, with gleaming brass rails, and here and there jardinières filled with plants that flourished, green and verdant, in the steamy atmosphere. Sunlight streamed through huge windows, making everything bright and cheerful. Most of the area was taken up by a steaming saline pool, in which people soaked away the aches and pains of gout, rheumatism and over-indulgence.

'This is the most popular treatment area,' stated Frau Arlberg, somewhat unnecessarily, then she regarded Cassie critically. 'I think now it is time we went into the pump-room,' she said, with undisguised satisfaction.

As Cassie hurried along after her she knew exactly why the other woman was so triumphant. She was all too well aware that the hem of her cream skirt was stained with damp, her silk blouse clung limply to her with perspiration, and long strands of wayward hair hung down from under her hat. In this state she was to enter the pump-room, the fashionable centre not only of the spa, but of Bad Adler itself. Frau Arlberg, in contrast, was as immaculate as when they had begun their tour; not one golden strand of her perfectly coiffured hair was out of place.

It must be one of the tricks of the trade, decided Cassie. Nevertheless, she had to admit that Frau

Arlberg had won the trick this time. It also proved her
to be a cunning adversary.

When they entered the pump-room they were almost
overwhelmed by the hum of voices. The really serious
drinkers of Bad Adler spa water arrived soon after
dawn for the privilege. Those that were imbibing at this
late hour were the more frivolous sort, whose minds
were far more occupied with the goings-on in society
and recent scandal than the state of their internal
workings.

That most of them knew who she was became
immediately apparent to Cassie. The women gazed at
her with interest. Even those who made a show of
snubbing her by turning away only did so after they had
had a good look at her first. The men were more
forthright. Their regards held only interest and appreciation. Frau Arlberg's ploy of making Cassie appear in
public dishevelled and at a disadvantage proved a
failure. It was something to do with the silken-straw elf
locks that framed her face, the cheeks flushed by
exertion and steam, the vulnerable mouth far too wide
ever to be compressed into a prim, fashionable rosebud.
Hats were raised politely to Frau Arlberg, but it was
the enchanting waif-like creature following in her wake
who attracted all the attention.

Blissfully unaware of the disintegration of her strategy, Frau Arlberg strode through the vast, elegant hall,
skirted the twin lines of people waiting patiently for
their daily dose of salty water, and avoided potted
palms numerous enough to have forested a moderately
sized Pacific island. Her goal was the long polished
mahogany desk which dominated one corner.

'This is where you will work!' she declared. 'In here
is the office!' Frau Arlberg went on, entering through a
glass door. 'That desk in the corner is yours. You will
be responsible for all correspondence coming from
England or English-speaking areas. You will at all times
be attentive that no visitor is waiting at the desk. You
will begin work promptly at six o'clock in the morning.

You will be neat and tidy at all times. You will be responsible for the uniform generously provided by the governors of the spa, which will be one blue linen skirt and two white cambric blouses for summer, and for winter. . .' Frau Arlberg paused in her litany, and her eyes narrowed. 'I do not think I need go into the uniform for winter,' she said. 'Somehow I do not think it will concern you.'

Cassie looked at the place where she was to work. As she had expected, her desk was in the darkest and no doubt draughtiest corner of the office. The type-writer on it was a monument to heavy engineering, and if the Arlberg creature was half the adversary she purported to be then Cassie was confident it would prove to have stiff keys and a defective space bar.

'Well?' demanded Frau Arlberg. 'Have you any questions?'

'No', replied Cassie drily. 'I think I know exactly what to expect!'

She was at work by five-thirty the next morning, not that she wished to impress anyone by her over-punctuality; there were preparations she wanted to make before her day began. She was determined to be efficient. As she worked, a stout woman with a moustache came and also took up her station behind the desk.

'*Gruss Gott*,' said Cassie politely. 'I'm Cassie Haydon.'

'Frau Willendorf!' was the abrupt reply.

'I'm sure we'll enjoy working together,' Cassie continued hopefully.

'Fräulein Haydon, we are here to work, not to gossip!' snapped Frau Willendorf.

Cassie moved a little further along the desk. Frau Willendorf had surely been hand-reared by Frau Arlberg, she decided. They both had the same stamp of easy charm.

The cleaners departed, having polished the potted palms to everyone's satisfaction, and the visitors began

to arrive. Outside, the area set apart in the grounds for
carriages began to fill up as a procession of people
made their way up the steps and into the pump-room.
These were the serious invalids and the serious hypo-
chondriacs, come to begin their day with a large dose
of Bad Adler water. From her post behind the desk
Cassie could hear the shudders of the drinkers and the
gurgles as the salt water reached empty stomachs. Then
the imbibers walked, limped, hobbled, or were pushed
away again. Cassie suspected that the trick was to get
home as quickly as possible before the salts in the water
began to do their worst.

Somewhat to her surprise she spotted the upright
figure of Dr Sommer moving through the crowd. Just
about everyone seemed to know him, for he could
hardly move two yards without having to stop to talk to
someone. Eventually he came over to the desk. At first
he ignored Cassie.

'Is everything in order for the day, Frau Willendorf?'
he asked.

'Oh, yes, *Herr Doktor*,' she gushed in reply. 'I've got
everything under control. You know no detail slips past
me.'

Cassie regarded her companion's swift change of
character with astonishment. She had never seen
anyone with a moustache simper before. Now it was
her turn to be under the doctor's scrutiny.

'Fräulein Haydon, you are here,' he said heavily.

'Yes, I am, *Herr Doktor*,' she replied. 'Sorry to
disappoint you.'

Presumably he could not think of a suitable reply, for
he snorted angrily and stalked away.

Throughout the rest of the day Cassie was kept busy.
There were a few English visitors at the spa, and they
all seemed to think a receptionist of their own nationality, for their own special benefit, to be an excellent
innovation. Fortunately, her weeks of searching for
work had given her an exceptional knowledge of the
town, so she was able to answer questions which varied

from where could one find a reputable umbrella repairer to what were the times of services at the Protestant church.

It was too much to hope that Frau Arlberg would leave her in peace for long. Before the morning was over the familiar voice was stating reprovingly, 'Fräulein Haydon, you are improperly dressed!'

Surprised, Cassie looked down at her neat grey and white poplin.

'Isn't it expecting rather much of the dressmaker to have finished my uniform already?' she queried. 'I only went to her yesterday afternoon.'

'I am not commenting on your lack of proper dress,' answered Frau Arlberg, 'but on your choice of alternative. Stripes! Have you nothing less loud and vulgar?'

Cassie brushed an invisible speck from her skirt.

'I had never realised that narrow grey and white stripes were loud and vulgar,' she commented. 'Oh, dear! Do you think we should tell Dr Sommer?'

'About what?'

'I happened to notice this morning that he was wearing a loud and vulgar shirt.'

Frau Arlberg's mouth opened a few times, but nothing came out. When speech was restored to her all she could snap was, 'Get on with your work!'

She did not bother Cassie again for the rest of the day.

'I say! Where did you spring from?' remarked a very English voice.

Cassie looked over the desk to see an elderly gentleman in a Bath chair. He looked frail, and she saw that the joints of his hands were badly distorted with rheumatism, but his eyes were bright and lively, and he sported a pink carnation in his buttonhole.

'Good afternoon,' she said. 'I'm here to be of assistance to all English visitors. Can I do anything for you, sir?'

'You've considerably brightened up my day already just by being here,' he said appreciatively. 'If there's one thing puts new life in me it's the sight of a pretty girl. The Ice Dragon slipped up when she appointed you.'

'The Ice Dragon?'

'Anna Arlberg. The frostiest female I've ever come across.'

'She's very beautiful,' she observed.

'So's the Schwarzenberg.' The old gentleman waved an ebony walking-stick in the direction of the mountain that dominated the town. 'But I wouldn't want to cuddle it on my lap on a dark winter's evening.'

Cassie could not help laughing.

'You shouldn't say things like that.' She tried to sound reproving.

'Yes, I should. At my age I can say what I like; it's the only privilege of growing decrepit. That's why I say you've brought a breath of spring into this place, my dear. I wonder what the Ice Dragon was thinking of when she took you on. The females she usually chooses have a sad tendency to look like drill sergeants. All that's missing is the clink of campaign medals.'

'You're exaggerating,' she chuckled.

'I'm not! Look about you! There's not a female employee in the place who isn't middle-aged and built as if she could go ten rounds with the Lambeth Mauler. She doesn't like the competition—the Ice Dragon, I mean. She's setting her cap at Dr Sommer, and she means to have him. That's why she must have had her eyes shut when she picked you.'

'I don't think Frau Arlberg had any say in my appointment.'

'Ah, it came from way over her head, eh? So you're *that* little English *fräulein*. Now don't look daggers at me, my dear. Live and let live, say I. Any lass who's been unfortunate enough to catch the eye of that oaf, Pentransky, doesn't need my disapproval. Perhaps we should introduce ourselves. George Lindholme, at your service.' He stretched up a gnarled hand.

She knew at once who he was. Sir George

Lindholme, Baronet. One of her first moves had been
to memorise the names and details of all the English
visitors in the visitors' book.

'I'm pleased to make your acquaintance, Sir George,'
she said, shaking hands. 'I am Cassie Haydon. I hope
you are enjoying your stay at Bad Adler. Your accommodation at the Alpenrose is comfortable?'

'You've done your homework, I see, young lady,'
replied Sir George appreciatively. 'Always did like a
woman with a decent brain. Much more entertaining
than the fluffy empty-headed variety, in my view. And
in answer to your question, yes, I am extremely
comfortable at the Alpenrose, thank you. I would not
have stayed there every summer for the last twelve
years if I were not. Now, I have a question for you.
Can you tell me, please, does history record that Attila
the Hun had any female relatives?'

'I'm afraid I can't answer that one. Why?'

'Well, if I'm not mistaken one of them is heading in
my direction. I fear I'm about to be subjected to
unspeakable torture.'

He was right, the woman approaching did present a
forbidding profile, with her sturdy body held ramrod
straight and her large feet presented at ten to two.

'It's only Frau Willendorf, come to tell you it's time
for your treatment,' chuckled Cassie.

'That's what I mean. A fate worse than a fate worse
than death! Goodbye, my dear. We who are about to
suffer the descending douche treatment salute you!
Forward, Markham! Let's meet the foe with a stiff
upper lip!'

Cassie was still laughing as Sir George was wheeled
away by his dour, lugubrious servant.

'Something has amused you, Fräulein Haydon?' Dr
Sommer's voice made her start.

'Sir George Lindholme's jokes, *Herr Doktor*,' she
replied.

'Ah, yes, a very courageous gentleman. He suffers a
lot of pain but never lets it dim his spirit. He is a

frequent visitor to Bad Adler.' The doctor paused, and
Cassie braced herself for his criticism—she could think
of no other reason for Anton Sommer to have come to
speak to her. To her surprise he continued, 'I have
heard good reports of you. We have very few English
visitors at the moment——'

'Twenty-seven,' supplied Cassie promptly.

'Yes, quite so. Only twenty-seven. Not all of them
have visited the Kurhaus today, but those who have
have been unstinting in their praise of you. They say
you have been helpful and efficient. You have made a
good start.'

Cassie was surprised into silence by such unexpected
praise.

'And how are you getting on with Frau Willendorf?'
went on Dr Sommer.

Cassie looked at her fellow worker, who was busy
with a customer and out of earshot. 'I think we have
reached an understanding,' she said ambiguously.

'Ah, yes. I know what you mean.' Dr Sommer gazed
at her steadily. 'An excellent woman. True Germanic
stock. Her lineage goes right back to Attila the Hun, I
believe; at least, according to Sir George.'

Was she mistaken or was there laughter sparkling in
those hazel eyes? Cassie could not believe it. His face
was as impassive as ever, yet she had a definite
impression that laughter lurked beneath the surface. . .
Humour from Dr Sommer *and* praise?

Before she could think of a reply a patient claimed
her attention, and when she looked back the doctor
had moved on.

Not for the first time she wondered if she had
misjudged him. Everyone else seemed to like Dr
Sommer. The men considered him to be a first-rate
fellow and, as for the ladies, one had simply to see the
way heads turned as he walked across the pump-room
to realise his attraction to the female sex. She alone
disliked him, for only with her, it seemed, was he prone
to quarrel, yet for a few short minutes he had been

both agreeable and humorous. Somewhat bewildered, she marked his progress among the palm trees and leather-upholstered sofas. As she did so another, unpleasantly familiar figure caught her eye, progressing arrogantly towards her with a total disregard of those unlucky enough to be in his way.

When he drew level with Anton Sommer, Count Pentransky paused. No words passed between the two men, just a look of such bitter enmity that it silenced all about them. Then Pentransky's face curled into a sneer, and he deliberately turned away to let his gaze wander about the pump-room. It was inevitable that he would see her. The moment his eyes alighted on her he bellowed out, 'Ah, there you are!' in a voice that echoed right up to the great curved roof, then he headed in her direction.

This was the moment Cassie had dreaded. She had guessed it would only be a matter of time before he came. Swallowing hard, she opened her blue eyes wider, and let her generous lower lip protrude slightly. All it needed was a flutter of her long eyelashes as the Count approached the desk for her to take on the appearance of a simpering innocent.

'So you are working at the Kurhaus at last!' he stated. 'Are you pleased? It's all because of me, you know.'

'Yes, Dr Sommer told me. You are so kind to me. Thank you very much, Count.'

'Say "Thank you very much, Bobo!"' he instructed.

'Thank you very much, Bobo,' she repeated, managing to put a girlish inflexion into the idiotic name.

'There! I do things to please you, yet you run away from me. Why?'

Cassie had to think hard. It was not easy, not with everyone in the place taking note of their conversation and Dr Sommer glaring away in the background.

'I thought you liked me to run away,' she said, pouting ever so slightly. 'Are you cross? Don't you enjoy hide-and-seek?'

'I'm not cross, and I enjoy hide-and-seek very

much—when I win! And I intend to win this little game with you, you know.' He leaned over the desk and pushed his face towards hers in a gesture she presumed he thought was appealing. 'But I haven't come to play now. I must go away for a few days; the Emperor has invited me to go hunting, and even games with little English birds must take second place to our Emperor. Never mind, I'll be back in a few days. And just so that you won't forget me I've brought you something pretty. I promised you pretty things, didn't I?' He placed a leather case on the desk. 'Go on, open it,' he urged.

Reluctantly she did as she was told. Inside the case was a gold bracelet set with a huge ruby surrounded by emeralds. As a piece of jewellery it was gaudy, ugly and very expensive.

'I couldn't possibly accept this,' she protested, trying to give it back.

'Yes you can. I want you to have it. It's so that I can shackle my little English bird when I return.'

Everything he said seemed to have an undertone of menace. He pushed the case back towards her. Repeatedly she tried to return it to him, until finally sheer embarrassment made her give up. Everyone in the place was already convinced she was Pentransky's mistress; she did not need to add to their afternoon's entertainment by having an undignified tussle with him into the bargain.

'Now I must leave you.' The Count snatched up her hand and planted a slobbery kiss on the back. 'I will see you when I return, won't I? After all, I now know exactly where to find you, don't I?'

His final words struck a chill in her that stayed long after he had left the Kurhaus. It even blotted out the buzz of excited voices which erupted at the Count's departure. She had been so occupied with tackling her new post and its attendant problems that she had overlooked the greatest problem of all; Pentransky indeed now knew exactly where to find her!

'Fräulein Haydon!' Dr Sommer's voice broke

through her trance. He was standing in front of the desk, his face dark as a thundercloud. 'Fräulein Haydon!' he repeated, fairly spitting out her name. 'I would be obliged if in future you could desist from making assignations with your followers while you are on duty. This is a spa with an unsullied reputation, not a rendezvous for amorous ventures. Please remember that!'

She made no reply. What could she say? With such overwhelming circumstantial evidence against her, who would believe her if she tried to plead her innocence? Certainly not Anton Sommer for one. Of that she was absolutely sure.

CHAPTER FOUR

FOR the next day or two Cassie seriously considered leaving Bad Adler. Working at the Kurhaus seemed too fraught with difficulties to be worthwhile. After her latest encounter with Pentransky there had been complaints to Dr Sommer.

'Both Mrs Weston and her sister, Miss Duckworth, were quite appalled that a person of your doubtful reputation should be employed here,' Frau Arlberg informed her, with ill-concealed satisfaction.

'Oh, so my reputation is still doubtful, is it?' Cassie replied. 'That's a relief. After the gossip-mongers of this place had finished with it I didn't think I had any left.'

Frau Arlberg was disconcerted by this response. She had been expecting floods of humiliated tears at the very least.

'Have you no shame?' she demanded.

'Yes,' answered Cassie. 'But I have no cause to employ it at this moment. Now, if there is nothing else you require I do have a lot of work to finish.'

'The old biddies have been stirring it up, eh?' asked Sir George, as Frau Arlberg departed angrily.

'You overheard? Yes, I suppose I should have expected something of the sort.'

'Hey, there's no need to sound so gloomy! You aren't thinking of throwing in the towel, or anything appalling like that?'

'The thought had crossed my mind,' she admitted. 'As far as I can see, working here is going to be a continual battle against Frau Arlberg, against Pentransky, against Dr Sommer, and now against the visitors.'

'Not against this visitor, I assure you. And as for the

two old crows who complained, I know them, and
believe me if you did leave they'd be bitterly disappointed. You're the nearest to any excitement they are
likely to get.'

At this Cassie could not hold back a smile, and Sir
George nodded approvingly.'

'That's better,' he beamed. 'You see, you've nothing
to worry about.'

'You would cheer anyone up, Sir George, but unfortunately there are not many people like you. Everyone
seems to think the worst of me.'

'I don't think the worst of you!' The old gentleman
was quite indignant. 'And young Sommer will soon
come round, you mark my word.'

'Dr Sommer?' She was incredulous. 'Why, he's absolutely convinced that I'm a scarlet woman! There's no
hope of changing his mind.'

'I beg to disagree, my dear. He's a bright fellow, and
as fair as they come. It won't take him long to sort the
rumours from the facts. When he does you'll have a
formidable champion, believe me. So let's have no
more thoughts of leaving, otherwise there's no hope of
persuading the old battleaxes that they're wrong! You
stay and fight, if only to brighten the days of one
miserable old wreck.'

'I don't know which old wreck you are talking about,'
said Cassie, a sudden lump in her throat at such
encouragement. 'But I promise you I'll stay.'

'Splendid!' Sir George edged nearer in his chair.
'And on the subject of gossip I heard some odd tale
about you giving Pentranksy the slip at the Hotel zur
Post. Now, my dear, tell me exactly, what did
happen. . .?'

One unwanted souvenir of Pentransky's last visit was
soon disposed of. Cassie wrapped the hideous bracelet
in brown paper, and posted it back to the Count. Not
to his hunting-lodge! Instead, she reasoned that the
Count was certain to have a residence in Vienna, a
place to which he was unlikely to return until the end

of summer. Finding the address was no problem; it only required a visit to the public library. Then, congratulating herself on her cunning, Cassie sent the parcel off to the capital, and promptly forgot it.

After a while Cassie was glad she had taken Sir George's advice and remained in Bad Adler. She found she was growing increasingly fond of the place, and the work was even more interesting than she had anticipated. Her relationship with Dr Sommer grew no better. Not so long ago she thought she had glimpsed humour and a certain warmth in his manner towards her. Now she knew she had been mistaken. That he still disapproved of her presence was perfectly obvious. He was too conscious of maintaining a calm and dignified atmosphere in the Kurhaus ever to express his disapprobation in front of the visitors, but Cassie could see it in his eyes. He did not speak to her more than was absolutely necessary.

One morning he did go so far as to remark, 'I do hope you haven't forgotten the other aspect of your duties, *fräulein*. Soon I shall be expecting a report from you on how we can best appeal to English visitors.'

'I haven't forgotten, *Herr Doktor*. I have the matter well in hand,' Cassie was able to reply honestly, conscious that in her pocket was a notebook in which, from the very first day, she had been recording her ideas, suggestions and possible innovations. When she gave that report it was going to be brilliant! Something about Anton Sommer's lack of belief in her spurred her on to work even harder. He might hope to find her wanting, but he was doomed to disappointment.

The Kurhaus was open all week; Cassie had quite a wait for her first day off. By the time it came she had to admit she was more than ready for it. There had been more strain involved with her early days at the spa than she had anticipated.

'You should get out into the fresh air,' Trudi advised. 'Enjoy this lovely weather.'

Cassie liked the suggestion. She had had little opportunity to explore beyond the bounds of Bad Adler, and on a bright summer's day the mountains beckoned appealingly. Armed with a map and a substantial picnic provided by Trudi, she set out.

Bad Adler was a compact town, having little tendency to straggle over the flat wide valley floor in which it was situated; because of this Cassie soon reached the open countryside. Following the map, she struck off on a path which led her away from the main road.

Farmhouses studded the landscape like scattered toys, with their long low roofs, their balconies and their ornately carved eaves. But it was the meadows which delighted her the most: rose-coloured primulas, yellow-eyed asters, anemones with white petals tinged with violet, and here and there clumps of wild cyclamen, their small pink flowers as delicate as butterflies. So enchanted was she by the sight that she hardly noticed her path begin to climb. Only when the flowers grew scarce and pines began to dot the scene did she realise she was reaching the more tree-lined slopes. A lifetime's dreams were being realised; she was in the mountains at last! Exhilarated, she climbed higher and higher until fatigue and hunger forced her to halt. Finding a pleasant patch where the sun slanted through the tall firs, she settled down to enjoy her picnic. By the time she had finished her feast her eyes were definitely growing heavy and she drifted off into sleep.

She awoke feeling stiff and rather cold. The sun had gone and a grey mist was drifting through the trees from the valley below. Shivering, she began to wish she had brought a more substantial coat; when she had set out her thin jacket had seemed more than adequate.

A bit of brisk downhill walking, that'll get the circulation moving, she told herself, and set off at a sharp pace. Unfortunately, the further she descended the thicker the mist became, dampening her jacket and making her feel colder still. The single path through the trees was clearly defined, so she was in no fear of getting lost. When she reached the meadows, however, matters were very different. Paths criss-crossed the open slopes and, with the edges of the meadows shrouded in mist, visibility was very limited. Decisively she took what she considered to be the main track, then unexpectedly it forked. She could not remember such a junction on her way up. She was tired, chilled to the bone, and beginning to feel rather miserable. If this mist did not lift she foresaw herself having to spend the night on the open hillside. Not a pleasant prospect!

It was then she saw a movement in the fog. A shape was coming towards her, large and frighteningly indistinct in the haze. When she finally identified the shape it did nothing for her peace of mind.

'Shoo!' she cried, her voice shaking shamelessly.

The cow stood still and regarded her with curiosity.

'Shoo! Go away!' she cried again, with no better result. Never had Cassie felt so alone or so vulnerable. Of all things which struck terror into her heart, cows had to head the list. She knew all about their gentleness and how they were benefactors of mankind, but her town-bred heart was not inclined to put such theories to the test. The cow, on the other hand, was an adventurous spirit and began to approach. What was more, it was encouraging its sisters to do likewise— Cassie could see their silhouettes emerging from the gloom.

'Oh, do go away!' she wailed, close to panic. Only one thing prevented her from taking flight and beginning to run—the thought that she had two legs, while each cow had four. It was an uneven contest from the word go.

Fear, confusion and indecision were emotions usually alien to Cassie, but she was experiencing them all now. Then a miracle occurred. She heard music! To be more accurate, she could hear someone whistling a tune.

'Help!' she called, relieved to find she was not alone in the world. 'Oh, please help me! I'm over here!'

The whistling stopped.

'I'm coming!' shouted a voice, and she heard the regular thud of boots running over the grass.

The figure that approached was male, and looked reassuringly vigorous. Thankfully he was a farmer, judging by his dress. Just the sort to handle a bunch of recalcitrant cows.

'Thank goodness you've come!' she cried.

The figure stopped abruptly.

'Fräulein Haydon! What the devil are you doing here?' demanded a familiar voice.

For a brief second Cassie thought this must be part of a nightmare.

'Dr Sommer?' she said hesitantly. 'Dr Sommer, can it be you?'

'It can and it is!' The doctor came closer.

It was not the effects of the mist which caused Cassie to doubt her eyes; it was Dr Sommer's clothes. She was used to seeing him dressed most formally, the epitome of elegant tailoring. There was nothing formal or elegant about him now, though. He wore leather breeches, a jacket of thick grey wool, with lapels and cuffs faced in green, and buttons made of stag's horn. His linen shirt was open at the neck, and his stout boots were caked in mud. His face glowed with exertion, and his dark brown hair was ruffled and dampened by the mist. He might have been any farmer or woodman who had spent the day out of doors.

'Well?' he demanded.

'Well?' she repeated, bewildered.

'Fräulein Haydon, I came running up because I heard cries for help. I presumed you were in some sort of danger. Perhaps you would be kind enough to tell me about it now that I'm here.'

'I was in danger,' she protested. 'There's no need to be sarcastic about it.'

'I can't see anything.'

'Yes you can! Those!' And she pointed to where the cattle were innocently grazing.

'Cows? You gave me the fright of my life because you encountered some cows eating grass?'

'They weren't eating grass then,' she observed. 'They were looking at me in a threatening manner. At least, that one was.' She waved a hand towards the nearest animal.

'Are you telling me you are afraid of cows?' he demanded irritably.

'This is a very lonely hillside, and they might have been bulls.'

'You are afraid of cows?' he repeated, his voice sounding rather odd. 'The intrepid Fräulein Haydon, who shows no terror of anything or anyone, not even directors of spas, is afraid of a humble cow?'

'Directors of spas don't have horns!' Cassie snapped.

'Oh, I was sure you thought they did,' he retorted, then quite unexpectedly he grinned.

Cassie had seen him smile before, of course. No successful director of any spa could survive for long without having to recourse to smiling politely at regular intervals. But this was no obligatory social smile; it was a full-blown grin which threatened to develop into a chuckle at any moment. Cassie found it strangely disturbing. Suddenly she could understand what other women saw in Anton Sommer. This was more than any mere physical attraction, though the way his features had softened and his eyes lit up with humour certainly added to his appeal. No, it was the revelation that beneath the cool, sophisticated charm he exhibited every day there was something else—an impish humour, which when coupled with an unsuspected warmth proved to be a very potent force. It produced an irresistible urge to know this hidden Anton Sommer better, to discover what other latent qualities might lurk within him. . . Here Cassie stopped herself sharply. She was not sure she wanted to delve into Anton Sommer's latent qualities.

'Has something amused you?' she demanded.

'Your pardon. I suddenly recalled an incident which

happened when I was a boy. Our kitten fell into the goldfish pond.'

'You must have an odd sense of humour to find such a thing amusing, not to mention a bizarre memory to have thought of it just at this minute!'

'I must deny both charges.' His grin was growing wider. 'No harm was done; the pond was shallow and I soon fished the poor little thing out. It looked very much as you do at this moment—damp, bedraggled and not at all grateful for being rescued.'

'Oh!' For a moment Cassie was struck speechless by such an unflattering comparison, then she retorted, 'You said yourself that I was in no danger.'

'Not from the cows, certainly. The risk of pneumonia however is another matter. You're shivering. Here, put this on.'

He took off his jacket and put it round her shoulders.

'No!' she protested. 'Your shirt will get soaked in this mist.'

'Only if you insist upon continuing this conversation in the middle of the meadow. There's a farmhouse close by. I suggest we go there and get you dry. Come along.'

She had no alternative but to follow him. His jacket still held his warmth, and it smelled of good-quality soap and woodsmoke. She was glad of its protection, yet at the same time the intimacy of wearing something of his made her feel uncomfortable.

'You are right, I have not yet thanked you for rescuing me,' she said, eager to cover her unaccustomed awkwardness.

'There is no need. I told you before you were in no danger.'

'So you say, but if cows are harmless why do they have horns?'

'Pure ornament,' he assured her. 'We decorate those horns with flowers each year, when we take our cows up from the valleys to spend the summer on the mountain pasture. That is the sole function of their horns.'

Cassie was still not convinced. 'I didn't know you owned cows,' she said.

'I was speaking as an Austrian, not as a cow-keeper.'

'Well, as an Austrian you could hang flowers in garlands round the cows' necks. Then there would be no need for horns at all.'

'You don't think their heads would look rather unfinished without horns?'

He spoke with an absolutely straight face, but his eyes were still glittering with laughter. Cassie was not sure how to cope with his unexpected banter. A joking Anton Sommer seemed a contradiction in terms. She decided to stick to cows as the safest topic of conversation.

'No, I don't!' she retorted. 'And I don't see why they have to stare so. Look, they are doing it now.' She flapped a hand at some of the cows who had stopped grazing to watch them pass.

'You must excuse them if their manners slip a little. They don't get much excitement up here; they lead very dull lives.'

In spite of herself Cassie gave a snort of laughter.

'Now it is my turn to say "Has something amused you?"' he said.

'It was simply that Sir George Lindholme said a similar thing the other day, only he was referring to some of the ladies who frequent the Kurhaus.'

The Dr Sommer she knew, the one who strode through the Kurhaus with the authority of a god, would have reprimanded her for repeating such a thing, reminding her that visitors should be treated with respect at all times, even when they were out of ear-shot. The Anton Sommer who was striding across the meadow, his hair all dishevelled and his shirt growing increasingly damp, burst out laughing.

'I sometimes think they do have certain similarities,' he chuckled. 'And there are days when, given the choice, I would prefer the company of cows.'

Such a revelation from the director himself silenced

Cassie with amazement. They were approaching the farmhouse now. Much to her mortification she realised it was only a few hundred yards from the place where she had encountered the horned beasts—and Anton Sommer. There was no chance of their arriving unannounced—a gaggle of geese and a pair of noisy dogs saw to that. A middle-aged woman appeared at the open door, peering into the mist. As they drew closer, however, her suspicious look faded and her face became wreathed in smiles.

'Dr Sommer!' she cried with delight. 'Now, this is a lovely surprise!'

'Good day to you, Frau Strauss,' he greeted her. 'Can I please ask a favour? Would it be possible for us to dry off beside your kitchen fire for a half-hour? Fräulein Haydon here is quite wet.'

'Such a big favour to ask!' Frau Strauss flung up her hands in mock disgust. 'Of course you can come in. This way, if you please. My, to think of seeing you today, *Herr Doktor*! Ernst is up in the barn. He'll be back in a minute, and won't he get the surprise of his life?'

As she talked, Frau Strauss led the way into the kitchen. In a minute she had the pair of them ensconced by the fire, and was ladling them bowls of steaming meat broth with dumplings from a large cauldron which sizzled over the logs.

'But we're taking your family's supper,' Cassie protested, trying to ignore the empty rumblings coming from her stomach.

'There's more than enough for them, never fear. Oh, but *fräulein*, your jacket is wet! Here, let me have it and the *Herr Doktor's* jacket too. I'll have them dry in no time.'

'Fräulein Haydon lost her way out walking, then she took fright at your cows,' Anton Sommer said mischievously.

'The *Herr Doktor* now expects you to make mock of

me for being afraid of such harmless creatures,' said
Cassie.

'As if I would do such a thing! And besides, they
aren't always harmless. Did you see the one with two
white forelegs? Kick you as soon as look at you, she
will. The bruises I've had when milking her. . .'

Cassie shot the doctor a triumphant look at this
unexpected support, but he only grinned and applied
himself to finishing off his broth. As for Frau Strauss,
she carried on talking, clearly enjoying the company.

'Not that I'm afraid of cows, of course, not after all
these years. . .'

At that moment the door opened and in came a wiry
ruddy-cheeked man. On seeing Dr Sommer his face
broke into a wide smile that rivalled his wife's, making
his weather-beaten features resemble one of the cheery
carved sprites that decorated some of the older houses.

'How are you, Ernst?' Dr Sommer rose to greet him.

'I'm fine, *Herr Doktor*, thanks to you,' beamed the
newcomer. 'I heard the dogs barking. I guessed we had
visitors, but I didn't expect a treat like this.'

'The *Herr Doktor* and the *fräulein* got caught in the
mist and came in to shelter for a while,' Frau Strauss
explained.

'I'm afraid we're imposing,' said Cassie, after introductions had been made.

Both the farmer and his wife looked shocked at the
idea.

'The day will never dawn when Dr Sommer isn't
welcome in this house, nor his friends,' said the farmer.

His wife nodded her agreement. They meant it too.
Cassie could tell from their faces that their pleasure in
seeing Anton Sommer went far beyond ordinary politeness. She could not imagine what the sophisticated Dr
Sommer could possibly have in common with these
simple country people.

'How is your shoulder, Ernst?' asked the doctor.
'While I'm here let me have a look at it.'

'It's as good as new, *Herr Doktor*. No bother at all!' said Ernst.

'Let's put it through its paces, all the same,' the doctor insisted. 'A consultation in exchange for your wife's delicious broth. That sounds fair.'

'The silly old fool was repairing the roof and fell off,' Frau Strauss confided to Cassie, as her husband proceeded to move his arm in different directions at the instructions of Dr Sommer. 'He dislocated his shoulder, and was told he'd never use that arm again. "Strap it down out of the way, and learn to use just one hand." That was the advice he was given! I ask you, how could he run a farm with just one arm? Then we heard about Dr Sommer, and there's not been a day since but we've mentioned him in our prayers.'

'Your shoulder is certainly much better.' The doctor was nodding with satisfaction. 'It still has some way to go yet, though. Don't think of giving up your treatment, will you?'

'There, you can't fool Dr Sommer,' said Frau Strauss with satisfaction. 'It does pain him at times, *Herr Doktor*, though he won't admit it.'

'I can manage well enough,' muttered Ernst.

'Now you can, but it would be another matter if you strained your shoulder again in any way.' Anton Sommer's voice was suddenly kind. 'I know it must be difficult for you, taking a whole morning off every week to come down to the treatment baths, but I do advise it. Another couple of months should make all the difference.'

'He'll come, *Herr Doktor*, supposing I have to use the hayfork on him,' promised Frau Strauss.

'There'll be no need for that, wife! I know good advice when I hear it,' said Ernst.

'See that you do come,' said Dr Sommer gravely. 'I've enough to do without repairing holes in your backside into the bargain.'

'Herr Doctor! What a thing to say in front of the

fräulein!' cried Frau Strauss in such shocked tones that they all laughed.

In fact the laughter continued, most of it prompted by Anton Sommer. Time and again Cassie was amazed at his unexpected sense of humour. Equally, she was astonished at how much at home he seemed in the farmhouse. At the Kurhaus she had seen him conversing easily with barons and princes and archdukes, yet here he was, talking equally happily with simple farming people. It was incredible.

'I think it's time for us to go, if we are to get back to Bad Adler before dark,' said Dr Sommer.

In truth Cassie was reluctant to move. It was more than the warmth of the fireside that held her; she was enjoying being in this comfortable room, with its plain simple furniture, its wooden beams hung with hams and cheeses and bunches of herbs. Most of all, though, she was finding it a great pleasure being in the company of the farmer and his wife, and being with Anton Sommer too. Yes, she had to admit it.

There was one thing which puzzled her a little. The doctor had spoken as if Ernst Strauss was a regular patient at the treatment baths, yet Cassie could not recall having seen him before. She wondered, too, at the expense. The farmhouse was snug and trim, yet she saw no signs of affluence. Sessions at the baths did not come cheap, and although she did not know how much Anton Sommer charged his patients she knew it would usually be a great deal more than a bowl of broth. Still, perhaps the Strausses had savings, and anyway it was none of her concern.

As they began to leave, Frau Strauss came up with a cloak in her hand. It was of the same thick grey loden cloth as the doctor's jacket.

'You wear this on your way home, *fräulein*,' she insisted, slipping it over Cassie's shoulders. 'You need something more substantial than that flimsy little coat of yours for walking in the mountains, if you'll pardon me saying so. This belongs to our eldest daughter. She works in Salzburg. She won't be needing if for a while, so don't worry.'

'How will I get it back to you?' asked Cassie, grateful for the cloak's warmth.

'Oh, just give it to the *Herr Doktor*. My Ernst can pick it up from him when he comes for his treatment next week.'

Cassie was a little nonplussed at this idea of using the spa's director as an errand boy. She waited for the doctor himself to make some objection, but he did not.

'It was worth getting lost and being frightened by cows to meet Herr and Frau Strauss,' she remarked as they set off once again across the meadows. 'They are such very nice people. Have you known them long?'

'I've been treating Ernst for about two years now.'

She was surprised. Two years as Anton Sommer's patient was surely an expensive enterprise.

'I wonder at your being able to continue in medical practice with all of your other duties at the spa,' she said.

'One can always do what one enjoys,' was the reply.

They continued on some way in silence, and she gained a distinct impression that the doctor had something on his mind. She was certain that she was right when he cleared his throat and said, 'Fräulein Haydon, there is something I must say to you, so please don't get angry.'

'Go ahead, though I make no promises about the state of my temper until I hear what you want to say,' she replied, somewhat mystified.

There was an almost imperceptible pause before he spoke again.

'You were very foolish to go up the mountain so ill-equipped,' he said.

Was this really what had been bothering him? She had her doubts.

'I know I was,' she said.

'You should have prepared yourself with adequate clothing.'

'Yes, I should.'

'And you should have made sure of weather conditions before you even set out.'

'Yes, that was stupid of me.'

He came to an abrupt halt.

'Fräulein Haydon,' he said, 'I think I'm hearing things. Here I am scolding you, and all you've done is agree with me.'

'That's because I do agree with you. Your criticism is perfectly justified. I know it is, and I will not be so stupid again.'

For a moment he was stunned into silence.

'No arguments?' he said at last.

'No arguments!'

'But aren't you always right?'

'No, and when I'm not I admit it. Mind you, when I think I'm right I say so, and no nonsense.'

'I've noticed.' There was another pause, then he said, 'At the risk of trying your patience, I suggest that before you embark on such an expedition again you ask old Jacob, the gardener at the Kurhaus, what the weather is going to be like. I find him quite infallible.'

'I'll remember that. Do you often walk in the mountains?'

'Every spare moment I get. It's the perfect antidote to the hectic life at the Kurhaus.'

'It must be.' Until today she had never imagined him in any setting other than the elegant confines of the Kurhaus, or against a background of spa society. She was still coming to terms with this active outdoor Anton Sommer.

'Can I also suggest that you always take a waterproof of some sort with you? A thin mackintosh cape is very practical.'

Why did she have the impression that he was talking for the sake of talking?

'I'll buy one immediately.'

'There's no need. I have a spare one.'

'No, thank you. It is kind of you, but I prefer to buy my own. Put it down to the independent streak in me.'

'Ah, yes. The independent streak.'

There was yet another pause, far longer than the previous ones. Cassie was conscious of how close they were to one another. It was a disturbing experience, yet she felt no urge to move away.

'Fräulein Haydon,' he said suddenly and decisively, and she knew that whatever was on his mind was about to be revealed. 'Fräulein Haydon, now I really am going to make you angry, by meddling in matters which don't concern me. Firstly, I must admit I do not understand you; you are like no young woman I have ever met before. First I think you are one type of person, then I think you are another. At times when I consider you are being more independent than usual I am tempted to let you get on with it, in your own sweet way. However, at other times, such as today, when you seem such a totally different character, I feel I must say what is on my mind, so now I will say it then that will be an end of it. I will never mention the subject again.'

'What subject?' asked Cassie, bemused by this rambling speech.

'Pentransky! I can't understand how you came to be mixed up with him.'

Suddenly—she did not know how—he was holding her by the arms. She could feel the firm pressure of his fingers through the thick cloth of her cape. When she looked up at him she found him gazing down at her with an expression of such intensity and concern that unaccountably her mouth went dry.

'Fräulein Haydon—Cassie,' he continued, his voice low and vibrant. 'Knowing your independent nature it is probably crass stupidity to warn you against anything, but I must warn you against that man. He is wealthy, and high-born, and can give you expensive presents, I grant you, but don't be taken in by his buffoonery. He is one of the most malicious creatures it has been my misfortune to meet. I beg you to be on your guard. He is dangerous! Far too dangerous for you to trifle with! I implore you to keep away from him. . .'

Slowly his voice faded to nothing, as if he had just become aware of how tightly he was holding her against him, so tightly that his hold became perilously close to being an embrace, so tightly that she could feel the beating of his heart. Cassie grew conscious of a surge in the throbbing of her own pulse. For a long moment there was silence between them, charged with an indefinable emotion. Then quite abruptly, as if coming to his senses, he stepped away from her, released his hold and let his arms fall to his sides.

'There, I have had my say. The subject is at an end.' He spoke in an odd, clipped tone. Then he turned on his heel and began to stride away.

Cassie watched him, completely stunned by what had happened. He had shown concern for her! He had called her by her Christian name! He had held her in his arms!

The doctor had gone quite a distance before she emerged from her stupor. The sight of his rapidly retreating back roused in her a desperate need to explain, to deny any involvement with the Count, above all, a need to gain Anton's approval.

'*Herr Doktor*!' she called, hurrying after him. '*Herr Doktor*! Anton! Wait!'

If he heard her he gave no sign, and she was obliged to hitch her skirts and run after him.

'*Herr Doktor*. . .' she panted, when she caught up with him. 'Please, listen to me. . .'

'The subject is closed.'

'But I must explain. . .'

'Explanations are unnecessary. I should not have mentioned the matter. It was impertinent of me.'

It was no use. He would not listen. He had suddenly reverted to being the starchy Dr Sommer she knew and loathed so well. The transformation was astounding. One moment he had been warm and concerned, the next he was showing complete indifference. She had to make him listen: it was suddenly very important that he should know the truth. For quite a distance she hurried after him, explaining away as best as she could. He simply strode further and further ahead. He even began to whistle tunelessly to himself, in an attempt to drown her voice.

She became so frustrated that she was sorely tempted to bawl out the full story at the top of her voice. However, they were reaching the outskirts of Bad Adler now, and she decided that such an action would not be wise. Seeing the upright figure of the doctor in front of her was maddening. It incited her to one piece of unseemly behaviour. If he could whistle, so could she! Putting two fingers into her mouth she gave a blast piercing enough to stop half the local dogs in their tracks. It also brought the doctor to a sudden halt, which was the object of the exercise.

'Yes?' he demanded haughtily. The other Anton Sommer, who had so recently held her in his arms, might never have existed.

'Now I have something to say,' she stated. Then, as he turned hurriedly away, she said with resignation, 'No, it's not about Pentransky. It's about this.' She unfastened the cape and gave it to him. 'Would you be kind enough to return this to Herr Strauss, with my grateful thanks?'

'I will, certainly. But won't you permit me to escort you to your lodgings?'

'No, thank you. I'm no distance away. Besides, I wouldn't want to besmirch your reputation.'

He flinched at her remark. 'I've offended you, and I apologise,' he said. 'Can I make amends?'

'Anything but listen to my side of the Pentransky story, I suppose?' She paused. 'All right, I do have one favour to ask you.'

'Very well, ask away.'

'I want your word as a gentleman you will never tell Frau Arlberg that I'm afraid of cows.'

'My word is given,' he said. His voice sounded

decidedly unsteady, and as he bade her farewell and walked away he was laughing. She guessed it was against his better judgement.

The complexities of Anton Sommer's behaviour occupied Cassie quite a lot that night. She found she preferred to concentrate on his peculiarities sooner than dwell upon her own. Not for all the world would she admit, even to herself, how much pleasure being in his arms had given her, nor the sense of loss she had felt when he had released his hold on her. One thing she could not suppress, however, was the happy anticipation she felt at the thought of the morrow, when she would see him again.

Cassie was at her desk bright and early next morning. She told herself that the lightness in her heart was due entirely to the bright summer sunshine. It was not true, however. She was forced to admit the fact the moment she became aware of Anton Sommer approaching her.

'Good morning, Fräulein Haydon. I am glad to see you at your post so promptly.' His remark was characteristic of the authoritarian Dr Sommer, but there was nothing strict or austere about the expression in his eyes.

'I am never late, *Herr Doktor*.' In turn, her response was typical of the independent, self-willed Cassie, but somehow she could not give her words their customary edge.

'Nevertheless,' he replied gently, 'my comment was an observation, not a reproof, you understand.'

How could she not understand, when he was standing there smiling at her in that disturbing way?

Before she could marshal her thoughts he continued, 'I hope you suffered no ill effects after yesterday? You weren't chilled after your little adventure in the mountain mist?'

'Not at all, thank you. I think Frau Strauss's broth was good enough to ward off all chills and ills.'

'I am glad to hear it. I confess I was concerned for you. The swift changes of weather in the mountains can prove treacherous for the unwary, and for those whose constitutions aren't used to it.'

'Don't worry, I have learned my lesson. I will never go up into the mountains so ill-equipped again.'

'Good, so now you are prepared for the climate. That's one problem solved. But how do you propose dealing with those savage cows, eh?' His face was bright with humour, making him look unexpectedly like a mischievous schoolboy.

'A gentleman should not remind a lady of her weaknesses in such an ungallant way,' she answered with mock disapproval.

'Ah, but you are not a lady, you are a New Woman. You admitted so yourself. And I am not a gentleman, I am a spa director—minus horns!'

'In that case, if ever I am confronted by cows again I shall merely tell them to behave themselves or I'll report them to the Herr Spa Director. If that doesn't terrify them I don't know what will, even minus the horns.'

At this Anton roared with laughter. Immediately heads turned in their direction. It was unheard of for the *Herr Doktor* to engage in conversation so early in the morning. As a rule, during his preliminary circuit of the Kurhaus his comments were terse and to the point. On this morning, however, he had been chatting to the English *fräulein* for several minutes in a most animated manner. Moreover he showed no inclination to move on and complete his usual tour.

Cassie was vaguely aware of numerous pairs of eyes turned in their direction. She paid them scant heed. She preferred to give her full attention to Anton.

Someone else, though, had other ideas. In a rustle of stiff taffeta Frau Arlberg came bustling up, a parcel in her hands.

'Do forgive me for breaking into your little *tête-à-tête, Herr Doktor*,' she gushed. 'But I have something for Fräulein Haydon.'

Anton made way for her with a stiff bow. He did not look pleased at the interruption.

'This came for you by special messenger.' Frau Arlberg thrust the square package across the counter almost gleefully. The coy way she said 'special messenger' gave the two words a certain emphasis.

'For me?' said Cassie with surprise. 'I wasn't expecting anything.'

'No? Are you sure?' It was there again, that note of simpering innuendo. 'I fancy the messenger thought otherwise. "Fräulein Haydon will know what it is," he said. "See that it is given into the *fräulein's* own hands and no other. If it goes astray my master will be extremely upset." Well, what could I do except bring it to you immediately? We don't want to upset his illustrious master, do we? Not a gentleman of his rank and standing.'

'Who is this gentleman?' asked Cassie, examining the paper wrapping. 'There's no name on the outside.'

She should have known better! The moment the words were out of her mouth she realised her stupidity. The happy banter she had been exchanging with Anton had absorbed her thoughts and put her off her guard. Of course Frau Arlberg would not be affable without a reason. Here was the Ice Dragon running errands for her without a word of complaint, not even a hint of censure for receiving personal matter at the Kurhaus or wasting valuable business time. There had to be an ulterior motive! Cassie could guess at once what it was. She knew who had sent the package.

She turned her gaze to Anton. The change in his expression was total. He was looking at her with disbelief and—yes, and with contempt. He knew too.

'Your unknown admirer is not so very mysterious, not when he sends his servant out in full livery and has his coat of arms stamped all over the parcel.' Frau Arlberg was still pretending to be coy. 'Anyone can tell it's from Count Pentranksy—oh, how foolish of me!

I've given the game away!' She looked anything but
contrite. Her grey eyes glistened with triumph.

Cassie scarcely noticed her. Her attention was all for
Anton. There was not a trace of humour in his
expression now. Instead his face was white and grim.

'Thank you, Frau Arlberg. Perhaps you would return
to your duties,' he said through stiff lips.

Clearly disappointed not to see the full outcome of
her scheming, Frau Arlberg withdrew.

Anton turned his gaze on Cassie.

'Fräulein Haydon, would you kindly inform your
admirers that this Kurhaus is not an extension of the
post office?' he said.

Never had she heard him so abrupt or so formal.

'I swear I knew nothing of this,' she protested.

'You knew who it was from, though, didn't you?
Don't deny it. It was written all over your face. Nor did
you show any surprise.'

'I wasn't expecting it, I tell you. Nor do I want it. I
want nothing from Pentransky.'

'An excellent performance. You are to be
congratulated.'

'It's true, I tell you.'

'So you say. I should have trusted my first
impressions.'

'I beg your pardon?' She looked at him in surprise.

'No, I beg yours.' His voice was low and angry.
'Yesterday I came close to listening to you, and hearing
your version of your relationship with. . .with that man!
Fortunately I blocked my ears. Just in time I remembered the occasions when I had seen you together,
occasions when you had been blatantly delighted to be
in his company. Yes, I was right not to listen to you.
You would only have told me how blameless you were,
and how Pentransky was nothing to you. Nothing to
you, yet you receive gifts from him, and you are pleased
to be seen with him. You are even happy to accept a
post here at the Kurhaus obtained for you through his
influence! If I had listened I would have heard nothing

but lies. Yesterday you talked very glibly of your
independent streak. Your brand of independence has
another name in this country!'

Angry and distressed, Cassie faced up to him.

'Now you are being insulting!' she cried. 'Not that I
care one jot about your opinion of me. Think what you
like! As for this, I want nothing to do with it!'

Furiously she knocked the parcel off the counter with
a sweep of her arm. The impact as it hit the floor at
Anton's feet split the paper wrapping to reveal a leather
jewel case. He picked it up and, placing it back on the
counter in front of Cassie, he pressed the catch to open
it. The hideous ruby and emerald bracelet lay on the
velvet lining. Alongside there was now a pair of equally
hideous matching earrings. Ugly they might be, but
there was no denying their quality or their value.

'Where is your independent streak now, Fräulein
Haydon?' he demanded.

Before she could think of a reply he had gone.

CHAPTER FIVE

'DR SOMMER wishes to see you in his office,' said Frau Willendorf one morning. Then she added, 'Now!' in a way which implied not only urgency but the prospect of an unpleasant time ahead for Cassie.

'Ah, yes, it will be to congratulate me on my work,' said Cassie.

In truth, she had no idea why she was being summoned to the director's presence, but it gave her spirits a boost to see the gleeful satisfaction fade from Frau Willendorf's face. As she trudged up the stairs she had to admit to herself she was unlikely to meet any praise at her journey's end.

Ever since the incident of the bracelet Dr Sommer had seemed to be going out of his way to criticise her. For a brief time she had found herself thinking of him as Anton, but these days that seemed singularly inappropriate. The light-hearted man who had come to her rescue on the mountainside and who had teased her about her fear of cows might have been nothing more than a figment of her imagination. Less easy to dismiss as a fanciful notion was the memory of his arms holding her and his eyes regarding her with warmth and gentleness. That particular recollection aroused in her an uncomfortable sensation which came perilously close to pain. She preferred not to think about it.

There was one point in his favour after that episode. He had kept his word and remained silent about her fear of cows. Frau Arlberg was still ignorant of this flaw in her defences.

'Just as well!' muttered Cassie, as she trudged upwards. 'Otherwise the wretched woman would have herds of them in here, drinking the waters and swimming up and down in the baths, just to annoy me!' For

Frau Arlberg had taken the hint from her beloved *Herr Doktor*, and was finding even more fault with Cassie than usual. At least, she was trying to; so far Cassie had managed to thwart her attempts by sheer efficiency.

As she expected, Anton Sommer was fairly glowering when she reached the office. There was no hint of sympathy about him, no trace of friendliness: he looked cold and angry, like authority personified.

'Ah, yes, Fräulein Haydon, I sent for you!' he said. 'Can you tell me what this is?' He waved a piece of paper in the air.

'Yes, *Herr Doktor*, it's a piece of paper,' said Cassie. 'If there's no other subject upon which you need my help I'll go back to my desk.'

She swung round angrily, her skirts swirling about her ankles as she made for the door. It was foolish of her to antagonise him, she knew, but she was tired of his constant criticism. In a dozen different ways he was showing his mistrust of her, and she had had enough of it. Let him believe she was Pentransky's mistress if he wanted to!

'Come back!' he roared, in a voice which sent shivers through the crystal chandelier above them. Lowering his tone half a dozen decibels he said, in the manner of a man controlling himself with difficulty, 'Fräulein Haydon, most people consider me to be mild-mannered. I have a reputation for remaining calm in any crisis. Why is it, then, that you have this ability to make me angry?'

It was an interesting question. She had to admit that she enjoyed aggravating Dr Sommer lately. Something about him, his self-assurance, his self-confidence, irritated her. She had only to look at him and she felt an urge to disagree. No one else had ever had this effect on her either, only him!

'Was that a rhetorical question, or would you really like an answer?' she asked.

'I would dearly like an answer.'

'It's because I'm not afraid of you. I question your

judgement,' she replied. If he could be curt and abrupt then so could she!

He nearly roared at her again, but held himself back in time.

'We will start this interview again,' he said through gritted teeth. 'Frau Arlberg has brought to my attention your indiscriminate and unauthorised use of the telegraph. I want to know why you have deliberately run up such an exorbitant bill.'

'It is extremely difficult to run up such a bill accidentally.' There, she was doing it again! Saying things guaranteed to make him angry. She did not seem able to stop herself. The words slipped out of their own volition. She made a belated attempt to give a proper reply to his question. 'Not long ago you told me you would soon be requiring a detailed report on my ideas for attracting English visitors. That is correct, is it not, *Herr Doktor*?'

'Yes. . .' The reply was cautious.

'I needed facts and figures for my report, and the quickest way to obtain them was by telegraph. I understood there was a certain urgency in the matter.'

'There is.' He stabbed at the paper in front of him with a well-manicured finger. 'But so much money and without authority?'

'I thought you had enough to do without me running to you every five minutes asking permission to go to the telegraph office, *Herr Doktor*.'

'Then you should have gone to Frau Arlberg.'

'I've tried going to Frau Arlberg. She questions every request I make, even for a new pen-nib or a sheet of blotting-paper. If I'd waited for her my report would never have got finished. Last week I asked for a new pen-holder and she replied, in writing, "Request refused. In my experience pen-holders do not wear out and need replacing." Do you wonder I don't consult her?'

'She has a point, though,' said Dr Sommer reasonably. 'Pen-holders do not wear out.'

'They do if Frau Willendorf treads on them.'

Just for a moment the doctor's icy demeanour cracked. The papers on his desk suddenly attracted his attention with a curious intensity. He bent his head over them, obscuring his expression from view, but not quite quickly enough to hide the grin which lit his face.

Cassie found him more irritating than ever. If he felt like laughing out loud then why on earth did he not do so? She had seen him laugh before and it had been a very pleasant experience. Swiftly she closed her mind to that particular line of thought. Perhaps it was better for him to remain serious.

When he raised his head again his features were once more set into their customary impassive gravity.

'Quite so,' he said. 'Under those exceptional circumstances you would certainly require a new pen-holder. I'll put the matter in hand.'

'There's no need, thank you. I've got one. I went to the stock cupboard and helped myself. Frau Arlberg mustn't have found out yet, otherwise they'd have heard the uproar as far as Salzburg.'

Dr Sommer's lips began to twitch again, clearly against his better judgement. 'Fräulein,' he began, trying to control them, 'taking stock from the cupboard is a serious breach of the rules.'

'It is, I agree with you, but I couldn't work without a pen, and you've just authorised me to have one, so everything is all right, isn't it?'

'Yes.' He sounded rather surprised. 'I suppose it is.' He shuffled his papers and extracted the telegraph bill once more. 'I suggest we get back to the matter in hand,' he said. 'I am willing to concede that you have a point in your favour. When matters are urgent the telegraph is a convenient method of communication. However, I would like more details of your expenditure. First of all, this message to Messrs Jackson, in London, Who are they?'

'Grocers.'

'Grocers?' The doctor's eyebrows shot up.

'Yes, Jackson's of Piccadilly. They are renowned suppliers of all sorts of foodstuffs. Have you never been to London?'

'Frequently, but I did not spend my time shopping for food. Can I ask what, on your shopping list, was so urgent you had to telegraph London for it?'

'The shopping list was not a personal one, I assure you. It may have escaped your notice, *Herr Doktor*, but the shops in Bad Adler are remarkably deficient in certain commodities.'

'They are? What, for example?'

'Tea, for a start.'

'Oh, come now. Tea is plentiful here. Why, it is even served in the Kurhaus café.'

'I am talking about real tea,' said Cassie disparagingly. 'Not a tasteless liquid resulting from putting three tea leaves in a muslin bag and drowning them!'

Dr Sommer regarded her loftily, as though he had taken this slur on Austrian tea-making personally.

'And how do you propose to rectify this deficiency?' he asked.

'By making sure good-quality tea is available here. That is why I contacted Messrs Jackson. They were most helpful in sending me price lists, freight charges and delivery times, not only for tea but other things on my list.'

At this point the door opened, after the briefest of knocks, and Frau Arlberg entered.

'Anton, do you have the letter——?' She stopped, her gaze resting on Cassie. 'Oh, Dr Sommer,' she amended, fluttering her eyelashes and clasping her hands as if in agitation at her gaffe. The effect was extraordinary, and unconvincing. 'I didn't know. . . I had no idea you were occupied.'

Dr Sommer accepted this use of his Christian name very calmly, though Cassie thought she detected a momentary spark of annoyance in his eyes. No doubt he was irritated at being disturbed while he was in full rebuke.

'Which letter do you require, *Frau Arlberg*?' he enquired.

'The one to the Hospital of Rheumatic Diseases, *Herr Doktor*.'

Efficient as ever, Anton Sommer reached for it unerringly, and handed it over.

'Thank you, *Herr Doktor*. I will see to the reply immediately, *Herr Doktor*. And. . .and I do apologise for entering in such an unseemly way. . . It was unforgivable. . . I'm very sorry. . .' She was being positively gushing in her penitence.

Cassie did not believe a word of it. Anna Arlberg had known she was in the office right enough, so why had she barged in? It could not have been her eagerness to hear Cassie being reprimanded; she could have managed that perfectly well with her ear against the keyhole. What other reason could she have had, apart from making sure that Cassie knew she was on Christian name terms with the doctor? It was very puzzling.

If Dr Sommer was equally bemused at the behaviour of his assistant he gave no sign of it.

'And, pray, what commodities are you proposing to import?' he continued, as if nothing had happened. 'I tell you now, I will not consider your setting up an English grocer's shop in the Kurhaus, no matter how high-class.'

'As if I would suggest such a thing!' Cassie was scornful. 'That is why I had a most valuable chat with Herr Flegel, who owns the excellent grocery and provisions store in the main square. Do you know him?'

'Not personally, though I believe my housekeeper shops there.'

For a moment Cassie was taken aback by the idea of Dr Sommer buying anything as mundane as groceries, even by proxy. She knew he occupied a house in the grounds of the Kurhaus, though she could not picture him relaxing in an armchair, wearing carpet slippers. But then she had never pictured him in leather breeches and a country jacket halfway up a mountain, either, yet there he had seemed to fit quite naturally into both the clothes and the scenery.

She became aware that he was speaking.

'I beg your pardon?' she said.

'I merely asked what was the outcome of this most valuable chat?'

'Herr Flegel was extremely interested. We talked for some time about expanding his stock and aiming for a specific market among the visitors. Naturally, he will need time to think it over and study the information from Jackson's. However, I think he'll be willing to stock English foodstuffs.'

In fact Herr Flegel had been as putty in her hands. She had recognised the ardent expression on his face all too well, and she guessed that if she had asked the portly grocer to stock elephants he would have given the matter serious consideration. It infuriated her. She would have much preferred to have persuaded him by the strength of her arguments and the logic of her business sense rather than the brilliance of her eyes.

'And may I ask what other items appear in your extensive shopping basket, apart from tea?'

'Lots of things. Digestive biscuits, golden syrup, Gentleman's Relish, Bath Olivers, Stilton cheese, Oxford marmalade, curry powder, kippers, Yarmouth bloaters. . .' She reeled off a formidable list. 'We need English-style bacon too, of course, but there could be problems over transportation. However, Herr Flegel knows a farmer who might be willing to cure his bacon the English way, if we can find out about the right method.'

'And how do you propose finding out?' asked Dr Sommer. 'I presume it meant another telegraph message?'

'Yes.' Cassie rose and looked over his shoulder at the bill. 'There it is. The item directed to the publishers of Mrs Beeton's *Book of Household Management*.'

'Not to Mrs Beeton herself?'

'I think she's dead.'

'I'm surprised you let that stop you.'

Cassie was about to make a stinging retort in answer to this sarcastic remark, but something prevented her. Something to do with noticing how remarkable his eyelashes were, so thick and dark. From this angle they gave a gentler aspect to his face, making its lines softer, more appealing. . . Hurriedly she returned to her seat at the opposite side of the desk.

'*The Times!*' The doctor read on, apparently oblivious to her swift retreat. 'But *The Times* already reaches Bad Adler. We have it in the Kurhaus, and I know that during the season it is available at several cafés and newsagents.'

'Yes, when it's two days old.' Cassie forgot her momentary awkwardness in the flush of her new enthusiasm. 'I sent to the management of *The Times*, suggesting a route which would get the newspaper here in little over twenty-four hours. They need to get the papers on the five a.m. Dover to Ostend ferry, which connects with——'

'Save me the details!' Dr Sommer put his hands to his head and groaned slightly. 'I don't think we need to go further into the telegraph bill. I accept that you have an answer and an explanation for everything.'

'Of course!' She looked at him with genuine surprise. 'Did you imagine I sent all those telegraph messages simply out of mischief?'

'No,' he said. Then he repeated, 'No, never that. I can see you have worked hard and paid great attention to detail. If you have finished your report I will be happy to read it.' As she was leaving the room he added, 'Fräulein Haydon, in any other circumstances I think I might be glad to have you in my employment.'

Cassie hurried downstairs, glad to get away from his office. The phrase 'in any other circumstances' and its accompanying note of regret had been too uncomfortable to dwell upon.

These days Frau Arlberg's behaviour mystified Cassie. The woman seemed to be dogging Dr Sommer's footsteps. Whenever the doctor appeared, so did she, demanding his attention on the flimsiest pretexts. She fussed about him, performing little duties for him that he clearly did not want performed—fetching his coffee, carrying the morning post for him, even renewing the carnation in his lapel long before the previous one had had time to wilt.

Shaking her head in bewilderment, Cassie observed Frau Arlberg's calling for an umbrella as if her life depended on its prompt arrival. The *Herr Doktor* was going out!

'It's not even raining,' she observed to Sir George, who had been watching with her. 'And Dr Sommer is going over to the town hall; it's just ten minutes away. He won't melt in that time. There's only one small dark cloud to be seen.'

Sir George gave a chuckle. 'Maybe Frau Arlberg can see a greater threat than one small cloud,' he said.

'I'm sorry, I don't understand.'

'Can't you see what she's doing, my dear? She's warning you off.'

'Off what?'

'Why, off the doctor! He's her property, at least, in her eyes. She's been pushing him towards the altar for a good year now, and she's got no intention of letting anyone get in the way. That's why she's staking such a hefty claim—just in case you get any ideas.'

'About the doctor?' Cassie snorted. 'I've plenty of ideas about him, but none that concerns matrimony. I presume there is no Herr Arlberg? No one ever mentions him.'

'The story she gives out is that she's a widow. My guess is that he's run off with some nice cuddly little barmaid, and is living very happily somewhere miles from here. It's what I'd have done in his place.'

'Frau Arlberg and bigamy don't seem to go together too well. She'd want the matrimonial knot tied tightly and irrevocably if I'm any judge,' said Cassie with a grin. 'Well, I'm no threat to her plans; she's welcome to him.'

'Pity.' Sir George gave a regretful sigh. 'You and young Sommer are the two people who make this place worthwhile, as far as I'm concerned. It would have been nice if you'd got together.'

'I'm sorry to disappoint you, Sir George. You know in the usual course of things I'd go out of my way to oblige you, but I have to draw the line at marrying Dr Sommer. Mind you, it might give the scandalmongers something to talk about, because I guarantee that within the first month one of us would have murdered the other.'

'Perhaps, in that case, it would not be worth it, no matter how interesting the outcome might have been.' Sir George gave a deeper sigh of exaggerated regret. . . 'Now we really must go, my dear. Talking to you does me more good than swallowing gallons of the foul brine they dish out here. Walk on, Markham, walk on.'

If Markham objected to being addressed like a cab-horse he gave no sign. In fact he rarely spoke, or showed any emotion at all, yet Cassie knew he and Sir George were devoted to one another.

Sir George's idea of a romantic attachment between her and Anton Sommer caused her bitter amusement all the way home. It was one way of diverting gossiping tongues from coupling her name with Pentransky's. On second thoughts, in view of the assured murderous outcome of any match between her and the doctor, it might defeat its own end.

Temporarily she had been free of all thought of Pentransky. The return of his bracelet had brought with it one blessing—a letter in which he informed her that his Emperor could not bear to part with him and had insisted on his staying for a few days more. Her heart went out to poor Franz Josef. Surely the man who ruled over one of the world's major empires could not be so desperate for company that he had to put up with Pentransky? More likely the Count had gained some small foothold at Court and was proving difficult to dislodge. He could be tenacious when he chose, as she knew to her cost.

She could breathe freely for a day or two more! It was a blissful feeling. Her one tangible link with the Count was his hideous jewellery. Its reappearance in her life had been a shock; however, she was still determined to get rid of it as soon as possible. The temptation to throw it in the river was great. Only her frugal soul rebelled at the wanton destruction of something so valuable. She tried offering it to Trudi.

'It's kind of you, really it is, but——'

'But what?' asked Cassie.

'To be honest I would sooner not have it. Everyone knows it came from the Count, and if I tried to sell it he'd soon come to hear about it. Then there'd be no knowing what he would do to me.'

'Why, what could he do?'

'For a start, he owns these apartments.'

'Oh, I didn't know.' Cassie was chastened. 'The last thing I want is to bring you trouble. What if I sell the bracelet and earrings and give you the money?'

'I'd still refuse, if you don't mind. It's very generous of you, and goodness knows the money would be useful. All the same, I would prefer to have nothing to do with it. I would feel much safer. Why not keep the money yourself?'

'Like you I'd prefer to have nothing to do with it, though for different reasons,' said Cassie wryly. 'Under no circumstances do I want that horrid creature thinking I'm obliged to him in any way. If you're sure you don't want the stuff I'll give it to some good cause.'

This proved to be surprisingly difficult. The description of the jewellery and its background must have spread through Bad Adler with astonishing speed and accuracy, because it was recognised wherever she offered it. Charity treasurers took one look and gave a regretful, 'No, thank you,' while the local jewellers practically hustled her out of their shops once they saw

what she had to offer. Such was the menace of
Pentransky's reputation that no one would even consider breaking the pieces and buying the gold and jewels
separately.

Disconsolately, Cassie put the leather case back into
her drawer until she could think of what to do with it.
Along with the disappointment of still owning the
hideous pieces came news that was just as depressing.
Franz came one evening expressly to tell her that the
Count had returned to Bad Adler.

All the next day and the day after she was tense and
watchful. When, by the third day, there was still no
sign of Pentransky, she allowed herself to relax a little,
but her vigilance was as sharp as ever. Meeting Count
Pentransky again was absolutely the worst thing that
could happen to her, she decided.

In fact, another event was to run this disaster a close
second. Dr Sommer's opinion of her report. The conflict it caused could be heard all over the Kurhaus.

'Advertise?' the doctor had bellowed at one item.
'You are proposing we advertise? Let me remind you
that this is a select spa, not a packet of backache pills. I
am not going to have the name of Bad Adler spread all
over the English Press.'

'Then how do you think the English are ever going
to hear of Bad Adler?' demanded Cassie, equally
angry.

'As they do now, by personal recommendation.'

'In that case I can see Bad Adler's having a good
name and no business!' she retorted. 'Now, to what
other items do you object? There's sure to be more. I
can see it in your face!'

'How right you are! I object to this!' Dr Sommer had
waved the sheet at her like a favour at a carnival. 'A
special price on the railway for visitors coming from
England? I've never heard the like!'

And so the argument had raged on. By the time the
last page of Cassie's report had been reached there was
not a single item upon which she and the doctor had

agreed. In the end she had ripped the report in two and stormed out of the office. Admittedly she had restrained herself from throwing the torn pages in Dr Sommer's face; nevertheless, she was not surprised when an hour later she was summoned back to his presence. To her surprise he did not mention the report. Instead, he indicated a flat, square package propped against his desk.

'This has just arrived for you, Fräulein Haydon,' he said, with exaggerated civility. 'Not knowing its contents, I thought it more prudent for you to open it here, sooner than downstairs in the pump-room. And if you could drop a hint to your friend Count Pentransky not to use this as a parcels' office I would be most grateful.'

At the name Pentranksy Cassie went cold. Would she never be free of the man? 'Is it from him?' she asked in alarm.

'Are you telling me you have more than one admirer who sends you gifts?'

Cassie ignored this remark, although it stung.

Then the sight of the postmark made her go limp with relief. 'It's from England!' she exclaimed. 'I'm surprised you didn't notice!'

'I've learned to be suspicious of all parcels left here for you,' he retorted.

'Oh, really, that remark was quite uncalled for——' she snapped. She would have said more, but he interrupted her.

'Yes, you are quite right,' he said quietly. 'I was abominably rude. I apologise.'

His swift change of attitude and the sudden softening of his expression overwhelmed Cassie with confusion, a very uncharacteristic emotion where she was concerned. She speedily turned her attention to the package, in order to hide her glowing cheeks.

'How kind!' she exclaimed, as she ripped off the wrapping-paper. 'How very kind!'

'What is it?' demanded the doctor, as a square of green-painted wood was revealed.

'It is a score-board for putting up the the results of the county cricket matches.'

'A what?'

'A score-board. It was sent by a sporting magazine, *Sporting Weekly*. See, it's got "Results supplied by the *Sporting Weekly*" in gold letters at the bottom. The magazine has agreed to provide us with the latest results of county cricket matches, test matches. Oh, and the varsity matches, too. And they will pay half of the telegraph bill, which I think is very reasonable of them.'

'Cricket?'

'Yes, a game not popular in Austria, I believe. . . Now there's an idea! We could start a cricket club——'

'No, we could not!' The doctor's words were emphatic. 'I am not having that piece of wood hung up anywhere in the Kurhaus.'

'Dr Sommer, let me explain,' she said, as if talking to a not too intelligent child. 'The thing the Englishman abroad misses most of all—even more than a decent cup of tea—is being able to keep up to date with the progress of his county cricket team. Now, in Bad Adler, he will know exactly how things stand with Surrey or Hampshire or wherever, so he will be perfectly happy and content.'

'No, he will not, because I am not having that thing here!'

'We could put it in the gentlemen's changing rooms?'

'No!'

'The gentlemen's lavatory?'

'*Definitely no!*'

Cassie's patience snapped.

'Why did you have me write out a report if you had no intention of taking of my suggestions seriously?' she demanded. 'Or are you turning them down simply because they *are* my suggestions?'

'Come back!' bellowed the doctor, as she headed indignantly for the door. With a superhuman effort he lowered his voice. 'Fräulein Haydon, yet again you have made me lose by temper.' Here he took a deep, calming breath. 'On one thing I am adamant. I am not having the walls of the Kurhaus decorated with cricket score-boards advertising vulgar sporting magazines. . . Not under any circumstances!' he added more loudly as Cassie opened her mouth to argue. He took another breath and moderated his voice yet again. 'Now, having considered your ideas for the gentlemen, surely you have some schemes for the ladies?'

'Yes, but you'll say they are vulgar and outlandish.'

She was still angry with him. His quiet tone was not going to soothe her ruffled feelings! She had worked very hard on this report, and he was rejecting everything out of hand.

'Tell me anyway.'

'I thought that one or two days a week the ladies' card assembly could be given over to bridge. It's a very popular game in England at the moment. Also, I've made some enquiries about ladies' magazines being made more readily available in Bad Adler, publications such as the *Lady, Ladies' Realm, Vogue*. This is all in my report, you know,' she added sharply.

'Yes, I do know!' His voice was rising again. 'I've read it most carefully. It was simply that I could not believe you wanted so little for your own sex. I was expecting something controversial, such as lectures on votes for women, or deep-sea diving for women, or blacksmithing for women.'

'What a good idea. . .' began Cassie, then she caught the rising fury in his face. Instead she said demurely, 'I think the bridge and the magazines will do for a start. English ladies are very easy to please.'

'Oh, no, they're not!' said Anton Sommer with a groan. 'I know from bitter experience they are awkward, difficult, opinionated and argumentative! In fact, if we ever succeed in making this spa popular with the English, it is my fervent hope the ladies will stay at home and only the gentlemen will come to Bad Adler.'

'In that case, *Herr Doktor*,' Cassie said angrily, 'you will definitely need the county cricket results!'

Once more she made to storm out, but his angry roar of, 'Don't do that!' brought her to a halt.

'Do what?' she asked in surprise.

'Flounce out like that! You do it every time, swirling your skirts and showing your ankles in that provocative way! Isn't it enough you make me lose my temper?'

'I do not flounce!' She was highly indignant. 'And as for being provocative! That, *Herr Doktor*, is nothing more than your masculine vanity! I have not the slightest——'

She got no further, for in one swift movement Anton Sommer had leapt to his feet. The next thing she knew, his hands were about her waist, lifting her, and his lips were crushing hers, dispelling her words, her breath, and every rational thought in her head in one fell swoop. She was so disconcerted that she made no attempt to fight him off. In fact, resistance was the last thing which entered her mind. Her fingers closed instinctively over the lapels of his morning coat, drawing him ever closer instead of repulsing him.

When at last he set her on her feet again, he took a step back, his face flushed.

'That's one way of stopping you from arguing,' he said, breathing hard. 'Now get out!'

Such was Cassie's confused state of mind, so great was her degree of bewilderment at what had happened, that she went—without saying another word!

CHAPTER SIX

ANTON SOMMER'S extraordinary behaviour had an unsettling effect upon Cassie. It was as if her view of life, normally so precise and clear-cut, had unaccountably wavered. She tried to persuade herself that her opinion of the man had not altered one jot, she still found him intensely aggravating and far too proud and haughty by half, yet constantly she found she was watching out across the crowded pump-room for the sight of his familiar upright figure or a glimpse of his dark head.

It was early morning in the Kurhaus when she encountered him again. The commissionaire had not yet opened the huge oak doors to the public, yet the pump-room was far from quiet. The cleaners were laughing and joking as they gave the leather banquettes a final polish, the under-gardener was whistling cheerily as he watered the potted palms, and a steady clanking came from the pump itself as two women filled stoneware jugs with health-giving Bad Adler water, ready to dispense it to the visitors. Above all this noise Cassie knew that Dr Sommer was approaching. Despite the racket she recognised his tread—firm and decisive—coming in her direction.

He greeted her with his usual, 'Is everything ready, Fräulein Haydon?' without a hint of embarrassment.

'Yes—yes, Herr Doktor. I–I think so. . .'

It was she who stammered and was ill at ease. He nodded curtly and walked away without another word. As she watched him go she reflected that he had not even offered her an apology. What was worse, she had made no attempt to demand one. On previous occasions when a man had kissed her against her will she had registered her disapproval. Her methods had varied from sharp words to an even sharper hat-pin, but at least her emotions had been consistent. With Anton Sommer there had been no such consistency. Instead, she had been able to pick out his footsteps from among all the others. This unlooked-for ability seemed to have some underlying significance and it bothered her. She closed her eyes and tried recognising other people's movements, but failed abysmally. Even Frau Willendorf's heavy plod did not register. Only Anton Sommer's. She did not like it.

'Fräulein Haydon, this is no time to sleep! In one minute exactly the doors will open, and you still have not seen to the post!' Frau Arlberg's voice caused Cassie's eyes to fly open. She had failed to recognise her approaching steps, too.

Her gaze went down to the pile of letters in front of her. The envelopes all bore English stamps and postmarks and not one of them was open.

'I'll attend to them at once,' she said.

'You will stay at your desk,' boomed Frau Arlberg. 'Can't you see the doors are opening and the visitors are coming in? No, you must deal with the letters in your spare time—if you get any spare time!'

The other woman's evident triumph did nothing to restore Cassie's ruffled peace of mind. This was the first time her efficiency had been found wanting. It was very upsetting.

In the days which followed it was quite extraordinary how aware of Dr Sommer's presence she became; she did not want to observe him, of course, but she did not seem able to help herself. It was as though her senses were drawn to him like a pin to a magnet. She could not raise her head without seeing him in her line of vision, and almost always Anna Arlberg was hovering somewhere in the vicinity. They were always together, far more than was necessary for their business relationship.

If they're having an affair they are welcome to each other as far as I am concerned, Cassie told herself. She

had just been watching the pair of them walking across
the Kurhaus garden, deep in conversation. For some
reason the sight of them shortened her temper. The
scandalmongers had been quick enough to tear *her*
reputation to shreds; why had they nothing to say about
the doctor and Frau Arlberg? Irritably she turned back
to her letters, refusing to let her attention stray any
more.

The pump-room was closed now and the visitors all
gone, but still she worked on. Recently she had felt
that her own rigid standards of efficiency were slipping,
and she was determined to rectify matters. Above the
clatter of her typewriter she heard footsteps that were
all too familiar.

Dr Sommer entered the tiny office. 'You are working
late, Fräulein Haydon.'

'I have some letters to finish. I want to get them in
tonight's post,' she said. Surreptitiously she looked past
him for some sign of Anna Arlberg. There was none.
He must have parted from her in the garden.

'Are you so overworked that you need to stay so
late?'

'No, *Herr Doktor*,' she replied swiftly.

'There's no need to sound so defensive. I was not
suggesting that the work was beyond you. If you've too
much to cope with then you must say so and we will see
what can be done about extra clerical help.'

She looked at him warily, not able to believe the
amiable note in his voice.

'I can manage competently without any help, thank
you, *Herr Doktor*,' she replied.

'And wild horses wouldn't get you to admit it even if
you couldn't, eh?' He spoke lightly, in a gentler tone
than Cassie had heard for some time.

She was not sure how to reply.

'We've had quite a lot of queries from England this
week; it has taken me some time to find answers to
them all,' she said, by way of explanation.

'You don't have to account for your presence here in detail. I accept that you are conscientious.'

Was she mistaken—was there approval in his tone?

'Have I actually done something right, *Herr Doktor*?' she asked.

'You sound surprised. Maybe you have good reason.' He paused, as if choosing his words carefully. 'You said something to me a few days ago which has lingered in my thoughts. When I was commenting on your report, somewhat adversely, as I recall, you accused me of turning down your suggestions simply because you had made them. At the time I was convinced I had not been so unjust. After a while, however, I began to reconsider, and now I confess that I may not have been quite fair. In fact, I have re-read your report, torn though it was, more carefully and am willing to admit that some of your ideas have possibilities. . . Not the advertising, though!' he said quickly as she showed signs of interrupting. 'And certainly not having a cricket score-board hanging on the wall! But some of the others are worth further study.'

Cassie had never expected such magnanimity.

'May I ask which of my suggestions you approve of?'

'Certainly the one about having bridge at the ladies' card assembly. In fact, it should be brought into being quite soon. I've just been talking to Frau Arlberg about it, since I, as a mere male, am not allowed to set foot in the ladies' salon. Really, I don't know why your sex wants the vote. Put a pack of cards in your hand, a coffee-pot by your side, and it would appear you rule the world. You even exclude me from one of the rooms in the Kurhaus!'

He was teasing her! She listened, bemused at the bantering tone in his voice. He had a point, of course. The nightly ladies' card assemblies were strictly all female, and heaven help the man who tried to enter, upon whatever pretext.

'Why should any male want to enter the ladies' salon?' Cassie replied in kind. 'There are plenty of other places where men can play cards. The only advantage would be the certainty of keeping up with current scandal.'

'Ah, yes, scandal!' He suddenly became serious. 'There's never any shortage of that in Bad Adler. I'm afraid it is the cause of much needless trouble and distress.'

He did not look at her as he spoke. The omission was so pointed that Cassie wondered if he was referring to her own case. Was it possible he had begun to doubt the gossip linking her with Pentransky? Before she could question him he spoke again.

'But I digress,' he said briskly. 'To go back to the game of bridge, Frau Arlberg is enthusiastic about it and says she will see it is introduced as soon as possible.'

It was a good thing Cassie had not got too excited at the prospect of one of her plans coming to fruition. With Frau Arlberg in charge she doubted if she would see bridge being played at the ladies' card assemblies within her lifetime.

'And is that the only one of my ideas to have your approval?' she asked.

'No. The special railway fare for people coming from England to Bad Adler seems to have great possibilities. I think we should go further. Why not have one price to include railway fare and subscriptions to various facilities at the Kurhaus, say entry to the pump-room, the card assemblies and certain concerts?'

Cassie could not believe it. He actually sounded enthusiastic.

'I presume the railway fare would be first-class?' she said.

'Of course.' He grinned mischievously. 'I have no wish to encourage third-class visitors to the spa, even if they are English! Naturally there will be much careful costing to be done before I can give my approval, but I intend to consider the matter. Now, *fräulein*, I think you have worked late enough. It is time you went home.'

'I haven't finished. . .'

'At the risk of making you lose your temper, Fräulein Haydon, I say you have finished!' Gently but firmly he picked up the typewriter cover and placed it over the machine. 'Now for once do as you are told without argument and go home!'

Cassie smiled. 'It seems I have no option but to obey,' she said.

'Exactly. . .! At last, I have gained a little obedience from you!' He spoke with a mock severity which was almost a parody of his formal self. He went on more softly, 'We cannot have you overworking. If you keep on at this rate you will make yourself ill. And then where would we be?'

It was as well he did not appear to require an answer, for Cassie's concentration was all at once in sad disarray. It had suddenly become apparent to her that they were very much alone in the small office; no outside sounds penetrated the silence. They might have been the only two beings on earth at that moment. Other things began to fill her consciousness—the fresh, clean scent of his cologne, the line of his mouth, not hard and stern as she had once thought it, but generous, with corners ready to tilt with humour. This preoccupation with Anton's mouth brought with it disturbing recollections; the memories of his lips on hers made colour flood into her cheeks.

Similar thoughts must have been passing through Anton's head, for he seemed at a loss for words. . . Then he gave an abrupt cough, as if determined to break the silence which had settled upon them.

'Home!' he said decisively. 'Off you go.' He opened the door for her.

'Thank you, *Herr Doktor*. . .' She could not think of an excuse to delay any longer. 'Good night.'

'Good night, Ca—— Fräulein Haydon.'

No, she had not imagined it—he had almost used her Christian name again! Only once before had that happened—after her encounter with the cows. As she made her way back to Elizabethplatz she was conscious of feeling happier than she had been for a long time. She did not try to fool herself that this was because her report was being appreciated at last. Her high spirits were entirely due to Anton's approval. He was beginning to believe in her. More than that, he was beginning to like her, she was convinced of it. . . And her opinion of him? For some reason that was something she tried hard not to think about.

Fortunately Cassie had no expectation that Frau Arlberg's opinion of her would change too; such hopes would have been doomed to a remarkably brief life.

The morning began as usual for Cassie with people waiting at her desk. Over the weeks it had become quite noticeable how much longer the queue was for her attention compared with that for Frau Willendorf's. Equally noticeable was the high proportion of men eager for a moment of her time, and not only Englishmen, either. Even races not noted for their ability to queue stood patiently in line for the opportunity of gazing into the azure-blue eyes of the little English *fräulein*.

On this particular morning the crowd waiting for Cassie must have been more remarkable than usual. Maybe it had something to do with the high content of colourful military uniforms. Whatever the cause, Frau Arlberg's attention was attracted. Within seconds she was behind the desk and bustling Cassie to a spot beyond the earshot of the waiting visitors.

'What is the meaning of this?' she hissed like a tea-kettle.

'Of what?' Cassie refused to be intimidated.

'Of this! I demand an explanation!' Frau Arlberg flung out her arm to encompass the small crowd at the other side of the desk.

'An explanation? Surely it is obvious enough. Frau Willendorf is dealing with the queries of one very deaf old lady, while I will, in time, deal with the queries of

. . .let me see. . .three ladies, one small boy, and eleven gentlemen.'

'And what sort of gentlemen?' demanded Anna Arlberg.

'What sort. . .? Well, I can see three gentlemen in civilian dress, one who looks like a clergyman, two hussars, a cavalry officer——'

'Their nationalities, Fräulein Haydon! What are their nationalities?' In her indignation, Frau Arlberg's voice was beginning to rise. 'There are Austrians waiting to see you, and Hungarians, and Germans, even a Frenchman! Fräulein Haydon, you are to restrict yourself to Englishmen only!' At this point her voice rose to such a pitch that her final sentence was audible over half the pump-room. Heads began to turn.

Above the interested hum of voices, footsteps rang out across the marble floor, clear and decisive.

'Is anything wrong?' asked Anton Sommer in a voice tinged with disapproval.

Anna Arlberg gave a visible start. She had not noticed him approaching.

'Oh, thank goodness you have come, *Herr Doktor*!' she said. 'I have been reprimanding Fräulein Haydon; her conduct has been most reprehensible.'

'And what has the *fräulein* done which merits such a commotion?'

'Surely it's obvious, *Herr Doktor*? You have just to look at the crowd waiting for her.'

The doctor regarded the lengthy queue at Cassie's section of desk, then the solitary old lady who was still at Frau Willendorf's.

'Fräulein Haydon would indeed seem to have a lot of people waiting for her attention,' he said.

'And most of them men, with scarcely an Englishman among them!' Frau Arlberg was indignant.

'Are you suggesting she is unfairly luring other nationalities to her section of desk?'

'No, of course not, *Herr Doktor*. But her duties are to attend to the English. That is why she is here!'

'Quite so, but how do you suggest that we deter other nationalities from seeking her help? Should we forbid her to speak to any nationality other than her own? Should we perhaps hang an "English Only" notice round her neck?'

'No, *Herr Doktor*, that would be ludicrous.' At the growing sarcasm in Anton Sommer's tone, Frau Arlberg was sounding more unsure of herself. Clearly she had expected him to support her in reproaching Cassie. She was quite taken aback when he did not.

'Indeed it would be ludicrous!' The doctor now sounded not only sarcastic but annoyed. 'Frau Arlberg, surely you are woman of the world enough to realise any man with eyes in his head would seek out Fräulein Haydon in preference to Frau Willendorf, even if all he required was a ticket on a river steamer? To have disturbed our visitors by making such an unnecessary uproar is not the conduct I expect from you! Now I suggest we leave the Fräulein Haydon to get on with her work. Goodness knows, she's got enough of it!'

Anna Arlberg was so stunned by this unexpected rebuke that she could only gasp. Anyone else would have turned crimson with mortification; she merely flushed the palest of pink.

'As you say, *Herr Doktor*,' she said at last, through gritted teeth, and stormed away.

Anton Sommer watched her go without further comment, then he bowed politely to Cassie and left also.

Cassie was nearly as astonished by the doctor's reaction as Frau Arlberg had been. To begin with, he had taken her part against the Ice Dragon for the first time ever. Also, if her ears had not deceived her, he had actually paid her a compliment. True, it was not much of one. To have one's looks compared favourably to those of Frau Willendorf fell short of lavish praise; all the same, it was another 'first'.

It was foolish to let a few trivial words of near-praise affect her, yet she could not help it. No matter how she tried, she could not rid herself of the feeling that something exceedingly pleasant had happened to her. And why? Because Dr Sommer had implied she was prettier than Frau Willendorf! It was idiotic! Nevertheless, she could not prevent a happy smile spreading over her face, tilting the corners of her generous mouth, and making her eyes glow like incandescent sapphires. The result was so devastating that several Hungarian officers, having already queued to ask her one lot of trivial questions, immediately dashed to the end of the line for a second turn.

Finally, the last visitor departed for the day, leaving the pump-room to the cleaners. Cassie, too, stayed on. As Dr Sommer had remarked, she had collected plenty of work, and now was a good time to catch up. There was no risk of interruption on this occasion, for she had seen the doctor leave for home unusually promptly. The happiness of her day seemed to spread into her toil; her fingers sped over the typewriter keys without a hitch, as letter after letter was completed. Eventually there was a very satisfactory pile of envelopes waiting for the post, and no enquiries left in her 'in' tray. Cassie put on her hat, picked up the envelopes and left the Kurhaus.

It was a glorious summer evening, perfectly in keeping with her mood. So much so that, after she had visited the post office, Cassie did not feel like returning immediately to Elizabethplatz. Instead she headed for the esplanade. The day had been hot and stifling, and now a walk beside the river was refreshing. The esplanade was a popular place, especially on such an evening. Cassie enjoyed being among so many smartly dressed people, happily promenading among the flower-beds. At the little pavilion, where the gas-lamps were already lit and diffusing a soft golden glow, folk were enjoying coffee and cakes. A group of musicians played Strauss waltzes and modern songs from operettas, seemingly oblivious to the fading light. It was all so delightful and perfect. Yes, she had certainly been right to come to Austria.

It was getting late, though, and she had had a long

day. Leisurely she turned her steps towards
Elizabethplatz. Her way took her past Bad Adler's
ornate theatre, and she noticed a small crowd outside.

'Is something special on tonight?' she asked a flower-
seller, who was waiting to cross the road, a basket
packed with blooms on her arm.

'It's the charity gala, *fräulein*, haven't you heard?
Everyone who's anyone will be there. And the
dresses. . .!' The woman raised her eyebrows appreciatively, then she grinned. 'There's something about a
charity performance which puts folk in a spending
mood. This is my second basket-load already and the
curtain doesn't go up for another half-hour. I've sold
every gardenia I could lay my hands on. And as for
Parma violets, well. . .'

Cassie never did find out what had happened to the
Parma violets; the flower-seller saw a gap in the traffic
and dashed across the road almost under the hoofs of
the oncoming cab-horses. Cassie followed at a slower,
more prudent pace, and joined the crowd of onlookers.
It was almost as good as a play itself, watching the
carriages draw up and disgorge their well-dressed passengers. She had never seen such wonderful gowns or
such jewels.

As she watched, a fiaker drove up, drawn by a sturdy
chestnut horse. The theatre doorman stepped forward,
opened the door and then stood aside, respectfully
touching his hat as a man alighted, a man in perfectly
tailored evening dress. Cassie froze with recognition.
Anton Sommer turned to help his companion down.
For once Anna Arlberg was not wearing her eternal
black taffeta. Instead she wore heavy white silk crêpe,
cunningly draped to show off her statuesque figure to
advantage. Her only ornament was a brilliant clip in
her immaculate golden hair, holding a single white
plume. She needed nothing more. With her plain,
almost severe gown perfectly complementing her classical beauty, she made the elaborate fashionable dresses
about her look over-fussy.

Cassie did not feel over-fussy. In her blue uniform skirt and her white cambric blouse, now limp and crumpled after a day's wear, she simply felt terribly dowdy. The sun seemed to have set abruptly; its light had gone from the sky and its warmth from the air. Frau Arlberg looked up and smiled possessively at Dr Sommer, then put one white-gloved hand on his arm. For Cassie the night grew a little colder, a little darker. As they walked together up the steps to the theatre she turned away.

She was angry! Angry with Anna Arlberg for claiming the doctor as her own quite so blatantly. And she was angry at herself for caring! Yes, most of all she was angry with herself! For falling in love with Anton Sommer! Because she was in love with him! She had tried, but it would not be denied. The misery she was feeling at that moment was proof of her stupidity. How could she have done such a thing? Her life was carefully mapped out! There was no room in it for love! How had it happened?

She could not remember when she had started to love him. Her love had been in full flower before she had been aware of it.

She was not even sure why she was in love with him. Arrogance, haughtiness, an overbearing attitude—all of the male characteristics she liked least he had in plenty. Yet, when she tried to dwell on them, to persuade herself that she could not possibly care for him, all she could think of was the glow of laughter in his hazel eyes, or the sharp attractive curve of his high cheekbones.

It was hopeless. She knew she could no more stop loving him than she could stop breathing.

It was such a useless emotion! No matter how much she loved him she knew there was no chance of his ever returning her affection. Recently she had thought he was softening towards her. But she had been wrong. The sight of him with Anna Arlberg tonight had proved it!

All at once she felt exhausted and totally disconsolate. She trudged back to Elizabethplatz.

Trudi grew anxious when she said she did not want any supper.

'You're too tired to eat, that's what's wrong with you,' she scolded fondly. 'All this extra work; it's not good enough. No wonder you're too worn out to hold a knife and fork. You can't work all hours with nothing inside you.'

Cassie gave in and agreed to have some supper. Perhaps Trudi was right—her despondency was nothing more than hunger. But the nourishing meal did nothing to lessen the knot of leaden misery which had settled round her heart. Sleep did not drive it away, either. When she awoke next morning it was still there, as heavy and dispiriting as ever.

A glance in her mirror before setting out had told her that her face was pale and that dark shadows encircled her eyes. She tried pinching her cheeks to bring colour into them, but the improvement was only temporary.

She did her best to absorb herself in her work, but it was very difficult. Even harder was trying to ignore Anton Sommer as he moved about the pump-room. As usual her gaze seemed drawn to him. She would turn away, yet her eyes would return to him as if of their own volition. Particularly when he was with Anna Arlberg! Oh, how it hurt to see those two figures standing close together. They made a fine-looking couple! Cassie had to admit it, though the thought twisted in her like a knife.

Grimly she bent her head over the railway timetable in front of her. Grappling with times of arrival and departure and working out convenient connections was just the sort of mental activity she needed. It would give her no time for thoughts of Anton Sommer. Even as the notion crossed her mind she became aware that he was coming towards her. Stubbornly she gave her attention more fiercely to her work, determined she would not acknowledge his presence. He reached the desk and stood there for some time, yet still she refused to look at him.

Eventually he remarked, 'You seem very absorbed. What are you doing?' She had no choice but to look him in the face.

'Mr and Mrs Blake wish to go to Berlin on Saturday. I am finding out the best route and convenient train times for them, *Herr Doktor*,' she said.

'I'm sure their journey will go smoothly with you arranging it for them.'

She replied, 'I do my best, *Herr Doktor*,' expecting him to walk away. Instead, he stayed, looking at her in a way which was disconcerting.

'Fräulein Haydon,' he said, 'forgive me for asking, but are you feeling well?'

'Perfectly well, thank you. Why do you ask?'

'Simply because you seem rather quiet this morning.'

'I'm in excellent health, thank you,' she retorted, determined not to betray any hint of the upheaval inside her.

'Then perhaps it is the weather that is making you look a little pale. It has turned decidedly sultry; I think we'll have a storm before nightfall. I trust the prospect of thunder and lightning doesn't worry you?'

'Not at all!'

'I didn't think it would, somehow. Only one thing bothers our intrepid English miss—the savage cow with its fearsome horns.' And he smiled.

That smile nearly overset her! It was warm and mischievous, hinting strongly at another more light-hearted Anton Sommer, and causing her heart to behave most erratically.

'Will you never let me forget it?' she demanded hotly, masking her emotions with anger.

It were as if a shutter had closed on his face, blocking out the teasing laughter, leaving only the stern haughtiness she knew all too well.

'Yes, you are quite right. I should not have referred to the incident. I apologise,' he said.

She had been so tense in his presence, struggling so hard not to show her feelings that it was only after he had moved away that she really considered what he had said. He had noticed she was looking pale, and been kind enough to ask if she was feeling unwell. Surely that meant he had some concern for her? And his teasing banter about cows. . . He did not usually unbend enough to joke with staff on duty. She had never heard him laughing with Frau Willendorf, for example. Or with Frau Arlberg, for that matter. He had singled her out, been considerate and humorous towards her. It had to mean something. How she regretted her sharp reply now, but it was too late. Much too late! Already he was talking to Anna Arlberg. As she watched, they walked off together, not exactly arm in arm, but close. Very close!

At this point Cassie grew really furious with herself. What on earth was she doing mooning hopelessly after the doctor? She had all her life before her; she did not want it cluttered up with unnecessary love-affairs. She was a New Woman, and New Women did not need love! They needed independence! Anna Arlberg was welcome to her precious *Herr Doktor*. Cassie decided she preferred freedom!

Such stirring thoughts rejuvenated the spring in her step and put a fresh determination in her manner so successfully that during the next few days she was able to forget she loved Anton Sommer for whole minutes at a time.

'Fräulein Haydon, your help is requested in the treatment baths.' One of the spa valets stood respectfully at the desk.

'Very well, I'll come directly, as soon as I have attended to the ladies and gentlemen who are waiting.'

'Your pardon, *fräulein*, but I understand the matter is urgent.'

'Oh, what's wrong?'

'I don't know, *fräulein*; I was simply told to fetch the English *fräulein* immediately.'

It was not unknown for Cassie's services as an interpreter to be required for patients receiving treatment.

'In that case I'll come at once. It does sound to be an emergency. Maybe one of the English visitors has been taken ill.' She turned to the waiting queue. 'I'm sorry to leave you, but I am urgently required elsewhere. I've no idea how long I will be, but I am sure Frau Willendorf will attend to your enquiries most efficiently.'

The effect of her words was to make the line of people melt away like snow in the Sahara. Cassie barely noticed, however, for she was hurrying after the valet. To her surprise he led her not to the grand bath, but downstairs to the subterranean chambers below.

'I was instructed to request you to go to room four, *fräulein*,' said the valet.

'Aren't you coming too?' Cassie asked in surprise, for the valet was showing every sign of returning rapidly the way they had come.

'I regret, *fräulein*. . .' he began, then seemed to forget what he regretted. At any rate, the last Cassie saw of him he was hurrying back up the stairs.

Mystified, Cassie walked along the gloomy corridor, looking for room four. Everything was remarkably silent. When she rapped on the door the sound echoed round the tiled walls.

'Hello,' she called. 'I'm Fräulein Haydon. You sent for me.'

There was no answer. She pushed at the door. It swung open and she took a step inside the room. At once she was enveloped in a sickly scent of funeral lilies, as the door slammed shut and a pair of clammy hands were clapped over her eyes.

'Guess who?' said an unpleasantly familiar voice.

She cursed herself. Yet again she had been caught off her guard. Would she never learn?

'Guess who?' repeated Pentransky, rather impatiently.

'Good day, Count Pentransky,' she said wearily.

'You guessed!' He sounded peeved, but he did take his hands away from her eyes, only to slide them tightly about her waist.

The sight of Pentransky did nothing to calm Cassie's taut nerves. He was clad in the usual manner of a gentleman undergoing treatment at the spa—a dressing-gown over striped bathing-drawers—a state of undress too compromising for her comfort.

'Please let go of me, Count.' She tried unsuccessfully to push his hands away.

'Let go of you? Why should I do that? And you're not to call me Count, you must call me Bobo. Had you forgotten that you're my little English bird?'

How she mistrusted him when he was in this infantile mood; there was something beneath the baby talk that made her flesh creep. For a moment she wondered if she should play up to him, then decided firmly against it. That ploy had been effective enough in the short term, getting her temporarily out of Pentransky's clutches; in the long term, however, it had proved a failure. Instead of discouraging him, her actions seemed to have inflamed his interest.

'Count Pentransky,' she said, speaking firmly. 'This nonsense has got to stop. I have no wish to be your little English bird or to call you by any silly pet name. In fact, I want you to stop pursuing me in this fashion.'

The fingers grasping her waist tightened painfully.

'You don't mean that.' His tone was no longer childish.

'I do! To put it bluntly, I am not interested in being your companion, your mistress, or anything else you may have in mind. I want you to leave me alone.'

The fingers tightened more, making her gasp.

'How quickly you've forgotten what you owe me. I'm not a man who forgets his debtors,' he said with menacing softness.

'I've tried time and again to return your jewellery!' she protested.

'So you have! But what of your post at the Kurhaus, eh? Have you forgotten what you owe me for that?'

'I owe you my thanks, and nothing more! But if that is the only reason why you keep hounding me, then I'll give in my notice immediately!'

'It will do you no good, little English bird. I will make sure it is not accepted.' The threat in his voice was growing by the minute, causing her fear to grow. How to get out of this lonely room and back among the crowds? That was Cassie's principal thought. In the distance she could hear voices echoing faintly from the direction of the dressing-rooms, but it was not worth screaming. She doubted if anyone would hear her, or come to her aid if they did. Pentransky's hands were moving on her rib-cage, so that his thumbs were beginning to caress her breasts.

'Of course!' he cried unexpectedly. 'I know why you're in a bad mood! Why didn't I think of it before? It's because you imagine I've been neglecting you lately.'

'Count, your neglect is the one thing I pray for,' she said fervently.

He gave a silly, boyish laugh.

'Oh, you are cross,' he pouted. 'And all because I've not been to see you much of late. But you don't need to worry, it wasn't because I don't like you any more. It was because I had an accident. My horse threw me and I hurt my foot. It's not better yet. Look.' He stretched out one slippered foot, and sure enough it was heavily strapped.

Cassie decided the horse deserved a medal.

'I had the stupid beast shot, of course,' said Pentransky, as though he could read her mind.

She gave a shudder. 'What does it take to make you understand?' she cried. 'I don't like you! I never have and I never will! Now, let me go!' She began beating at his chest with her fists, but his reaction was to leer down at her.

'This is good fun!' he said, beginning to breathe

heavily. 'I like it when you're cross. We're going to have some good games now.'

'No, we're not!' retorted Cassie, bitterly regretting her momentary lack of control; it had made her situation even more perilous. 'You're going to let me go immediately.'

'All right,' he said, unexpectedly, and he grasped her more tightly to him.

Being clutched close to the Count's scantily clad body was not an experience Cassie relished. His next words sent a dread fear running through her.

'We're all alone here, you know,' he breathed, his flabby mouth against her neck. 'I've booked every one of the treatment rooms. . .we won't be disturbed. . . not even any servants. . . Just you and me. . .'

'Just you and me?' Her mouth went uncomfortably dry.

'Yes, I'm going to let you go. . .but only so I can catch you again!' He expressed an uncomfortable amount of lechery in that one phrase. 'You must run and hide, then I'll come looking.'

'How—how many are you going to count up to?'

'Ah, that's for me to know and you to find out!'

Cassie knew he had no intention of letting her get far, but somehow she had to get back upstairs and into the crowded pump-room—but how? In desperation she attacked, stamping hard on the Count's bandaged foot. His scream of agony was genuine enough—not that she waited for the results of her action. She pulled away from him and fled along the damp corridor as fast as she could. As she ran she tried to remember the layout of these treatment rooms. All too soon she heard his footsteps echoing after her. True, they were limping footsteps, but they carried with them a terrible menace. She dived into the nearest treatment room.

Her hiding-place behind the door was totally inadequate. She stood there, her heart pounding as he came closer. She would have to think of something—but what? Then she saw the brass tap. It was her only chance. Tiptoeing swiftly across the floor, she went across and stood in front of it, her back to the wall.

Pentransky flung open the door and a licentious grin spread over his face.

'Ah, I've found you,' he purred. 'Now the fun will really begin!' He stepped across the room towards her, already shedding his dressing-gown en route. It was then that Cassie turned on the tap with all her strength. It was no ordinary tap; it controlled the descending cold water douche. As its name implied, it shot a powerful cascade of icy water down on Pentransky so forcibly that it sent him gasping to his knees. She picked her moment, then ran. Such was the shock suffered by the Count that he was incapable of reaching out to grab at her skirts. It was not a situation destined to last long, though. He would recover and be after her. She shot up the stairs and into the corridor leading to the pump-room, but even here she did not feel safe. The service door at the top of the stairs gave her an idea. It was the attendants' room. Taking a deep breath, she entered without knocking and gazed round sternly.

'Who is responsible for administering the wet sheet treatment today!' she demanded.

'We are *fräulein*.' Two men rose.

'Then why are you not attending to your patient?'

'We didn't know we had any appointments this afternoon, *fräulein*, truly we didn't.'

'Well, you have, so you'd better go and see to him immediately. He's in the descending douche room; he may even be hiding from you. I think he's having second thoughts about the treatment.'

'You'll be surprised how many do, *fräulein*.' One of the men was swiftly gathering sheets from a cupboard as he spoke. 'Some of them even swear they aren't for the treatment at all, they've just got lost on the way from the dressing-rooms.'

'Well, don't believe any such stories from this gentle-man. He needs the treatment for his gout; you'll see his right foot is heavily bandaged.'

'We won't be taken in, *fräulein*, never fear.' The second man grinned. 'We're used to it. We'll have him wound up in nice wet sheets, unable to move a finger, before he knows we're there.'

In spite of feeling limp with relief, Cassie could not hold back a chuckle as the men hurried off. The thought of Pentransky wrapped as tightly as an Egyptian mummy was very pleasing; she only wished she could see him lying there immobile and helpless. Not that she was foolish enough to return downstairs. She decided to make herself scarce in the one place where she would be safe from the Count—the ladies' card assembly. Frau Arlberg would be presiding. This gave Cassie another idea. It was high time her suggestion of introducing bridge on the programme was put in motion. She would tackle the Ice Dragon about it now, while the light of battle was still in her eyes!

CHAPTER SEVEN

'THERE is a rumour concerning Pentransky going about town,' stated Sir George next morning. 'As far as I can gather, the story is that he was locked in one of the spa treatment rooms for several hours. One version of the tale says he had an assignation with a young woman down there, only things did not go as planned.'

'Goodness!' said Cassie, opening her eyes wide.

'Don't try that innocent look on me, miss,' Sir George grinned. 'I know only one young lady in this vicinity with enough spirit to get the better of that rogue.' He leaned forward confidentially. 'Come on, my dear, tell me the details before curiosity brings my grey hairs to the grave.'

'Very well, Sir George,' she agreed. 'But this is for your ears only, and Markham's too, of course. As usual, the gossip is inaccurate. There was no assignation. I went to the treatment rooms thinking I was needed as an interpreter; I had no idea it was one of the Count's nasty tricks. . . '

Cassie went on to relate all that had happened.

Sir George listened with growing astonishment and delight.

'The wet sheet treatment, you say?' he chortled, when she had finished. 'Pentransky was swathed in wet sheets, unable to move a finger? What wouldn't I have given to have seen such a sight! It's priceless, it truly is!'

The old gentleman was laughing so hard that he was obliged to mop his eyes, and even the lines on Markham's dour face rearranged themselves—the nearest thing to a smile the manservant could manage.

'There!' gasped Sir George breathlessly. 'The moment I clapped eyes on you, my dear, I knew you'd brighten things up. But, by Harry, I never expected anything as good as this! To think of him done up like a suet pudding! It's the best thing I've heard in years.' He was still chuckling as Markham trundled him away towards his own treatment.

Seeing him so amused made Cassie relax and smile too. She had to admit to herself that, ever since the incident, she had felt tense and ill at ease. Undoubtedly the Count would be in a vile temper over the affair. She was not sure which was worse—being his enemy or being his object of desire. Either way, she was going to have to be extra vigilant. Sir George's mirth and evident admiration had served to bolster her self-confidence. What if she did have to be more wary of the Count? She had already outwitted him several times. What she had done once she could do again.

Buoyed up by this optimism, she worked on happily. All the same, she kept a wary eye open in case Pentransky made an appearance. By the time her day's work was over there was still no sign of him. Determined not to let her vigilance waver, she scrutinised the gardens carefully before leaving the Kurhaus.

Early evening was usually a quiet time at the spa; the gravel walks and smooth lawns were almost deserted. Only one other person was in sight, approaching her with long, athletic strides.

Anton Sommer had been in Salzburg for two days, and now, as she saw him coming towards her, she realised how much she had missed him. She tried hard to school her heart not to lift at the sight of him, without success. To her chagrin she felt the colour rise in her cheeks. Of all the foolish, schoolgirlish things to happen, when she was telling herself so sternly that she must stop loving him! At his approach, illogically she experienced hope and happiness and a whole tangle of other emotions she could hardly identify.

As he drew closer, however, all these pleasant sensations subsided. She knew no other man who could register anger so emphatically without saying a word.

The tilt of his head, the set of his shoulders, even the angle of his back betrayed wrath. He came to a halt in front of her, his hazel eyes smouldering and cloudy with vexation. She wished she could detect just the slightest hint of humour in them, or some suspicion of warmth towards her, but there was none.

'Fräulein Haydon, you are exactly the person I wish to see,' he greeted her, his voice terse. 'No, that is not quite accurate. I have no wish to see you. Unfortunately it is a sad necessity, a disagreeable duty from which I wish I could free myself.'

'What have I done wrong now?' she asked with resignation, trying not to wince at his tone.

'You need to ask? Would it jog your memory if I mentioned an incident in the spa treatment rooms while I was away, involving a member of the Austrian aristocracy?'

'Oh, Count Pentransky.'

'Yes, Count Pentransky! I am relieved that you remember. I do not fancy having to relate the whole sordid affair in order to restore your memory.'

'It is not something I could easily forget. However, I fail to see why you should be angry with me.'

'You don't, eh?' He took a sudden step towards her, and when he spoke again his voice was low with fury. 'Then let me explain! I am perfectly aware that, at some spas, certain areas such as the dressing-rooms and treatment chambers are regarded as convenient rendez-vous for clandestine meetings and all sorts of immoral activities. Such things happen—but not at Bad Adler! I will not have the Kurhaus turned into a place of ill repute, not while I'm in charge. Do I make myself clear? If you attempt such a thing again I will run the pair of you off the premises, no matter what the cost to myself!'

His words hit her like blows, making her speechless.

'You've got it all wrong!' she protested at last.

'Have I? Do you deny that you were in the treatment

rooms alone with Count Pentransky? Completely alone?'

'No, of course not, but——'

'And are you denying you were there for purposes that, for want of a more delicate word, I can only call amorous?'

'The Count was. I certainly wasn't!'

'Are you saying you were carried, protesting, down to the treatment rooms? My informant says you went willingly enough.'

'Then I suggest you tell your informant to find out the truth before he or she comes running to you with tales. Upon consideration I think the little bird who whispered in your ear was most likely female. I am sure Frau Arlberg was only too delighted to pass on every juicy detail.'

'This matter does not concern Frau Arlberg!' His reply was so sharp that she knew her guess had hit its mark.

'It does if she has deliberately distorted the facts. For instance, I don't suppose she mentioned how Count Pentransky tricked me into going down there, did she? I was told I was needed. I thought someone required an interpreter. Do you think I would have gone if I'd known he was lurking there?'

'And you were not suspicious when you found the place deserted? You had no inkling that it was your friend, the Count, who had hired the entire suite of treatment rooms? I find it hard to believe. Other people seemed aware of the fact.'

'By other people you mean Frau Arlberg, I suppose!' cried Cassie angrily. 'I can't help what she told you! I did not know he was there!'

'A likely story! I was back from Salzburg for scarcely an hour before I was besieged on all sides by people eager to tell me what had happened.'

'And every account pure fiction, by the sound of it,' Cassie retorted. 'I suggest you vent your anger on Frau Arlberg instead of me. She was the one who approved the booking. Surely it must have aroused her suspicions?'

'Don't try to shift the blame on to my assistant!' he snapped. 'You were the one involved in playing lecherous games down there.'

'Lecherous games?' hooted Cassie. 'How much lechery do you think the Count could indulge in bound tightly in wet sheets? That was the whole point of it.'

'I've no idea what you were up to, and I don't want to know.' Anton's voice shook with fury. 'But I will not have you involving innocent members of my staff in your stupid pranks. Because of you I have been forced to dismiss two perfectly honest attendants. Men with wives and families.'

'Dismissed? Two attendants?' said Cassie in dismay.

'Yes, *fräulein*. Are you too besotted by the Count to realise he would vent his spite on the unfortunate fellows who bound him up? They are poor and friendless and vulnerable—just the sort of people he delights in persecuting. His instructions for their dismissal were on my desk when I got back from Salzburg.'

The two attendants! It had never occurred to her that Pentransky might punish them!

'You didn't have to dismiss them!' she cried. 'You could have ignored the order.'

'Oh, come! What good would it have done? Pentransky would simply have found some other way of ruining them. As it was, I was in a position to give them alternative work elsewhere immediately. Under the circumstances they were relieved to go. Unlike you, Fräulein Haydon, they have no misconceptions about Pentransky's character. All they want is to keep out of his way. Things may not work out so conveniently another time; I warn you, don't try my patience too far. Keep your amorous activities away from the Kurhaus. In fact, I suggest you and your amorous activities remove yourself to Pentransky's hunting-lodge as soon as possible, for all our sakes.'

She was stung by his injustice and by his lack of faith in her.

'You'd like that, wouldn't you?' she declared hotly. 'You aren't interested in hearing my version. All you want is to be rid of me. Well, I won't go! I won't! Do you hear me?'

For an awful moment, through her anger, she feared she might burst into tears. She had so hoped he had mellowed towards her of late, and come to trust her more. It had proved to be a vain hope. But there was no way she was going to break down in front of him, though it took a superhuman effort to control herself. When she felt capable of speech again she spoke quietly.

'Dr Sommer,' she said, 'you have made some dreadful accusations against me. The least you can do is hear my side of things.'

Anton had begun to walk away; now he paused and turned back to her.

'I suppose I must,' he said, his expression still unrelenting.

'All I am guilty of is an error of judgement. In the past, in order to evade Pentransky's attentions I have played up to him. The situations were invariably difficult, and I had to use what methods I could think of on the spur of the moment. I hoped he would become bored and go after someone else. Unfortunately for me this has not happened. When I found myself alone with him in the treatment rooms yesterday I confess to being afraid. I knew what was on his mind well enough, and telling him I wanted him to stop pestering me did no good at all. You may or may not have realised that Pentransky prefers his victims to be unwilling. . . ' She paused, the sudden memory of her unpleasant encounter sweeping back over her. Suppressing a shudder, she went on, 'Again I used what methods I could to evade him. I should have known he would have punished the two attendants, but I'm afraid that, under the circumstances, I did not. The men are all right, aren't they? I mean they truly have new jobs and everything?'

'I assure you the men have been well taken care of.'

'Good.' She gave a tired laugh. 'Probably you are right—I should leave Bad Adler—but all my life I've longed to come to Austria. I like the place and I enjoy the work I'm doing. Why should I be driven out by groundless gossip? I've done nothing wrong. If I go it will be a victory for Pentransky and for the idle scandal-mongers of Bad Adler and, to be honest, I'm reluctant to give them the satisfaction. Whether you believe me or not is up to you. I'm sorry if I'm making your life difficult by my actions, but that's how it is!'

She waited for him to say something. When he remained silent she gave a little shrug and walked away. With every step she hoped to hear him call her to stop, to have him beg her forgiveness and say he believed her. Such things happened only in dreams. Not until she had reached the gateway to the Kurhaus gardens did she look back. It proved a useless exercise. Her eyes were too blinded with tears to see if he were still standing there.

Cassie was grateful that she had the next day off. At least it would give her some respite from the pain of seeing Anton. Nevertheless, she awoke feeling heavy-eyed. For much of the night she had lain awake, his harsh words and accusations hammering relentlessly through her head. That they were unjustified made no difference. He had said them! At least she had no illusions now as to his opinion of her.

'And what are you doing today?' asked Trudi, as she placed breakfast in front of her.

'Nothing much, I suppose,' said Cassie, lethargically stirring her coffee.

'Nothing much? What a waste. You get so little free time.'

'I know, but I don't feel like exerting myself, that's all.'

Trudi regarded her with concern.

'You aren't letting the incident with Count Pentransky worry you too much, are you?' she asked. Trudi knew about her lodger's unfortunate adventure with the Count: Cassie had had to tell her in order to explain her tear-streaked face when she arrived home. The true cause of the tears Cassie had kept to herself, but Trudi was a perceptive soul.

'No, I'm not worrying about it,' Cassie assured her.

'I'm sure Frau Arlberg took that booking knowing perfectly well whom it was from, and what it implied,' said Trudi. She poured herself a cup of coffee and sat down at the table. 'She's no friend of yours, that's obvious.'

'Would she do such a thing?' Cassie wondered.

'What, Anna Arlberg? Certainly she would. Not the sort to let anyone get in her way is our Anna. She was just one of the pump girls a couple of years ago, you know. But she was determined she was going to run the spa before she was through. Quite a few people got trampled underfoot on her way up.'

'Dr Sommer runs the spa, though, not her.'

'Give her time. Everyone knows that to be Frau Sommer is her next goal. That's why she's trying to get rid of you.'

'If she wants Anton Sommer she can have him. I'm not standing in her way,' retorted Cassie a little too hotly.

'I only meant that pretty girls don't stay for long at the Kurhaus, not if Anna Arlberg has any say in the matter.' Trudi's words were conciliatory and her eyes were full of understanding. She noted the way Cassie was reducing her roll to crumbs and scarcely eating anything. 'If you're feeling a bit tired, why not go for a stroll along the river? What you need is a bit of sunshine and fresh air, and that wouldn't be too strenuous.'

Cassie managed a grin. 'A bit of sunshine and fresh air is your remedy for everything. I bet you'd even recommend it for a broken leg.'

'It takes a lot of beating as a restorative.' Trudi grinned back. 'And it has the advantage of being free.'

'Then I think I'd better take your advice,' Cassie said, though she felt it would take more than a walk by the river to restore her spirits that day.

Although she did begin by the river she soon wandered away from its bank, her path leading her into one of the few districts of Bad Adler she had not properly explored. In truth, Weissenbach was actually a village which was gradually being swallowed by the larger resort. It was very picturesque, and Cassie began to find herself enjoying her leisurely stroll.

It was a quiet road. For quite a way she walked without meeting another soul. Then she turned a corner and beheld a stout nun leading a tiny donkey, heading in the same direction. As Cassie approached she was surprised to hear the sister talking to the animal in English.

'Come on, my buck-oh, put your best foot forward,' the sister encouraged it in a lilting Irish accent.

'Good morning,' said Cassie as she drew level. 'Isn't this glorious weather?'

'An English voice! If that isn't a blessed sound!' A beaming smile spread over the nun's red, perspiring face. 'Though I confess the day's a mite too glorious for the likes of me and my friend here. We will both be heartily thankful when we reach the convent, so we will.'

'Is it far?' Cassie asked.

'Another half-mile or so. Would you be bound in that direction?'

'I'm not bound in any particular direction. I'm just out for a stroll.'

'Then would you mind if we walked together for a spell? You've no idea how grand it is to have a chance to speak English.'

'Of course not,' said Cassie with a smile. 'You speak only German at the convent?'

'That we do!' The nun mopped her streaming face with a handkerchief. 'Don't get me wrong! I love this

country and I love the people. But, oh, the language! I
just can't get to grips with it. How do you manage?'

'I had the advantage of an Austrian grandmother
who refused to speak any English.'

The sister gave an appreciative chuckle.

'She sounds like a woman after my own heart. So
you learned German young, eh? And now you're
holidaying here, are you, Miss. . . ?'

'Haydon. Cassie Haydon. No, I'm working in Bad
Adler, at the Kurhaus.'

'And I'm Sister Kathleen. You work at the Kurhaus,
you say? Now there's a thing! We're in the same line of
business, in a manner of speaking. Maybe, if you aren't
in a hurry, you'd like to come and see our baths? They
aren't as grand as the ones you're used to, but we've
got every facility that you've got at the Kurhaus, with
the exception of the potted palms.'

'I didn't realise there were other baths in this area.'

'We've only been open a couple of years, and we
don't attract the fashionable sort of folk who frequent
the Kurhaus.'

As they talked they had been steadily progressing
along the road until they reached a stand of pines, in
which stood a large house. Next to it was a much more
modern building.

'The old place is our convent; there are the baths
next to us,' explained Sister Kathleen. 'Now, why not
come along in for a lemonade? If you're like me you'll
be parched. Then afterwards I'll show you the baths.'

'I would like that, if you are sure I won't be intruding,' said Cassie, who was indeed feeling thirsty. She
was curious about the baths, too. She had had no idea
that they existed.

'Of course you won't be intruding. It'll be a pleasure
having you.'

Sister Kathleen led the way up the long drive to the
convent, talking non-stop. When they reached the
house she handed the donkey over to a novice.

'A bucket of water for his nibs and some lemonade

for us, eh?' she chuckled, ushering Cassie into a pleasant, simply furnished room.

Almost before they had sat down another sister appeared, bearing a jug and glasses on a tray.

'It's delicious, the best I've ever tasted,' said Cassie appreciatively, taking a sip.

'That it is, but just you try prising the recipe out of Sister Marie-Josef and see where it gets you.' Sister Kathleen gave a grin, and demolished half of her own drink in one gulp.

Eventually they had drained the last drop of lemonade from the jug, and Sister Kathleen suggested that they should go to see the baths.

'Oh, so it isn't actually built on to the convent,' remarked Cassie, as she was led across the garden and through a gate in the wall.

'No, it was while they were putting in our new waterpipes that the mineral springs were discovered. If that wasn't the Divine Intent, with us being a nursing order, then I'd like to know what is! Ah, here we are!'

The building was smaller than the Kurhaus, and far less ornate. Nevertheless, it was very clean and bright, with one large bath in the centre and various treatment rooms and dressing-rooms ranged around it. Colourful tiles and light woodwork gave it a cheerful air.

'There, what did I say?' demanded Sister Kathleen. 'We've got everything but the potted palms.'

Cassie had to agree with her, but she soon noticed some fundamental differences between these baths and the more well-known ones in the town. Most of the attendants were nuns, for one thing, but it was more than that. To begin with, the folk who sat waiting on wooden benches were simply dressed, some almost in rags. Also, there were far more people in the large bath than she had ever seen at the Kurhaus, and every one of them had some real disability. This was a treatment centre for the truly ill, not a fashionable diversion for the overfed.

'Your patients,' she said. 'Where do they come from?'

'Anywhere and everywhere. No one is turned away,' replied Sister Kathleen, with satisfaction. 'Some pay, whatever they can afford, but if they're really poor they're treated free. And what a benefit the poor souls get from it! For some it's the only time they're free from pain.'

'That is marvellous,' said Cassie, much impressed. 'It must be a wonderful thing for the people of the area. . . ' Her voice tailed away. She had been watching a male attendant helping a man much crippled with rheumatism into the water. There was something very familiar about that attendant; she had seen him before, at the Kurhaus. He was one of the men who had given the wet sheet treatment to Pentransky.

'Would you excuse me for a moment?' she said to Sister Kathleen. 'I've seen someone I know, and I would so like to have a word with him.'

'Certainly,' replied the sister cheerfully. 'While you're doing that, I'll go in search of the doctor. He should be here today, and I've a message for him.'

As Sister Kathleen bustled off, Cassie went over to the attendant.

He recognised her immediately, and smiled, 'Why, *fräulein*, I never expected to see you here,' he beamed.

'Nor I you. But I am glad I've met you. Is your friend here also, the one who worked with you at the Kurhaus?'

'He is indeed, *fräulein*. He's with a patient at the moment; he'll be sorry he missed you.'

'I'm sorry to have missed him, too, because I want to apologise to you both. I didn't mean to get you into trouble with Count Pentransky. I should have thought. . . I know what a vindictive wretch he is, and it was wrong of me to implicate you.'

'Don't worry yourself about it, *fräulein*. You did the right thing, getting away from that villain the best way you could. He should be locked up, that's what I think.'

The man gave a chuckle. 'Most enjoyable work we've ever done, giving him the wet sheet treatment. You can be sure we bound him nice and tight. There's a lot of folks who'd have paid good money for such a chance.'

'All the same, you lost your job because of me.'

'As for that, *fräulein*, you may have done us a favour. Of course, it's early days yet, but Klaus and I both think we're going to like working here. It's a lot less stiff and starchy than at the Kurhaus, no one's forever bellowing orders at us, and we've got a bit more authority. The money's the same, too—Dr Sommer saw to that—so by and large we reckon we've made a good move.'

Worrying about the fate of the two attendants had been one of the causes of Cassie's sleepless night. Now she was so relieved to find him cheerful that a beaming smile lit her face, making her huge eyes glow with a jewel-like brilliance.

'It is very kind of you to take it like this,' she said. 'After such an upheaval you would be quite justified in being really angry with me.'

'Angry with you, *fräulein*? Never!' said the man, dazzled by her smile.

'Ah, you're still here!' Sister Kathleen came bustling up. 'The doctor was busy, I'll have to catch him later.'

Before Cassie could speak a voice behind her said, '*Fräulein*? Fräulein Haydon? Is it you?'

The voice came from a short man. Only his head showed above the voluminous white cloak, which was the garb of most patients, and his cheeky gnome's grin looked incongruous against such an angelic style of garment.

'Herr Strauss!' exclaimed Cassie. 'Are you a patient here?'

'That I am, *fräulein*, but not for much longer. Look at this!' He proceeded to wave his injured arm about in a series of energetic contortions. 'Not much wrong with it, is there? It's nearly as good as new, all thanks to Dr Sommer. Have you seen him yet?'

'Seen Dr Sommer? You mean he is here?' she replied, startled.

'Of course. He's on duty here every Tuesday morning, didn't you know?'

Cassie could only shake her head.

'There now, that's a nice surprise for the pair of you,' said Herr Strauss, with satisfaction.

Surprise! That was an understatement!

'He comes here every week, you say?' She was still bewildered.

'Certainly! Without him these baths wouldn't exist,' broke in Sister Kathleen, in her dreadful German. 'Of course you must know the doctor! Didn't you say you worked at the Kurhaus? What a fool I was not to realise it before!'

'Know him? Fräulein Haydon and the doctor are very good friends,' declared Herr Strauss. 'Ah, I see I'm being summoned. I must bid you farewell, it's time for my physical jerks. It's high time you and Dr Sommer came to see us again, *fräulein*. My wife was only saying so the other day. Make it soon, before the winter snows come, eh?'

Fortunately he hurried off before Cassie needed to answer.

'You're a friend of the doctor?' Sister Kathleen lapsed thankfully into English. 'If that isn't the grandest thing!'

'I work for him; I'm not really a friend,' Cassie tried to protest, without success.

'Isn't he the loveliest man? And so gifted! How he manages to run the Kurhaus and still find time to help here I don't know. He must get thirty-two hours work out of very day. . . Will you look at that, now, here he comes himself!'

Sure enough Anton, clad in a white coat instead of his habitual morning dress, was making his way towards them. It was a slow process, for at every side people claimed his attention. Because of this he did not recognise Cassie until he was almost up to her.

'Look who's here, *Herr Doktor*!' announced Sister Kathleen, returning to torture the German language. 'I bet you didn't expect to see Fräulein Haydon, eh?'

Cassie steeled herself for their meeting. Remembering their last encounter and the harsh words he had thrown at her, she braced herself for a sharp reproof, or at best icy politeness. Certainly he was surprised to see her, and pulled up short in his astonishment, but he seemed disconcerted rather than annoyed.

'Fräulein Haydon, you are the last person I expected to see here,' he said.

'It was another case of Divine Intervention, sure it was,' said Sister Kathleen. 'Didn't Fräulein Haydon meet up with me by chance on the road? And wasn't I so pleased to speak English that I dragged her back to the convent? And now it turns out she's a particular friend of yours. Divine Intervention, nothing less! We've been singing your praises, Doctor, that we have! It's a wonder your ears aren't burning red.'

It was Cassie's cheeks which flamed, rather than Anton's ears. A particular friend! Singing his praises! What sort of stories will he imagine I've been spreading abroad? she wondered with mortification. He seemed uncharacteristically embarrassed by the nun's words, and this did nothing to help Cassie's peace of mind.

'I-I think Sister Kathleen exaggerates a little,' she said hastily, annoyed to hear herself stammering.

'I'm sure she does,' replied Anton, sounding oddly ill at ease as he gazed at Cassie. Then his attention turned to the stout nun, and his voice took on a bantering note. 'Isn't there a special word that's used in connection with the Irish? Blarney? That's it, isn't it?'

'Get away with you!' chortled a delighted Sister Kathleen.

'And what do you think of our establishment, *fräulein*?' he asked, becoming serious again.

'I think it's magnificent. I had no idea such a place existed.'

'We do our best, though we're always short of funds.

It was kind of you to come. We do not get enough visitors. You must let Sister Kathleen give you a full tour—I think you will find it interesting. I wish I could show you round myself, but unfortunately I have patients to attend to. I hope you will excuse my discourtesy.'

Cassie listened to him with astonishment. He sounded so agreeable, so genuinely regretful at having to leave her.

'You are not being discourteous,' she said. 'But I have taken up enough of everyone's time already. I think I should leave now.'

'There's no need for you to go yet,' protested Sister Kathleen.

'I agree,' said Anton. 'How do you propose getting home?'

'By the same way I came, I suppose. On my own two feet.'

'No!' He was suddenly emphatic. 'It's far too hot to walk. I will be finished in an hour. I will take you home in my chaise.'

Cassie tried to object, but he would have none of it.

'If it is imperative that you leave immediately then I will send for my chaise at once and take you home,' he said.

'But what of your patients?'

'I will come back this afternoon. I'm sure they won't mind waiting for once.'

She knew she was beaten.

'That won't be necessary. I don't need to be home by any special time, so I accept your offer of a lift with thanks.'

She was not happy about it, though. The thought of driving back to town with him was not a comfortable one. Her feelings for him were too strong. Being alone in his company, even for a short time, was not going to help at all.

'Good, so I'll leave you in the capable hands of Sister Kathleen, and you can talk English to your heart's content.' He smiled at her. It was not the bright humorous smile that had set her down the treacherous path of loving him, but it was close.

Sister Kathleen's shrewd eyes went from one face to the other.

'Off you go,' she said, giving the doctor a little push. 'I'll take good care of her until you're ready, never fear.'

Once he had gone Cassie found it unusually hard to concentrate as they continued their tour. Only when the nun mentioned Anton Sommer's name did she find her attention held.

'They're all his idea,' Sister Kathleen was saying, waving a plump hand at a basket filled with rubber ducks, cork rings and a variety of other floating toys. 'We get a lot of children here, poor little mites, and we found that some were afraid to go in the water. Now, with the doctor's collection here, we have the devil's own job to get them out!'

A compassionate Anton, a thoughtful Anton. Sides of his character she had rarely seen. More fuel for her hapless love.

'Dr Sommer does a great deal for the baths, it seems,' she said.

'He does that. Without him, all this would not exist.' Sister Kathleen encompassed the whole building with one sweep of her arm. 'When the mineral springs were found there were some who tried to seize them in order to fill their own pockets with gold. You'd not believe the scheming and skulduggery that went on. One man in particular. . . Oh, he's a whelp of Satan, that Pentransky! And I don't care who hears me say it.'

'Who?' demanded Cassie, startled.

'Count Pentransky. A man with birth, privilege, everything he could want, yet all it's given him is a black soul. . . You know of him?'

'Unfortunately, yes.' The vehemence in Cassie's voice made the nun regard her sharply.

'Then you know what sort of rogue he is. He tried

everything to get his hands on the land; I reckon his plan was to build up a spa to rival the Kurhaus, but Dr Sommer had other ideas. He felt that these healing waters should be for the benefit of the ordinary folk, those too poor to pay the fancy fees at the Kurhaus. Somehow he persuaded some wealthy charitable folk to help him. They bought the land from under Pentransky's nose, and this place was built in record time, and a true blessing it is to so many. Not that Pentransky cares about such things. There's no love lost between him and the doctor, I can tell you.'

So that was the root of the animosity between Anton and the Count! Cassie appreciated how difficult that must make life for the doctor, being in his vulnerable position. It was a credit to his ability and determination that he had held on to his post as medical director at the spa for so long. No wonder he resented her presence at the Kurhaus, seeing Pentransky had insisted she get the job. Now she understood better the reasons for Anton's dislike of her; however, it did not make it any easier for her to bear his disapproval.

Later, when Anton handed her into the chaise, he showed remarkably few signs of dislike. Sitting beside him, with Sister Kathleen's entreaties to, 'Come back soon, do you hear?' ringing in her ears, Cassie had her work cut out to not feel happy. Such an emotion would be useless, and ultimately painful, and quite without hope; she sternly told herself these harsh facts in an attempt to bring her wayward sentiments to heel. Unfortunately the tiny glow of happiness within her obstinately refused to be quenched, causing her to despair of ever being in control of her emotions again.

At first Anton was very quiet, so that only the steady 'clip-clop' of the horse's hoofs and the rumble of the chaise wheels filled the silence.

'Have you had lunch?' he asked suddenly.

'Why, no,' she replied.

'Then would you care to join me?'

'Oh!' she exclaimed, taken off guard by the unexpectedness of his request. 'I don't know. . . . I mean. . . . Why?'

'We got little time to talk, back at the Weissenbach baths, and I have things I wish to say. Also, I am sure we are both hungry.'

'Aren't you afraid of a scandal, if you're seen with me?' Why she said those words she did not know. Her sharp-tongued response came from somewhere in the past, from a time before she had loved him.

He gave a sigh. 'I can be seen with you now,' he pointed out. 'We're very much in the public gaze at this moment. But, that apart, I think maybe scandal has had too much free rein of late. That is why I wish to talk to you.'

She looked at him in puzzlement, not knowing what he meant. At the same time she regretted her snappish words.

'I'm sorry,' she said. 'That was an ungracious reply to your invitation. If you can overlook it, I would be delighted to have lunch with you.'

'Good.' A brief smile lit his face. 'I know of a place not far away. It is simple and far from luxurious, but the food is excellent. Besides, it is quiet and we can talk.'

He flicked the reins, and the bay between the shafts increased its pace from the leisurely amble it had adopted. They followed a side road taking them away from town. The inn, when they reached it, was far out in the country, an ordinary plain chalet-style building which seemed to have little to recommend it. Anton helped her down, then handed horse and chaise over to an ostler.

'Would you prefer to eat indoors or out?' he asked.

'Oh, outdoors, please.'

'I hoped you would say that.' The brief smile brightened his face again, then taking her arm he led her round the inn to where simple wooden tables and chairs were set out under leafy chestnut trees.

Cassie could not hold back an exclamation of

pleasure. The place was idyllic, on the bank of a stream where woods and meadows seemed to intermingle. It was certainly peaceful, and she suspected that the only way this place could prosper was as a lovers' retreat. The two or three couples who were already dining showed not the slightest interest in the new arrivals, which made her suspect all the more that it was a clandestine meeting-place. Pushing such disturbing thoughts from her head, she allowed herself to be led to a shady table. A waiter came out to them, quiet and discreet.

'I promise you the trout here is particularly good,' said Anton.

'Then the trout it shall be,' she said.

The food was delicious and the wine was excellent, but all through the meal Anton talked only of trivialities. Not until they had been served with coffee, fragrant and strong, did he lean forward to her and say, 'Fräulein Haydon, I want to discuss something with you: your encounter with Count Pentransky in the treatment rooms.'

Cassie's heart sank.

'I thought we'd said everything there was to be said on the subject,' she declared.

'So did I, until I went to bed last night. Then I began thinking, and the more I thought the more convinced I became that I had misjudged you.'

'You did?'

'Yes, and I beg you, just for once, let me speak without interruption. I know we have had our differences, but two things I have never underestimated about you are your intelligence and your courage. While I was fuming over your having the audacity to make assignations in the dressing-room. . . Pray hear me out,' he said, as Cassie spluttered with indignation. 'While I was fuming it began to occur to me that no female with a grain of common sense would go down there, knowing she would be alone with Pentransky. Now, I know you are not stupid, and once having found yourself in such a difficult situation I am convinced you would use your last ounce of ingenuity to extricate yourself. To have thought of employing the wet sheet treatment to your own ends was inventive in the extreme. Not one woman in a thousand could have accomplished it.'

'Dr Sommer,' Cassie said, 'I'm not sure I follow your thread of conversation. What are you trying to say?'

'I think I am trying to say I apologise for having doubted you.'

'You mean you believe me?' she said in wonderment.

'I do. I said some very hard and unjust things to you yesterday, and I beg your pardon most sincerely for them. Again, many women would have used tears to sway my opinion, but not you. You argued your own defence most ably. I was a fool not to have realised you were telling the truth, not just then but from the very first day.'

'You believe me?' She was still numb with bewilderment.

'Yes, belatedly, to my shame.'

'W-what changed your mind?'

'Several things. My own deliberations, for one. Your own steadfastness, for another—you have never wavered in one detail when pleading your innocence. Sir George's good opinion of you, for a third. He's nobody's fool, and an excellent judge of character. Lastly, I know Pentransky. He's perfectly capable of hounding you, as you claim, and I know all too well that few people would come to your aid against him. You would be forced to protect yourself as best you could. I should never have allowed myself to be swayed by false first impressons and scandal; I should have had more sense. I ask your forgiveness.'

'Oh!' Cassie's breath was quite taken away.

'Do you forgive me?' he insisted.

'Yes, of course I do.' She knew she sounded eager and ardent, but she did not care.

'Good, that is a weight off my mind.' He did indeed

seem relieved. Obviously it had all weighed heavily upon him. 'Of course, some other things are unchanged between us,' he said more briskly. 'I still find you argumentative. And the New Woman business is nonsense in my opinion. And there are many of your ideas for attracting English visitors to Bad Adler that I will resist with the last breath in my body. But I acknowledge you are honest.'

His words were brusque, almost abrasive, but somehow Cassie was not fooled. Something told her that he did not mean them, no matter how decisively they were uttered.

'It's a step in the right direction,' she said, unable to stop herself smiling up at him.

She found herself looking deep into his eyes. They were such fascinating eyes, clear like dark amber, flecked with a deeper, richer brown. She felt she would be happy to go on gazing into them for ever and ever; she could never get enough of staring into their depths. Anton, too, seemed mesmerised, his regard never wavering. His hand stole across the table to enfold hers. The gentle touch of his fingers became part of one long, enchanted moment, when all else was forgotten and nothing else mattered.

'Are you in a hurry to get back to Bad Adler?' he asked. The question seemed of vital importance.

'No.'

'Then, perhaps, if you would care to. . .it is such a beautiful day—too lovely to waste—maybe we could take a stroll?' His hesitant, hopeful words were far removed from his normal assured manner.

There was no indecision in Cassie's reply. 'That sounds delightful,' she said.

They rose and took the path which bordered the stream. The way was narrow and rocky; it seemed natural for Anton to keep hold of her hand, enfolding it protectively in his. As they strolled they talked. The summer sun shone down on them as if determined to show them approval. In the brilliant blue of the sky, swallows skimmed relentlessly. Cassie had never known so perfect a day. Afterwards her only recollection of the conversation was that they had laughed a lot—she could not remember a single topic they had discussed. Such an idyll had to come to an end. Eventually Anton consulted his pocket-watch and reluctantly suggested that they go back.

The return path sloped sharply downwards—far more difficult for someone of Cassie's height to negotiate than scrambling uphill, at least with any degree of decorum. At the top of one particularly steep fall of rocks she hesitated for a moment, trying to decide on the best route. Then the need for decision was taken from her: seeing her predicament, Anton took hold of her by the waist and lifted her down. Whether it was by accident or design she did not know, but the next moment she was in his arms and his mouth was on hers. These were not the harsh angry kisses she had experienced in his office. These were soft, and tender, and offered the promise of untold happiness. Cassie's own arms went eagerly about his neck, drawing him close. . .

'I should ask your forgiveness for my behaviour,' said Anton when at last their lips parted, 'but it would be a lie. I'm not sorry. Not sorry at all!'

Cassie was too befuddled by happiness to do more than beam with joy. In fact, she beamed all the way back to Elizabethplatz.

As the chaise rumbled away, taking Anton with it, one thing became certain. New Woman or not, it was now useless for her to try to stop loving him. Such an attempt was doomed to complete and utter failure!

CHAPTER EIGHT

'My word, the fresh air and exercise have done you far more good than I anticipated.' Trudi regarded Cassie with approval. 'Where did you go?'

'Oh, only to Weissenbach,' said Cassie evasively. 'The oddest thing happened—I met an Irish nun on the road and she invited me back to the convent for the best lemonade I've ever tasted. It was very welcome, I can assure you. It was sweltering, walking.'

'Well, I've never known a visit to a convent produce such an effect before.' Trudi was still wondering at her lodger's brilliant eyes and glowing cheeks. Then she said casually, 'Weissenbach, you say? I don't suppose you happened to notice the new baths?'

'I could scarcely miss them.' Cassie busied herself with taking off her hat. 'In fact, Sister Kathleen showed me round.'

'Ah,' said Trudi. 'And it's Tuesday.'

'What has that got to do with anything?' Cassie demanded, although she could guess. Did the entire country know Anton Sommer was on duty at the Weissenbach baths each Tuesday?

'Oh, nothing,' said Trudi innocently. 'Nothing at all. But seeing that today's outing in the sunshine has been so beneficial, you have made sure your next day off will be on the fifteenth, haven't you?'

'Yes, it's all arranged.'

'Good. If a few hours at Weissenbach can do you this much good I can't wait to see what the country air at St Leopold will do for you.'

'It might rain,' said Cassie.

'What, on the Emperor's birthday celebrations? Never!' Trudi gave a happy sigh. 'I must say, I'm looking forward to showing you my home. What a

marvellous day we'll have. There'll be music and a
procession and dancing and. . .'

Cassie held up a hand.

'Stop!' she said, laughing. 'It sounds wonderful. I
don't know how I'll be able to wait two whole weeks.'

'It might be more wonderful than you think. I fancy
there'll be a surprise waiting for you when you
come. . .'

'A surprise? What sort?' Cassie was intrigued.

'If I told you, then it wouldn't be a surprise, would
it?' And Trudi refused to be drawn further.

Cassie had no time to dwell on her landlady's little
mysteries; she was too occupied with thoughts of
Anton. Time and again she went over their meeting at
Weissenbach, reliving every precious moment, treasur-
ing his every word.

Oh, how she loved him! And, incredibly, she was
beginning to think that he cared for her in return. Love
and hope! They formed a heady mixture. Yet, for all
her burgeoning happiness, she was aware she had
problems: what about her plans to have a career, to be
independent, to control her own destiny? How did
these equate with a future which included Anton?
Already she had found it impossible to bar him from
her mind, and once he was in her thoughts he had a
disturbing way of taking over, to the detriment of
everything else. Worse still, she found that she was too
much in love with him to care. What had happened to
her clear decisive intellect? To her ambition and self-
will? They were there somewhere, if only she could find
them.

Surely she was not alone in grappling with this
dilemma? Other New Women must have fallen in love.
There was Mrs Pankhurst, champion of 'Votes For
Women', for one. She seemed to have it all—a family,
and a cause. But had love and marriage come to
Emmeline Pankhurst before her forthright and radical
ideas? Cassie did not know. What she did discover was

the powerful manner in which love could nibble away
at even the most independent female character.

Next day, at the Kurhaus, Anton's behaviour struck
further blows at her independence. He came to her on
his morning rounds, as usual, but where once he would
only criticise now he asked if she had enjoyed her visit
to Weissenbach, commented upon how much good the
outing had done her to bring such colour to her
cheeks. . . He even joked about the continuing queues
of gentlemen who lined up every morning to consult
her, whether they had a query or not.

'We'll have to penalise any man who comes back to
ask you more than two questions per day,' he grinned.
'What would be a suitable deterrent?'

'Having to drink two beakers of spa water instead of
one?' she suggested.

He flung back his head and laughed, causing the
other occupants of the pump-room to look in their
direction.

'That should do it,' he chuckled. 'Though don't tell
anyone else I said so.'

'I won't say a word,' she promised.

The pleasure of sharing even so minor a secret with
him would have been enough to brighten the day for
her, but he came back to her again and again throughout the morning. His reasons were trivial, matters
which normally would only have warranted sending a
messenger. Now he came in person, attentive and
charming, not just on that day, but on those which
followed. She tried to tell herself he was making
amends for having doubted her for so long. She did not
succeed very well. Hope and happiness had a way of
intervening.

Other people began to remark on his attentiveness.

'Would you oblige me by giving this book to Dr
Sommer when next you see him, my dear?' asked Sir
George, one morning. 'I promised to lend it to him
most particularly. I can't see him anywhere, and Attila

the Hun's maiden aunt will be here to claim me at any moment.'

'Certainly, Sir George. I'll give it to him when he does his rounds first thing in the morning.'

'You'll see him before that!'

'What makes you say such a thing?'

'Sheer observation, my dear. I've noticed the way our handsome doctor's begun to gravitate towards this corner of late. Not that I blame him. I always knew he was a man of good sense and excellent taste.'

'If you'll pardon me for saying so, Sir George, you are talking nonsense.'

'I'll pardon you all right, my dear. Don't just take my word for it. The Ice Dragon's noticed it too. That's why she's striding round the place with a face like thunder, frightening timid mortals such as myself half to death.'

'You? A timid mortal, Sir George?' chuckled Cassie. 'That's an inaccuracy if ever I heard one. And as for the Ice Drag——And as for Frau Arlberg, there is nothing for her to notice, therefore she is in a bad temper for no reason.'

'If you can say "nonsense" to me, then I can retaliate and say "nonsense" back,' Sir George insisted. 'You are perfectly aware of the fact that young Sommer's attention is straying in your direction, you minx, and you aren't indifferent to him! Oh, no, or you'd not be getting prettier and prettier with every day that passes. Now don't go saying "nonsense" to me again,' he declared, as Cassie framed the word on her lips. 'I didn't believe you first time, and I won't believe you now.'

'Sir George, you are incorrigible!' laughed Cassie.

'Yes, I am. An incorrigible romantic, so you'll oblige me by not trying to disillusion me. Seeing two of my favourite people growing fond of one another is giving me the greatest of pleasure, and I'd not have it spoiled.'

'Oh, Sir George, what can I say?' Cassie said softly, touched by his sincerity.

'Say nothing, my dear.' The old gentleman patted her hand. 'Just go on being your delightful self, and giving ancient relics like me the enjoyment of looking at you. My word, if I were forty years younger then our doctor friend wouldn't stand a chance.'

'No one would,' she assured him. 'Not against such unfair competition.' And he went away beaming.

Only after he had gone did she realise she had as good as admitted her love for Anton. Not that it mattered—Sir George was her friend and very discreet, and anyway he had guessed the truth of the situation. Certainly he had been right in observing how short-tempered Anna Arlberg was these days. Cassie had to acknowledge that she herself had been on the sharp edge of the Ice Dragon's tongue rather a lot recently. The more Anton approved the more his assistant disapproved, or so it seemed.

Cassie had to admit she was surprised not to have seen the Count again. Daily she had been expecting him to take reprisals against her, but so far all had been quiet. It was what made Pentransky such a tricky adversary; his habit of seeming to disappear for ages, then reappearing when least expected.

Not again, though, she vowed. I'm being extra vigilant now; I won't be caught unawares by him again.

It was difficult to dwell on anything as unpleasant as Count Pentransky. Her thoughts tended to turn, far more agreeably, towards Anton. The mere fact of knowing he now trusted and believed her made an extraordinary difference to her life. She felt as if some dark cloud had been dispelled, making each day she worked at the Kurhaus filled with bright sunshine.

The one occasion when the actual sunshine failed was on the fifteenth of August. Trudi's prediction that it never rained on the Emperor's birthday seemed destined to prove false, because the day dawned with heavy clouds and an ominous stillness which threatened thunder.

'What if it does rain? A few raindrops won't hurt us!' Trudi declared. 'We'll still have a wonderful time.'

This expedition back to her home village was the great yearly treat in the Meyer household. True, St Leopold was only a few miles from Bad Adler, but it was too far to walk, and Trudi had little money to spare for train fares. Now she had Cassie and the children up and astir almost before it was light. They had barely finished dressing when Franz, the last member of their party, arrived.

'My word, won't we turn some heads today?' he said proudly.

Everyone did look smart. The Meyer family were dressed in traditional costume. Trudi and little Anna wore embroidered aprons over bright dirndl skirts, with tight bodices and snowy white blouses. The two boys wore miniature versions of the costume worn by Franz—leather breeches with embroidered braces, white shirts, and high-crowned hats of felt. Their grey loden-cloth jackets brought a smile to Cassie's lips, for they reminded her of the one Anton had worn when he rescued her from the cow.

'Why are you smiling?' demanded Anna.

'Because I'm happy,' said Cassie truthfully, though unwilling to admit the entire reason.

'And so you should be. You look a picture!' beamed Trudi with approval.

Cassie had a new dress. Although she always chose her clothes with care, she had always been influenced by what would look smart, or efficient, or make her look older. Now, for the first time, she had bought something simply to make herself look pretty, and she had succeeded. It was of pink muslin. The leg-of-mutton sleeves were perhaps a little old-fashioned, but the delicate fabric cried out for such soft fullness. Old Frau Schroeder, who lived next door, had made up the dress very simply, with none of the fancy trimming which was now in vogue. The reason was economy— Cassie's purse would not stretch far—but the neat tucks put in by Frau Schroeder instead suited her far better than heavy embellishments of lace or braid. Her one other extravagance had been a new hat—a plain leghorn straw which she had trimmed herself with swirls of pink tulle and ribbon.

'You look like a pink blancmange!' exclaimed Johann, Trudi's elder boy. And everyone laughed.

'Knowing how much you enjoy pink blancmange, I shall take it as a compliment,' smiled Cassie.

'It won't be the only compliment you get today,' Franz assured her. 'Now, if we don't get going we'll miss the train.'

Such a disaster was not to be contemplated; they hurried out of the apartment, much laden with umbrellas—for the sky was looking more threatening with every minute—and baskets of food.

The pleasures of the day began with the train journey, for Cassie as much as for the children. The countryside was new to her and she gazed out of the window with delight as the small engine puffed out of the valley, then chugged its way through the mountains. The line ended at the head of the Waldsee, the lake in the next valley.

'St Leopold is halfway along the lake,' said Trudi, as they alighted on the platform. 'It won't take us long to walk there, it's only five kilometres——'

'Not today!' announced Cassie, producing a handful of tickets. 'Today we go by steamer. My treat. I was told the best way to approach St Leopold was across the lake, and I want to see if it's true, so I booked ahead for all of us.'

'We're going by steamer! We're going by steamer!' The children went wild with excitement, and their mother had to issue dread threats before they would calm down.

Cassie was glad she had thought of her surprise. For one thing the sheer delight of the children pleased her, and for another she was thankful that she did not have to walk far on such a hot, airless day. Above all, there was the beauty of the lake itself; there was not a breath of wind, making it like glass. Round it were ranged high mountains, exactly reflected in the lake's mirror-like surface. So perfect was the image that Cassie almost regretted the way the steamer was forced to disturb the picture with its churning paddle-wheels.

Gradually the village of St Leopold came closer, nestling at the water's edge, the white column of its church tower standing out like a sentinel. Even before they disembarked she could see that it was a very pretty place, the balconies of the neat chalet-style houses ablaze with flowers. Everywhere was gaily decorated in honour of the day, with the rather sombre black and yellow colours of the Emperor's family, the Hapsburgs, being offset by strings of brilliant bunting.

They landed at a jetty just beyond the lakeside inn, and as soon as her feet touched dry land Cassie could sense the excitement and bustle in the air. Like Franz and the Meyer family, all the inhabitants were dressed in their best, and already the lively 'oom-pah-pah' of a brass band could be heard in the distance.

'It's the procession! They'll be making for the market square,' said Trudi, now as excited as her children. 'We must go and see them. It's not far.'

In distance it was not far, but it took them a time to get there, because Trudi was greeted on every side by friends, acquaintances and relations. Cassie's head began to spin at the endless introductions to cousins, uncles and aunts. Somehow they managed to find a vantage point where they could see the procession go by—the dignitaries of St Leopold, the priest and elders of the church, and representatives of every club and society the village could boast, each carrying a gaily embroidered banner.

When everyone had cheered themselves hoarse at the colourful spectacle the crowd fell in behind the procession and followed to the market-place. It proved to be a rather small square, and Cassie wondered how the brass band managed to continue playing, hemmed in as it was by such a crush. At one time she feared that the weight of numbers was pushing them all into the lake, for the square sloped quite steeply towards the inn and the water. After a little while, though, she realised that everyone was going into the church.

'We'll go to Mass first—it's the Feast of the Assumption too, you see—then we'll call on my parents, then. . .'

What came next Cassie never discovered, for she was borne bodily towards the church and out of earshot of Trudi's words.

It was a very large church for so small a village—a relic of an earlier, more prosperous time in St Leopold's affairs—but it was not the imposing size of the building, nor the magnificence of the interior decoration which made her take in her breath sharply. It was a brief glimpse of a dark head above the crowd. When she looked again the familiar outline had gone, lost in the crush. It could not have been Anton, could it? Was her imagination beginning to see him everywhere? Then she remembered! He came from St Leopold too! Trudi had told her long ago that they were from the same village. She remembered, also, her landlady's more recent coy comments and promises of a surprise if she came to St Leopold for the celebrations. Was Anton the surprise?

Jammed in an ornately carved pew with Trudi, Franz and the children, Cassie tried very hard to concentrate on the service. To her shame, time and again she found her eyes straying round the congregation, searching for another glimpse of that elegant dark head. Her search was in vain; she could see no sign of Anton. That earlier sighting must have been of someone else.

The mass came to an end, and everyone began to stream out of the church, but it was a slow process, for every pew had been filled and folk had been standing at the back. Cassie tried to keep up with Trudi and the others, then, as more people squeezed into the aisle, decided to give up the unequal struggle. St Leopold was not a large place—she would find them outside somewhere. Her slow progress gave her a chance to admire the decorations of the church more fully; it really was exceptionally beautiful with its ornate gilding. . . It was then that she saw him! Anton! He was on the opposite side of the church, being pushed inexorably along by the crowd.

At the same moment, as if drawn to her, he looked in her direction. So great was his surprise as he recognised her that he stopped dead, only to be propelled onwards by a hefty push from the extremely stout matron behind him. Cassie was gratified to note that, as well as surprise, his face registered pleasure at the sight of her.

There was no chance of speaking—distance and the rich harmonies of the organ saw to that. Anton looked speculatively at the pews, as if intending to cut across to her, but this was not possible. No expense had been spared on the church furniture—it was solid, high-backed, and practically impenetrable. He was now being swept through one door, while Cassie was being forced through another. Before he disappeared from sight he gave a wry grin, shrugged his shoulders, and mouthed three words that she interpreted as, 'See you later.' At least that was what she hoped he had said.

She had no opportunity of finding him outside in the market-square, for the moment she emerged she was pounced on by a relieved Trudi.

'There you are!' exclaimed her landlady. 'We thought we'd lost you. Come along, we're going to my parents' house for lunch now.'

At any other time Cassie would have been delighted to meet Trudi's mother and father. On this occasion, however, she could not help giving a regretful look or two behind her, in case there was any sign of Anton. Then she told herself not to be silly. She had already observed that St Leopold was not a large place; she was bound to meet up with him later in the day.

Trudi's family were just what she might have

expected—warm and courteous. Delighted as they were to see their daughter and grandchildren again, they were nevertheless genuinely pleased to welcome an English *fräulein* into their neat little house, making such a fuss of her that she felt completely at ease in their company.

After they had eaten they all went to the meadow in one large, jolly party but, enjoyable as it was watching the running and the games, Cassie was conscious that this was a family occasion. Franz was clearly regarded by the old couple as a future son-in-law, but she was an outsider. To give them time to be together and catch up on family gossip she excused herself, saying she would like to explore the village.

'That's it, you have a good look round,' Trudi encouraged her. 'We'll still be here when you get back. You can't get lost, not in St Leopold.'

It was a picturesque place. Cassie enjoyed her trudge up the steep main street of small shops, in spite of the clammy heat. Views of the lake were never far away, so she had no problem in getting her bearings. An interesting lane going downhill promised to return her somewhere close to her starting point, so she took it, and as she descended she began to catch the strains of music in the air. Not the cheery blasting of the brass band, but a more delicate sound of strings being plucked. Someone was playing a zither. This, she felt, was the true heart of Austria, the Austria she had heard about in her grandmother's stories and had come to love.

Attracted by the sound, she hurried on until she emerged, quite suddenly, to find herself right beside the lake. In fact, it was a landing area for boats, with a small jetty, and a wide slipway sloping into the water. Now, though, in the open space at the head of the slipway couples danced to the music of the zither played by a man sitting at the door of the inn. This was clearly an impromptu affair, not part of the organised celebrations, and she watched, entranced by the scene and the music and the dancing.

Absorbed as she was by what was happening, she was aware of Anton standing at her side even before he spoke. She turned and looked at him, hoping she did not betray her pleasure at his presence too obviously. He was wearing traditional costume, just as he had on their encounter on the mountain. Only his thick hunter's jacket and hat had been discarded because of the heat. In his shirt-sleeves and with his hair slightly ruffled he looked younger, less dignified. Cassie decided she preferred him like this. He also looked uncharacteristically diffident, as though he was not quite sure how she would react to his presence.

'Where did you disappear to?' he asked. 'I looked for you after church, but there was no sign of you.'

'I-I went with my landlady to her parents' home.'

'Your landlady. . .? Oh yes, you lodge with Trudi Meyer, don't you? I had forgotten. So you went visiting. I thought that perhaps you were hiding from me.'

'Oh, no!' said Cassie quickly.

His air of diffidence disappeared, to be replaced by a smile.

A silence followed. She would have said something witty or interesting, if only she could have got her brain and her tongue to work in harmony. Sadly, the only comment that came to her was trite in the extreme.

'Are you enjoying the music?' she asked.

'Are you enjoying the music?' asked Anton simultaneously.

Any awkwardness between them was dispelled by their laughter.

'In answer to your question, yes, I am enjoying the music.' Cassie smiled. 'Very much indeed.'

'Enough to join in the dancing?'

'Oh, I couldn't! I don't know the steps,' she replied in some alarm.

'You could manage this one though, surely. It's a *ländler*. Listen to it.'

Obediently she listened to the lilting tune.

'It's almost like a waltz,' she said.

'You are right. It is the parent of the waltz and, as all good parents should be, it is a little slower and more sedate than its offspring. If you can waltz you can certainly dance the *ländler*.'

In the face of such persuasion how could she refuse, especially since her feet were longing to move to the rhythm. His arm went about her, drawing her into the dance. His touch evoked memories of their embrace at Weissenbach. Now he was holding her in a way which was perilously close to that embrace. Admittedly it was part of the dance, but she was very conscious of his arms holding her about the waist. She could feel his warmth and the cording of his muscles through the fine linen of his shirt sleeve. At first she was tense, disturbed by his nearness, then gradually the sensation of his body so close to hers began to have an electrifying effect. Somehow she began to feel they were no longer simply dancing. A change had come over them, a heightened awareness that made her blood flame and charged every nerve in her with an unknown volatile force. Anton was affected, too. He had begun by smiling down at her, then slowly the smile faded and his face grew intense. His eyes never left hers, his gaze seeming to devour her. His encircling arms tightened gently, possessively, and she gave to their gentle pressure, wanting to be closer to him. . .and closer. . .and closer. . .

So engrossed were they in each other that they were not even aware of the music coming to an end. It was the burst of clapping from the other dancers that brought them rudely to their senses. For a moment they simply stood where they were, quite bewildered.

'Would—would you care to dance again?' asked Anton eventually. 'I could ask for another *ländler*. . .'

'No, thank you,' she replied swiftly. The sudden onslaught of emotions had shaken her. She needed to grow calm again.

'Perhaps you are right. . . It is too hot for dancing.'
He, too, sounded quite disconcerted. 'Shall—shall we
stroll along by the lake?'

'Yes, please.' That would be cool. It would give her
time to gain control of herself. She knew the sensible
thing would be to bid Anton farewell and walk away
from him. That would give her an even better chance
of regaining her self-control, but in her present state of
heightened emotions she was past doing anything sensible. Certainly she felt that to go away from him was
beyond her capabilities.

They walked along a path which skirted the lake,
Cassie mindful all the while of Anton's tall figure at her
side. They did not talk. Each seemed too absorbed by
their own thoughts for conversation.

It was not cool by the lake, nor was it silent. Distant
thunder was already rumbling through the far mountains. The sky had taken on a more sulphurous hue,
making the lake's surface like old pewter. The flags and
bunting hung limp and unmoving in the heavy air.
Beyond the village nothing stirred; even the flocks of
coots in the lakeside reeds were still. Cassie wished the
threatening storm would break soon. She felt that not
only would it clear the oppressive atmosphere, it might
also dispel the disturbing emotions that were building
up inside her.

The rain came suddenly, in fat, heavy drops, followed
almost immediately by flash after flash of lightning.
They were beyond the village now, in an area where
the trees fringing the lake were interspersed with
meadowland.

'There's a summer-house!' yelled Anton above the
peals of thunder. 'We'll make a run for it.'

He did not wait for her reply. Instead he grabbed her
hand and set off into the face of the now teeming rain.
Cassie, clutching at her hat with her free hand, kept up
as best she could. The summer-house loomed ahead of
them. It was modest enough—a simple wooden con-
struction with a small veranda facing the lake. There

was a short wooden fence surrounding it, but Anton ignored such a barrier. He flung open the gate for her and together they charged up the two shallow steps into the shelter of the veranda.

They had not run far, but it was far enough for Cassie's leghorn straw hat to droop and for her new pink muslin to be clinging damply about her legs. Her hair had long since begun to tumble from its pins and fall in pale strands on her shoulders. Anton, too, had suffered from the elements. His hair was soaking, plastered to his skull by the rain, and his skin glowed through the semi-transparency of his wet shirt. For one brief moment they stared at each other, their laughter rising as they surveyed the damage, then, as quickly, the laughter died and they were in each other's arms.

That first stunning moment was explosive, echoing the force of the tempest outside. Anton's mouth covered hers, and for a brief second she tasted rain on his lips, then the cool sweetness was gone, dispelled by a sudden eruption of passion as sharp and as electric as the lightning which shot across the heavens. She had known for some time that she loved Anton, of course she had, but she had never before admitted to herself how much she wanted him. Her need for him, her hunger for him, made her giddy and oblivious to all else, even the gust of torrential rain that swept in over the veranda, soaking them once more. Anton did not flinch at the drenching, nor did his mouth cease its passionate quest for hers, but he did stretch out one hand and open the door behind them.

'Won't—won't the owner mind?' Cassie managed to gasp, between kisses.

'Not. . .in. . .this weather.' Anton punctuated his words with caresses as his lips softly touched her cheeks, her eyes, her throat. 'Do. . .you. . .care?'

'No,' she admitted.

'Good.' His fingers went up into her hair, freeing it of the last confining pins. Gently he drew her closer, but his kisses were not gentle; they grew more demanding and ardent until Cassie was forced to cry for mercy. He eased away from her, and for the first time she realised that they were lying on a couch in the single inner-room of the summer-house. How they had got there she had no recollection. She was aware only of Anton.

Now, at her gasp of protest, he looked down at her.

'Cassie. . .' he said in a stricken voice. 'Oh, Cassie, I'm sorry!'

At once her hands went up to cradle his face.

'I'm not!' she said. 'I needed to breathe, that's all.'

He did not seem to believe her, for his eyes searched her face urgently, as if looking for reassurance. Then slowly the remorse faded from his expression, to be replaced by relief.

'Oh!' he said. 'Oh, thank goodness! For a moment I thought. . . I was afraid. . .'

'I'm not the least bit sorry. Why should I be?' Her fingers began to trace the curve of his cheekbones, the line of his jaw. Now that the storm of passion had eased she needed time to savour what was happening to her. It was unreal, like something out of a dream. . . But Anton's arms still encircled her and they were real, and the warmth of his body was still against her.

'Why? I could think of a dozen reasons, but I'm so glad you've no regrets.' He gave a rueful smile. 'What is this terrible effect you have on me? I used to be such a calm, self-controlled sort of fellow, and now look at me! I shout, I lose my temper, I lure young women into compromising situations. . .'

Cassie's fingers stopped their exploration.

'Perhaps I should ask you if you're sorry,' she said.

He bent down and kissed her full on the lips, not with the desperate hunger of before, but with poignant tenderness that made her eyes fill with tears.

'There, does that answer your question?' he asked.

'Yes. . . Well, almost.'

'Only almost?' He gave a laugh and kissed her again. 'There, will that do?'

She nodded, and he relaxed on to the couch, drawing her closer so that his cheek rested against the top of her head.

'I must have been mad,' he said.

'Mad? In what way?' She nestled her head against him, too happy to be really bothered about his late insanity.

'To have thought that you were involved with Pentransky. You! The idea is laughable! I see that now, why didn't I see it earlier?'

'Well, we did rather get off to a bad start, didn't we?' Secure in his arms, she was prepared to overlook their earlier misunderstandings.

'A bad start that looked likely to go on and on. We've wasted so much time! What a criminal waste!'

'We aren't wasting time now, though.'

'No, we're not, thank goodness!' She felt the soft touch of his lips on the top of her head. 'This is perfection, but I still feel as if I'm suffering from some form of madness.'

'Why? Because you are here with me?'

'Yes,' he admitted. 'This is the sort of circumstance in which I never expected to find myself. I don't claim to have led a particularly celibate life, but I've never been swept away by my feelings quite so completely.'

Cassie sat up abruptly.

'You *are* sorry you're here with me!' she said, in distress.

'No, not that! Never that! Believe me!' He reached out for her, pulling her back against him again, comforting her with light kisses and gentle caresses. 'Never that!' he repeated. 'It's just that I'm having trouble coping with this effect you have on me. As I said before, I used to be such a calm, self-controlled sort of fellow—I was quite proud of the fact—but now look at me! What a way for an eminent citizen of Bad Adler to conduct himself! I've never before behaved in such a shameful way with a young lady, yet I could no more stop myself from taking you in my arms than I could

stop the thunder and lightning outside. I've lost all
control over my emotions, and I'm finding it
bewildering.'

He spoke jokingly, yet beneath his teasing words she
sensed an unexpected seriousness. It had never
occurred to her that he, too, might be having difficulty
in coping with the force of emotion between them. She
knew that she was confused and perplexed by the
tumult of her own feelings, but somehow she had never
expected Anton—cool, self-assured Anton, who was
hardly ever without a beautiful woman by his side—to
be suffering in the same way. Perhaps they were more
alike in temperament than she had ever appreciated. It
was an intriguing idea. She had always considered
herself and Anton to be conflicting characters—that
was why they quarrelled so much. Now she thought
about it, the idea of them being closer to twin souls was
much more appealing.

'Perhaps it is the electricity in the storm affecting
your brain,' she suggested.

'No, it's your presence affecting the whole of me.'
With his fingers entangled in her hair he tilted her head
so that he could gaze into her face more easily. 'Yes,
it's you,' he insisted, his voice growing suddenly hoarse.
'From the first time I saw you, at the station, I've not
been able to stop thinking about you. No matter how
hard I tried to force you out you kept creeping back
into my thoughts, until there wasn't room for anyone
or anything else. You're driving me mad, do you know
that?'

To Cassie his words were unreal, too beautiful to be
heard in anything but a dream, but his gentle caresses
were becoming more vigorous and insistent, making
her gasp with sudden urgent longing, and she knew that
this was reality. Involuntarily her body curved to his in
an instinctive expression of her love. The conflict
between them was over now; all that was left was
happiness and sweet, sweet passion. . .

It was a single ray of sunshine, beaming bright and

warm through the summer-house window, that brought them back to reality. When the storm had stopped they had no idea, but now, outside, the lake shimmered calm and tranquil beneath a cerulean blue sky. They gazed out at the perfect summer's day, and burst out laughing.

'Goodness knows how long it's been like this,' chuckled Anton, then he glanced at his watch and his smile became a grimace of dismay. 'Three o'clock! It can't be as late as that! I was supposed to meet the two o'clock steamer!'

'Oh, dear!' Cassie tried to sound stricken at being the cause of his missing his appointment. 'What will you do?'

'I'd better call at my father's house, to see if a message has been left for me there. *Himmel*! I was looking forward to going back to the village with you, and joining in the fun.'

'Never mind, there's always another time.'

'That's true. We've the rest of our lives. . .'

The sentence was never finished. It was lost as they clung together in one last lingering kiss.

Making themselves presentable again was not easy. It took a while for them to collect up Cassie's discarded hairpins and her hat. Finally Anton opened the door to the summer-house and said, with a bow, 'May I escort madam back to the ordinary world?'

Ordinary! She knew that life for her would never be ordinary again. She had Anton's love. It was incredible, impossible, unbelievable, but it had happened. She had Anton's love! Her own love for him, she was convinced, must be shining from her like a beacon light, and she was glad of the quiet walk back to the village. It gave her a chance to compose herself a little. Not that she cared about her own reputation but this was Anton's home, he was well-known here, and she did not want to do anything that might embarrass him among people who had known him all his life.

Ahead of them, the sound of cheering wafted on the

breeze. 'Ah, they've started the races again by the sound of it,' said Anton. 'I wish I could stay, but I'm afraid I'll have to hand you back to Trudi, then bid you farewell.'

'You don't need to come with me, if you are in a hurry,' said Cassie, though she did not want him to go. 'I'm sure I'll find Trudi easily enough by myself.'

'It's no use, you can't get rid of me as easily as that,' he grinned. 'I'm walking you back to the village. Don't argue!'

'Very well, just this once I won't.'

As they made their way towards St Leopold, Cassie was convinced she was not walking—she was floating, drifting, light as a cloud, borne up by her happiness. They were approaching the landing-stage just as the paddle-steamer was mooring.

'That's the four o'clock, dead on time,' Anton observed.

Only a handful of passengers disembarked, but among the few who hurried down the gangway was one who looked disturbingly familiar.

'Anton!' Frau Arlberg came rustling along the jetty, a cool vision in pale green silk, with a matching parasol. 'How sweet of you to come to meet me. Have you been waiting long? Poor darling, you must have thought I was never coming. These wretched summer storms! Everything stops because of them. Never mind, I'm here now, and we can still have a lovely, lovely time together, just the two of us.'

Flinging her arms about Anton, she kissed him full on the mouth. If she noticed Cassie she gave no sign; she was too busy gazing adoringly into his eyes. With a gloved hand she brushed an importunate insect away from his sleeve, then she gently smoothed back a single lock of hair from his brow.

Cassie watched in uncomfortable silence. She recognised these little gestures, and she knew their significance. They were saying very clearly, 'This man is mine! Keep off!' She could not see Anton's reaction to this display, because his head was turned away from her, but she heard his greeting well enough. He said, 'Anna! Thank goodness you've come! I thought I'd missed you.'

Anna Arlberg was the person he had been expecting to meet! What was more, he was glad she had arrived—his tone, as well as his words, confirmed it. Cassie's happiness, new and precarious, teetered.

'Ah, Fräulein Haydon!' Frau Arlberg's tone chilled a few degrees as she noticed Cassie, apparently for the first time. 'I did not expect to see you here at St Leopold. What is this? A works outing for the staff of the Kurhaus?'

'Scarcely that,' laughed Anton. 'Fraülein Haydon and I met quite by chance.'

'I'm here with friends,' Cassie said.

'Ah!' Was there the tiniest hint of relief in the Ice Dragon's voice at hearing this? Whatever her emotion, she promptly turned away from Cassie, dismissing her as unimportant.

'How delightful of you to suggest that I come. You know how much I enjoy a day in the country, and to be in St Leopold, a place that means so much to you. . .' Frau Arlberg slid her arm through Anton's, neatly excluding Cassie. 'Shall we go now? I'm so looking forward to meeting your father again. I do hope he's in good health.'

She would have propelled Anton away, but he stood firm.

'One moment, Anna,' he said. 'Fräulein Haydon——'

'Oh, I'm sure Fräulein Haydon can find her friends again easily enough. She's such a competent young woman.' Frau Arlberg's words were civil but the dismissal beneath them was razor sharp.

'I would prefer——' began Anton again, but Cassie interrupted him.

'Frau Arlberg is right, there's no need for you to escort me,' she said, in a tight voice. 'I am quite capable of finding my friends by myself.' She swung round on her heel and stalked away, Anton's cries of 'Fräulein Haydon! Cassie! Wait!' ringing in her ears. Afraid lest he might come after her she hastened her stride, then plunged herself thankfully into the crowd which packed the church meadow. He would not find her—small as she was—among the tight crush of bodies.

All about her people were cheering enthusiastically about something—running-races, or wrestling, or it could have been a troup of performing elephants for all Cassie knew or cared. She stood there isolated by sudden numbing misery. How could he? How could Anton behave in such a way? To have been so loving to her, so tender, so passionate; yet all the time he had been waiting for Anna Arlberg. It had been the Ice Dragon whom he had invited, who had been his special guest—and Anna Arlberg had made no bones about how special! What did that make her? A brief diversion while he waited for the steamer to come in? Had he simply been making the most of his opportunities— seclusion and a more than willing female?

No, he's not like that, she protested to herself. He's gentle and courteous, and considerate.

And cold and self-controlled? demanded a harsh inner voice. That wasn't the way he behaved in the summer-house, was it? And he's certainly no novice where women are concerned. Go on, admit it, there are sides to Anton's nature that you just don't know. You thought he was being loving and adoring, but what if it was nothing more than a bit of lust with him? A romp in the hay? What if he's been making a fool of you?

'No!' she cried aloud, unable to bear it. Fortunately her voice went unheard in the roar of the crowd. 'No,' she repeated in a whisper. 'He loves me. I know he does.'

But she found it impossible to convince herself completely. The phantom of Anna Arlberg stalked her thoughts, Anna's confident possession of Anton, her kiss, the fact that she was his guest, that he had made no attempt to deny he had invited her. Worst of all, no matter how hard Cassie tried she could not recollect Anton saying that he loved her. The more she thought of it, the more she realised that the word 'love' had never been mentioned. She had only imagined it had. Cassie's insecure happiness tumbled and fell beneath the onslaught of doubt and humiliation, causing her to bend her head and weep silently, unnoticed by the noisy crowd about her.

It took her some time to compose herself enough to face Trudi and her family.

'We thought you'd disappeared,' declared Franz. 'We were about to send out a search-party. Where did you get to?'

'I took shelter from the storm, then had a bit of a struggle getting back to you in this crush,' she replied. It was no more than the truth.

Fortunately Trudi was too absorbed by being among her family and friends to be as observant as usual; Cassie's pale face and red eyes escaped her notice.

'Well, you're here now, and that's the main thing,' she said with satisfaction. 'Now let's just find ourselves a good spot for our picnic, shall we? We'd better get a bit of nourishment inside us because all the fun isn't over yet by a long chalk.'

But for Cassie all the fun was definitely over. As if anything more was needed to shatter her last vestige of happiness, when the steamer churned its way past them, later in the evening, she saw two figures on deck, one in pale green, the other tall, upright, unmistakable. The last vague hope, that Anton might come looking for her, withered and died. The day began to seem interminable, but she made a valiant effort not to spoil things for the others. Somehow she managed to talk and smile and even laugh, but deep inside her heart felt bruised. Anton did not love her. What a fool she had been to think that he did.

CHAPTER NINE

Dawn found Cassie wide awake, and she wondered how many sleepless nights she had endured since coming to Austria, all of them with the same root cause—Anton Sommer. This time was worse than any of the others, though. This time the hurt was much deeper, and she had humiliation and a sense of betrayal to add to her other miseries.

It was ironic, she thought bitterly, that ever since leaving the schoolroom she had been aware of the perils of being attractive to men. Suitors she had had in plenty, but she had rejected them, growing skilful in avoiding their attentions because the idea of love and marriage had never appealed to her. Until now! And now, when it really mattered, she had proved herself to be as weak and vulnerable as the most dim-witted of females. Worse, she had proved that she could be easily fooled by sweet words and gentle caresses. Since time began woman had been duped by that fatal combination, and she had fallen right into the honeyed trap.

Remembering the eagerness with which she had shown her love for Anton in the summer-house caused her to go hot with bitter shame. How he must be laughing at her, especially after all her fine declarations about being independent and career-minded!

During the long, tear-stained night she reached one definite conclusion. She would have to leave her job at the Kurhaus; she could no longer bear to work there, knowing she must encounter Anton every day.

As soon as it was light enough to see she rose and wrote a letter of resignation. The cool, formal words were stark on the page. Not once did she betray the distress she was feeling, and it gave her some satisfaction to know she could at least keep her pen under control.

When she arrived at the Kurhaus she slipped her letter in among Anton's morning post, then went to her desk. She was dreading the time when he would come on his usual rounds and she would have to face him again. But it turned out to be Frau Arlberg, a triumphant Frau Arlberg, whom she had to brave first.

'You are looking peaky, Fräulein Haydon. I hope you aren't suffering from the after-effects of yesterday's celebrations at St Leopold?' Anna Arlberg's voice was calm, almost solicitous, but her hard grey eyes were gloating.

'I'm just tired. Late nights don't agree with me,' replied Cassie.

'Ah, yes, you were with friends, I think you said? It must be quite wearing, taking part in the rustic revels with the peasants. Such activities don't appeal to me. I much preferred dining quietly with Dr Sommer at his family home. You have been there?'

'No,' Cassie was forced to admit.

'It's a delightful house close to the lake. It does show the lack of a woman's touch, perhaps; still, as Dr Sommer's father said, that's something he hopes his son will rectify before long. Such a charming old gentleman! He does so like to tease me.'

Cassie knew she was expected to ask some pertinent question at this point, but she refused to rise to any bait dangled by Anna Arlberg.

The Ice Dragon continued, 'Of course I'm a frequent visitor, quite one of the family you might say.' And she lowered her eyelashes in an attempt to look coy.

'How very nice for you.'

'Yes, it is. Now, I must not stay here gossiping all day, or Dr Sommer will have stern words to say to me.' Frau Arlberg gave something that almost resembled a girlish giggle and swept away, her black taffeta skirts fairly crackling with satisfaction.

'My, Frau Arlberg is in a good mood today,' commented Frau Willendorf, sidling up to Cassie's elbow. 'I've never known her be so affable. Of course, she's got good cause.' The older woman lowered her voice conversationally. 'Dining with Dr Sommer's family! That's got to mean something. Did you notice that necklace she was wearing?'

'Yes.' Cassie could scarcely have avoided noticing it, for Anna Arlberg had been fingering it continually during their conversation.

'Such a lovely thing. I do like filigree silver, don't you? It looks so good against black. And you'll never guess who gave it to her. Dr Sommer! Yes, this very weekend! That's got to mean something too, don't you think? I say there'll be wedding bells before long, you mark my word!'

'I think they should suit each other admirably,' said Cassie acidly, wishing Frau Willendorf would stop her prattling. Every word was an agony to her and she longed for a bit of peace. Her one consolation was that, so far, there had been no sign of Anton.

At that moment one of the valets came up.

'Excuse me, Fräulein Haydon, Dr Sommer says would you be kind enough to go to his office at once?' he said.

The thought of any sort of private interview with Anton made her feel sick with dread. There was no way she was going to his office, even though it would mean getting away from Frau Willendorf. Fortunately, just then the Kurhaus doors were opened, and people came hurrying in—a fair number of the male visitors heading straight for her.

'Please give Dr Sommer my apologies. I regret I'm not free to come at the moment,' she said.

The valet bowed and went away, clearly not relishing the prospect of delivering such a message, while Frau Willendorf stared at her with undisguised disapproval.

'You aren't going? When the *Herr Doktor* wants to see you?' she asked in awe.

'The *Herr Doktor* doesn't realise how many people

we've got to deal with this morning,' Cassie retorted. 'He can't possibly have meant me to desert my post with such a queue waiting for my attention. . . Now, sir, how can I help you?' She turned to her first client, an ageing English colonel, and dazzled him so much with the brilliance of her smile that he quite forgot what he wanted to ask.

Anton would not be happy at such a brusque refusal, she knew, and while she dealt with the stream of queries and problems she waited tensely for him to summon her a second time. When it came it was not delivered by any humble messenger but by Anton himself. A tense and angry Anton.

'Fräulein Haydon, I wish to see you in my office immediately,' he said.

'As you can see, *Herr Doktor*, I'm rather busy at the moment.' She refused to look at him, preferring to concentrate upon a harassed gentleman who was attempting to get the various members of his large and argumentative family to choose an excursion.

'Your work can wait,' Anton snapped.

'But I'm busy.'

'Now! At once!

'I'm sorry, *Herr Doktor*. I'm in the middle of making some very complicated arrangements. I can't possibly leave at the moment.' Doggedly she stuck to her post, knowing that Anton would never make a scene in public, no matter how incensed he was by her defiance. Instead, he came round to her side of the desk.

'What the devil do you mean by this?' he demanded in a low voice, thrusting her letter in front of her eyes.

'Didn't I make myself clear? It's a letter of resignation. I no longer wish to work at the Kurhaus.' Or for you, she added silently.

'But why? You give no reasons!'

'The terms of my contract do not require me to give reasons.'

'No, but I do! Cassie, what has happened? Yesterday. . .' He paused, realising that he had an attentive audience on the other side of the desk.

'Ah, yes, yesterday.' She turned to face him, aware that she could no longer fend him off. 'A day of amusing diversions, as I recall, but nothing of any lasting importance.'

'Nothing of lasting importance? How can you say such a thing?'

'Quite easily, because it is the truth.'

'No, it's not! Oh, for heaven's sake! Can't we carry on this conversation somewhere more private?'

'I prefer to remain where I am, thank you.'

'Then let me say, if you have had second thoughts . . .if you now regret the time we spent. . .'

'Oh, that!' Cassie spoke in a casual manner, because she did not want memories of the summer-house to return. 'That was nothing, as I said before.'

'I don't believe you. Something has happened to upset you, and I'm determined to know what. Are you angry because I left you to go with Anna?'

'Certainly not,' she retorted too emphatically.

'Then let me explain——'

'Explanations are not necessary.'

'Yes, they are. Anna's visit was important to me. I'd been waiting for her all day. Until I met up with you I'd been watching every steamer coming in for her arrival——'

'There's no need to go on. I understand the importance of Frau Arlberg's visit to you, and its significance.'

'You do? I don't know how you found out.'

'Surely it's obvious. This is Bad Adler, after all. Would it be in order for me to offer you my felicitations?' she said, struggling to keep her voice steady.

'It's a bit early for that, but thank you all the same. Nevertheless, I don't understand why you want to leave here.'

'You don't?' She stared at him aghast. Did he imagine that she wanted to stay when he had as good as admitted his engagement to Frau Arlberg? What sort of a female did he think she was? Then suddenly she knew she could not continue, she had to end this conversation. 'I got a better offer,' she said. 'It's as simple as that.'

'Oh!' He seemed stricken by her explanation. 'Then I suppose I must accept your resignation?'

'I don't see that you have much option. I intend to leave at the end of the month, whether you accept it or not.'

'Do—do you require me to give you a reference?'

'It will not be necessary, thank you.'

'In that case there is nothing more to be said.'

He stalked away, his face white and tense, leaving Cassie struggling to hold back her tears and the occupants of the pump-room wondering what piece of drama they had nearly overheard.

Cassie's 'better offer' had, of course, been fictitious, so she was obliged to begin the long, wearisome chore of searching for employment once more.

'Remember how hard it was last time?' pointed out Trudi, who did not approve of her resignation and made no bones about saying so.

'Things might have changed since then.'

'And they might not! What will you do if you haven't found anything by the end of the month?'

'Then I will have to return to England and go to live with my brother and his wife, like a dutiful little sister.'

'It doesn't sound much of a life to me,' Trudi commented. 'I'm sure there was no real need for you to throw up your job at the Kurhaus. Just because you and Anton Sommer had a tiff——' Then she caught sight of Cassie's stricken expression and stopped in mid-sentence. 'You'll find something,' she continued, with false enthusiasm. 'You won't have to leave Bad Adler, never fear.'

'Perhaps I *should* leave Bad Adler. It would be the sensible thing to do.'

'Leave. . .!' Trudi was aghast. 'But this is your home now. How can you think of going somewhere among

strangers. . .? Here's the local paper. Let's go through
the adverts like we did before. We're sure to find you
something suitable.' She pushed the newspaper into
Cassie's hands, determined to divert her mind from
thoughts of quitting the town.

Obediently, though she had little optimism about the
outcome, Cassie sat down with a pencil and notebook
and began the laborious task of going through the
'situations vacant' column.

The weeks while she worked out her notice were the
most difficult she had ever endured. There was no
avoiding Anton, and to see him day after day was an
agony to her, made worse by the fact that, in public,
they had to speak to one another and be polite.

Difficult though it was encountering Anton regularly
in the pump-room, her worst fear was that at some time
she would meet up with him in the gardens or a
secluded corridor or somewhere where they would be
alone, away from everyone's gaze. He had not totally
accepted her explanation for her departure. Time and
again he hinted that there was no need for her to leave,
that they should talk the matter over calmly and rationally. Calmly and rationally! Cassie knew she could
never achieve that! What she dreaded most was if he
badgered her for the truth until she gave in and
confessed her love for him. This was something she was
determined not to do. It was the one scrap of self-
respect she felt she had left.

In the pump-room and public rooms she was safe—
Anton would never make a scene in front of the
visitors—but elsewhere, at every step she was always
on her guard. At the slightest sign of him in the Kurhaus
gardens or in the street outside, she would double back
and leave by another route. Sometimes she suspected
he was lying in wait for her behind a corner, or in a
shop doorway, but she always managed to evade him.
And so she should! She had had plenty of practice
avoiding Bobo Pentransky.

These days she seldom thought of the Count. She

had quite enough to trouble her with Anton without worrying about Pentransky too.

'Where's your pretty smile gone?' demanded Sir George one morning when she had been feeling particularly miserable.

'I think I forgot to put it on when I got up this morning,' she tried to joke.

'Well, this won't do! Your smile is the only thing that puts any life in this old carcass of mine. Twice as beneficial as a tank of spa water, that it is! Now come on, make an effort.'

To please him she attempted a smile, and he regarded her efforts critically.

'Not too good, but it's better than nothing.' He leaned towards her, and gave her hand a fatherly pat. 'You know, you mustn't take these rumours seriously. Such tales have been floating round town for ages and never come to anything. In my opinion they never will.'

'And what stories are these, Sir George?' she asked.

'Why, that the Ice Dragon has collared poor Sommer at last, and is frog-marching him towards the altar. My guess is she is putting the rumour about herself, in the hopes that, if enough people are stupid enough to believe it, the unfortunate fellow will be honour-bound to marry her. Foolish creature! As if young Sommer isn't bright enough to see through such a ploy. So you see, you've no need to look so woebegone.'

For once Sir George's reassurance had the opposite effect. If he had heard that Anton and Anna Arlberg were to marry then the story must be well-known indeed. She only hoped that she was well away from the Kurhaus before it became established fact.

One thing she hoped her new situation would provide her with, apart from escape from Anton, was rather more spare time. Her time off from the Kurhaus was so scant, and frequently at such awkward times, that doing even the simplest shopping proved quite a problem. Usually she had to forgo food and rush out in her brief lunch-break. The imminent approach of her sister-in-law's birthday meant that instead of eating she would be forced to do a round of the shops yet again. Nor was she confident one lunch-break would be enough. Finding something which would suit both Maud's taste and her pocket was not going to be easy.

When she had assured herself that the coast was clear of both Anton and Pentransky she hurried into town. As she turned into the esplanade, however, she saw a very rotund, very welcome figure ahead of her.

'Sister Kathleen!' she exclaimed.

The nun swung round, and at the sight of Cassie her face became one beaming smile.

'Why, who better could I meet today? And who better could I talk to, seeing as I can use a civilised tongue with you?' declared the sister.

'Now that is what I call a fine greeting,' Cassie smiled.

'And there's a fine welcome to match if you ever care to come up to the convent again.'

'I'd like that, thank you, though I don't get much time off.'

'And here I am wasting what little bit of it you have. No doubt you're off somewhere important.'

'No, I'm only shopping. We can walk together if you're going along the esplanade.'

'That I am. I've some business to do with Herr Heller who keeps that nice gifts and haberdashery store by the bridge. I'm taking him these.' She lifted the cover on the basket she was carrying and displayed the contents.

'Oh!' Cassie gave a gasp of pleasure. The items in the basket were all small—purses, comb cases, wallets and things of a similar nature—but they were all of *petit point* embroidery, exquisitely executed in the most delightful colours.

'They're beautiful. Did you do these?' she asked.

'Ah, no. A bit of darning and plain seaming's all I'm fit for. They were done by two old ladies who live near the convent. They like to support our baths, and so this is their contribution. They do this wonderful embroidery, which I take down to Herr Heller, who gives us a very nice price for it. The visitors fairly snap them up, he says.'

'I don't wonder. The work is exquisite.' Cassie looked thoughtfully at a purse decorated with alpine flowers. 'I suppose I couldn't buy one now, could I? I came out to buy a birthday present for my sister-in-law, and this one with the posy of gentians and edelweiss would be exactly right.'

'Of course you can, and to you it'll be a special price.'

'Oh, no, I'll pay whatever Herr Heller would have given you,' Cassie insisted. When at last Sister Kathleen had named a sum, she went on, 'Are the baths in need of funds, then?'

'Indeed they are,' said the sister, accepting the money and handing over the purse. 'They're run entirely by charity, you see. We nuns accept no payment, of course, and Dr Sommer, the darling man, never charges a penny piece for his services, but the other staff must be paid, and the building maintained properly. Then there's equipment and medicines and a deal more. Oh, we're always in need, right enough.'

'Where does the money come from?'

'Everyone and anyone. The dear doctor's a rare one for persuading his rich friends to contribute money or jewellery, and the less wealthy, such as my two old ladies, they'll make things for us to sell or give us a copper or two when they can. It's wonderful how it all mounts up.'

'It must be.' Cassie wished she could do something to help, then she had an idea. 'Jewellery?' she said. 'You accept jewellery?'

'We do. Why, have you got something you can spare?'

'I can more than spare it,' Cassie said. 'I'll be glad to get rid of it.' Then she had second thoughts. Might she be bringing trouble to the good sisters and to the baths if she donated Pentransky's jewels?

'You think about it, if you aren't too sure about

parting with your jewels,' said Sister Kathleen, noting her change of expression.

'I want to part with them, never fear. It's just that . . .well they were an unwelcome gift from a so-called gentleman—a ruby bracelet with matching earrings. I want none of them, but he won't take them back, and because he has a nasty reputation no one will take them off my hands. Nothing would please me more than for you to have them, but it's only fair to warn you that there may be problems.'

'And would this so-called gentleman be Count Pentransky?'

'You know about that?' asked Cassie in astonishment.

Sister Kathleen laughed at her surprise.

'We aren't one of these closed orders, you know, we hear what goes on in the world,' she grinned, then her cheery face grew serious. 'We heard that you'd had a bit of bother with that imp of Satan.'

'How. . .? Oh, yes, the two attendants who came from the Kurhaus. They'd have told you.'

'Well, they did have a wondrous tale to tell about the Count being bound up in wet sheets. It would have been a pity to have kept it to themselves.'

'I suppose so. And in that case I expect you know that most of Bad Adler thinks I'm Pentransky's mistress.'

'Do they now?' said Sister Kathleen calmly.

'I'm not!' said Cassie fervently, scarcely hearing her. 'And never have been, though I can't prove it.'

'You don't have to prove anything to me, mavourneen. That's a matter between you and the good Lord, no one else.'

'Thank you for having faith in me. I appreciate it,' Cassie said with relief.

'There, I'm sure I'm giving you no more credit than you deserve, and if you're sure you want to donate those baubles I'm certain we could make good use of the money. There's no need to trail up specially. You could give them to Dr Sommer.'

'No!' said Cassie with vehemence. 'I don't want him to know anything about this.'

Sister Kathleen looked at her shrewdly.

'Maybe you're wise,' she said. 'There's enough bad blood between Pentransky and the doctor without stirring up more.'

'Yes. . .yes, that's the reason.' Cassie regained her composure. 'But are you sure the Count won't cause trouble for the baths or the convent?'

'He could try,' said Sister Kathleen thoughtfully. 'Count Pentransky versus the Reverend Mother! Now there's a fight that'd be worth seeing!'

The town hall clock struck the half-hour, warning Cassie to return to work.

'I'll see you again soon,' she assured Sister Kathleen, after bidding her goodbye, then she hurried back to the spa.

As she stepped through the great doors she felt her spirits plummet, as they always did now whenever she entered the Kurhaus. There was too much of Anton's influence about the place for her peace of mind, even when he was not there. She told herself that with every passing day the hurt inside her would grow less, but it did not. How did you learn to stop loving someone? she wondered frequently. Sadly, no solution came to her, any more than she could find a way of soothing the hot pain of the humiliation she had suffered. How she longed to find a new job and leave.

Anna Arlberg was another reason for her wishing to quit the Kurhaus. The Ice Dragon had always been overbearing; now there was a triumphant gloating in her manner which cut Cassie to the quick. That Frau Arlberg was soon to become Frau Sommer became common knowledge. It was all too evident from the way Anna Arlberg was conducting herself. She grew even more domineering in her work, making sure everyone knew, by implication rather than words, that soon she would be controlling the spa alongside Anton, instead of merely being his assistant.

Anton himself did not look happy these days. There was a grim tightness about his jaw, and a dark misery in his eyes which pulled at Cassie's heart, in spite of herself.

'That's what he gets for letting himself fall into the clutches of that Arlberg female,' commented Sir George. 'I confess I'm disappointed in the fellow. I thought he had more sense than that.'

Sir George's remarks did nothing to improve Cassie's spirits; they merely served to make her more eager than ever to leave the Kurhaus.

When her day off eventually came—the last she would ever have while she worked at the Kurhaus— Cassie kept her word, and set off for the convent.

'There, and aren't we glad to see you!' Sister Kathleen welcomed her with a cherubic smile.

'I've come bearing gifts,' said Cassie. 'Though I'm still worried in case the jewellery causes you trouble.'

'I told Reverend Mother the whole story, and she says not to bother your head about it. She's to go to Salzburg next week, and she'll take your jewels with her and sell them there. She'll drive a hard bargain too, you mark my words.' Sister Kathleen gave an appreciative chuckle. 'I'm only sorry you can't see her at the moment, it's the monthly trustees' meeting for the baths.'

'Much as I'd like to meet her, I wouldn't want to disturb her if she's busy,' Cassie said. 'In the meantime I think you had better take charge of this.'

She handed over the jewel case. Sister Kathleen opened it and gazed down. In the sunshine the colours of the rubies and emeralds shone but the gold settings looked heavy and over-elaborate.

'These must have cost Count Pentransky a pretty penny, anyone can see that!' said the nun. 'Fancy, for a man to have so much money and so little taste! It only proves what I've thought all along—that the good Lord has a sense of humour. Well, these baubles will do a deal of good where it's most needed, and it'll be thanks to your generosity.'

'Not really. I admit I'll be glad to get rid of them. They have too many unpleasant associations.'

Sister Kathleen looked at her sympathetically.

'Have you been having any more trouble from that terrible man?' she asked.

'Not recently, thank goodness! I haven't seen any sign of him for some weeks, but I've learned from bitter experience that this is the time I must be most on my guard. He's liable to spring out on me when I least expect it.'

'You poor child!' The sister clicked her tongue in sympathy. 'What a situation for you to be in! Now, if ever you're in need of a refuge, you can always come here. Not even Count Pentransky would dare violate a convent.'

'You're very kind.' Cassie was touched. 'Up till now the only other place I've ever been totally safe from him is the ladies' card assembly at the Kurhaus.'

'Well, you've certainly got a bit of variety now,' said Sister Kathleen, and they both laughed.

Suddenly the laughter died on Cassie's lips as the door opened and in walked Dr Sommer.

She stared at him in astonishment.

'It's not a Tuesday!' she said accusingly. 'What are you doing here?'

'As far as I know my activities aren't regulated entirely by the calendar,' he said calmly. 'I believe I am entitled to come here on other weekdays. On Wednesdays, for example, when there is a meeting of the baths' trustees—of which I happen to be one.'

'Oh,' said Cassie, feeling foolish and embarrassed because she had let her ruffled emotions get the better of her.

'Would it be impertinent to ask what you are doing here?' he enquired, still maintaining his icy calm.

'Just visiting,' said Cassie.

'Ah, the generous creature's brought us some fine jewels to sell for the baths,' said Sister Kathleen simultaneously. Then she clapped her hand over her mouth. 'There, haven't I let my tongue run away with me again! You weren't supposed to know, Doctor dear.'

'Oh, and why not?' asked Anton, curiosity piercing his imperturbable manner.

Before Cassie could speak Sister Kathleen broke in with, 'Why, because Cassie here didn't want to cause any more trouble between you and Count Pentransky, these jewels being an unwanted gift from that awful man.'

'How considerate,' Anton said. Then more gently, 'How very considerate of you.'

Cassie found herself growing uncomfortable before his gaze. His eyes held a warm expression which was too familiar. It reminded her distressingly of a time when she had believed he loved her. For once she could think of nothing to say, and she was thankful when Sister Kathleen took over the conversation, showing Anton the bracelet and earrings and saying, 'There, Doctor, did you ever see anything like them in your life?'

'I have had the dubious pleasure of seeing these jewels before,' Anton said quietly. 'Unattractive as they are, it is most kind of Fräulein Haydon to part with them.'

'No, it isn't,' said Cassie vehemently. 'As you very well know!'

He did not reply, but simply looked very thoughtful at this, and she wondered if he were remembering the harsh words he had flung at her on the day Pentransky had given her the bracelet. If so he made no reference to them. Instead he said, 'I must leave now. If you, too, are ready to go, I would be pleased to give you a ride back into town.'

Cassie tried to refuse, but somehow Sister Kathleen managed to overwhelm her objections, so much so that she began to wonder if the nun's slip of the tongue over the reason for her visit had been truly accidental. Certainly the sister looked enormously pleased with herself as she waved them off in the chaise.

'In spite of all you say, I think it is very generous of you to donate those jewels,' said Anton. 'Anyone can see they are very valuable.'

'Not to me.'

'Yes, I see that now. There was a time when I did not, to my shame.'

'You still believe me when I say I dislike Pentransky and always have?' The words were out before Cassie could stop them.

'Of course.' He sounded surprised. 'Did you doubt me? Is that why you've decided to leave the Kurhaus?'

'Certainly not! I've already given you my reasons for leaving.' Her reply was curt. How could she tell him the truth?

'I wish you wouldn't go. There's no need.' He sounded so persuasive that she longed to agree with him. She could not, of course.

'I see a need,' she said.

He gave a sigh. 'It's such a pity. You've begun your work so well. The English visitors are very complimentary about the services and facilities we offer, and it's all your hard work. Are you going to throw everything away?'

'You'll find someone else easily enough.'

'No, not someone like you.' Something in the soft tenor of his voice warned her that at the slightest encouragement from her he would take her in his arms there and then, on the high road. One part of her longed for him to do so, but her bruised and battered heart dared not take the risk. He had betrayed her trust once before. Moreover, he was going to marry Anna Arlberg. She would be a fool to believe his soft words now. She sat very still, her hands clasped tightly, staring woodenly at the ears of the horse in front of them.

'I've even made a concession, in the hope that you'll change your mind and stay,' said Anton.

'Oh, what's that?'

'The cricket score-board. I had it put up in the smoking-room this morning.'

'You did that to make me change my mind?' Her voice was harsh in her effort not to weaken.

'Well, Sir George did explain to me just how important the cricket scores are to every Englishman,' admitted Anton, with a smile which normally would have conquered her heart.

'I thought so!' she said acidly. 'It took another man to persuade you to accept a woman's idea!'

'Ah, do I detect signs of the New Woman emerging?' His smile grew, tinged with bitterness. 'Very well, I accept defeat. You won't change your mind and stay! I regret it, though. I regret it very much.'

His words sounded genuine.

He wants me to stay, he really wants me to stay, Cassie told herself as she climbed the stairs to the apartment in Elizabethplatz. Then she laughed bitterly at her own gullibility. He was manipulating her again, using her to his own ends. What had he in mind? Establishing her in a modest love-nest once he was married to Anna Arlberg? It was very fashionable for a man in his position to have a mistress as well as a wife; it was almost expected of him. Well, she was not going to oblige.

But her strong will and determination could not keep the pain away. She still loved him very much. The trouble was she could no longer believe him.

CHAPTER TEN

IT DID not help matters that Cassie's search for employment was not going well. As she answered advert after advert, without success, she had a feeling of history repeating itself. She had done all this once before; the only difference was that there was an even greater sense of urgency this time, quite apart from personal reasons. The spa season was drawing to a close. The fashionable crowds would be leaving Bad Adler in another month or so, and with them would go her best chances of finding a new post. Whether it was because it was so late in the season or whether her unwarranted reputation still lingered among the gossips of the town, she could not tell, but the result was the same. No one would employ her!

Then, just as she was beginning to despair, a letter arrived for her. The sheet of expensive hot-press paper bore an impressive crest, and Cassie read the neat precise script with interest.

> Dear Fräulein Haydon,
> I understand that you are seeking employment. I am, at the moment, in need of a companion-secretary, a post for which I think you are suited. I shall expect you at three o'clock this afternoon, when we can discuss details.

There was a certain imperiousness about the letter, but then, Cassie observed, it was signed by a baroness, the Baroness von Hackenberg. Moreover it seemed to be offering her a job, which was strange, because she had not applied to the Baroness. In fact, she had never even heard of her. Trudi would undoubtedly know all about the von Hackenbergs; unfortunately she had already left to do the shopping. Not that it made much difference; Cassie knew she had no choice but to accept, whatever the terms, although keeping the three o'clock appointment was going to be a problem. If she asked Anton for time off it would lead to awkward questions, and there was no point in approaching Frau Arlberg. To play truant was the only solution. There was no help for it, even though it went against the grain to give someone else extra work.

The worst they can do to me is dismiss me on the spot, she told herself. Somehow she did not think Anton would do that.

The address given in the mysterious letter was some way out of Bad Adler, on a road which soon began to climb up a forested slope. Cassie was glad she had given herself plenty of time; she felt quite hot and tired by the time she reached the imposing gates of the Haus Hackenberg. The lodge-keeper who let her in was decidedly surly, and she hoped he was not typical of the household.

If she had felt hot and tired when she reached the gates then she felt even more so by the time she caught a glimpse of the house, for the drive was long and wound steeply up through the trees. She had a few minutes in hand, and thankfully she sank on to a fallen tree trunk to rest her weary legs and to repair the damage caused by her exertions. It would not give a good impression to meet the Baroness with a perspiring face and a skirt that was covered in dust from ankle to knee. When she felt presentable once more she rose and walked up to the house.

The architecture of the Haus Hackenberg did not fit easily into any one category. It was far from being in the comfortable chalet-style, yet it fell short of being a castle. It was such a collection of ill-assorted turrets and jutting wings that it was impossible to decide what had been the original structure and what had been added at the whim of an eccentric owner. The result was interesting, and could have been attractive if sombre paint and shuttered windows had not given the place a grim air.

Cassie did not find it at all appealing. However, she

was in no position to be choosy, so she rang the bell. It was answered by a butler as old and surly as the lodge-keeper, who established his superiority by the haughtiness of his expression.

'Yes?' he demanded, looking down his long nose.

'I am Fräulein Haydon. The Baroness von Hackenberg is expecting me.' Cassie handed him her visiting-card.

The butler took it gingerly between gloved fingers as if it had been recently dredged from some murky pond.

'I will see if the *Baronin* is at home,' he said, and would have shut the door, but Cassie was too quick for him.

If she were accepted for the post as companion-secretary in this household, one thing she would not tolerate was problems from a supercilious butler. Begin as you mean to go on was her motto; as he was closing the door, she slipped nimbly past him into the hall.

'I will wait here,' she said.

The butler drew in a long, indignant breath. Whether he meant to roar his objection or to explode by way of protest there was no knowing. Cassie did not wait to find out.

'Go along, man!' she snapped. 'My appointment is for three o'clock and it is exactly on the hour now. I do not relish being kept waiting, and I very much doubt if the *Baronin* does, either.'

The butler exhaled with something like a whimper and, placing the card on a silver salver, hurried off as fast as his rheumaticky legs would take him. He was back in a surprisingly short time.

'The *Baronin* will see you now, *Fräulein*,' he said, with more than a touch of servility. 'If you would kindly follow me.'

He led the way across the hall and up a wide oak staircase. Cassie wondered if the interior was as gloomy as it seemed, or had her eyes simply not adjusted after the bright sunshine outside? Hardly any daylight filtered in, causing her to stumble on the unaccustomed steps. Eventually she was shown into a room that was a little better illuminated. At least she was able to make out the Baroness von Hackenberg amid the over-ornate furnishings. To be honest the lady would have been conspicuous in even the poorest lighting, for she was overweight to the point of grossness.

'Ah, Fräulein Haydon, you are prompt,' said the Baroness. Her voice was surprisingly tiny, considering it came from such a girth. 'Sit down. I have heard much about you.'

'May I ask from whom?' Cassie asked.

'That is none of your concern,' was the terse reply. 'Tell me, can you type?'

'Yes, *Baronin*.'

'Is your handwriting good, both in copperplate and gothic script?'

'Yes, *Baronin*.'

'You are fluent in both German and English?'

'Yes, *Baronin*.'

'I was told you have some experience of home nursing. Is that true?'

'Yes, *Baronin*.'

'When are you free of your present commitments?'

'At the end of this month.'

'Then you can start on the first day of next month. I will expect you then. That is all. Good day.'

In all of her considerable experience, Cassie had never before been interviewed in such a manner.

'By your leave, *Baronin*, but it is not quite all,' she said.

The Baroness looked surprised.

'The situation is yours. What more is there to say?' she demanded.

'Firstly, I have references. Perhaps you would care to look at them?'

With a languid wave of one plump hand the Baroness dismissed the idea.

'Too fatiguing,' she said. 'Is there anything else?'

'The matter of salary, *Baronin*.'

'I'll pay you whatever you are getting now.'

'But in my present post I live out,' said Cassie.

'So?'

'Well, I presume that here I will be living in?'

'Of course. That makes no difference.'

Cassie opened her mouth to explain that when someone lived in it was usual for a sum covering board and lodging to be deducted from their wages, then she thought better of it. If the Baroness wanted to pay her over the odds why should she object?

'There is one more thing, *Baronin*,' she said.

The Baroness flopped back against the sofa cushion.

'What is it?' she demanded. 'Really, I had no idea that interviewing staff could be so exhausting.'

'What will my duties be, *Baronin*?'

The Baroness seemed nonplussed by this simple question.

'Why, write my letters, and read to me and. . .and look after me when I'm not well.'

'Is that all, *Baronin*?'

'All? It seems a lot to me. I'm often not well. I'm very delicate.'

Cassie felt this was an unfortunate choice of word, considering the woman's size. All the same, the Baroness had a fine pink and white complexion, and such soft blonde hair that she wondered if, inside that fat lumbering body, there were the remains of what had once been a very pretty woman.

'You will come here on the first of next month.' It was a command, not a question.

'Very well, *Baronin*. Thank you.'

As Cassie followed the butler out of the room she should have felt jubilant. She had a new job, her duties did not sound to be onerous, and she was going to be well paid. Yet instead of being elated she was conscious of a feeling of disquiet. Something was wrong. She had been given the job too easily. The questions she had been asked had been almost perfunctory. At every other interview she had ever attended the potential employer had scrutinised each word on her references and interrogated her most thoroughly on her experience, her education, her religion and her upbringing. The Baroness had done none of these things and, even allowing for her languid disposition, it was strange. Cassie got the oddest feeling that the Baroness von Hackenberg had made up her mind to give her the post long before they had met.

But why? That was what puzzled her. And how had the Baroness got to know of her, and the fact that she was seeking a new situation?

Cassie was at the foot of the stairs when the mystery was solved. The door opposite the staircase happened to be open, revealing a drawing-room illuminated by a single shaft of sunlight. The contrast to the gloomy hall was so great that she could not helping looking in, and then she saw it, above the marble fireplace—a huge portrait of Count Pentransky! It was a very idealised view of him. He was in full military uniform, with one hand resting artistically on the head of a deer-hound which—on canvas at least—gazed up at him with adoring eyes. Prudently the artist had diminished the Count's stomach and extended his shoulders; nevertheless, Cassie felt her flesh creep at the sight of him.

The butler had reached the front door and was holding it open for her. Cassie did not move.

'Why is there a portrait of Count Pentransky here?' she asked.

'Because the *Baronin* wishes it, *fräulein*.' He seemed bemused by her question. 'It is only natural for her to want her son's picture in her house.'

'Her son?'

'Yes, by her first marriage, to Count Otto Pentransky, a very noble gentleman, who. . .'

But Cassie was no longer listening, she was charging back up the stairs.

The Baroness looked up in mild surprise when she walked into the room.

'*Baronin*, I have come to tell you I decline the offer of the post in your household,' she said.

'Decline?' Obviously such an eventuality had never occurred to the Baroness. 'But you can't decline! I have told you to come at the beginning of the month.'

'Yes, you did, *Baronin*, but I refuse.'

'Refuse?' This was clearly another word unfamiliar to the Baroness. 'Why?'

'You can ask that? *Baronin*, when I came in answer to your letter I had no idea you were Count Pentransky's mother. If I had, wild horses would not have dragged me over your doorstep.'

The Baroness clapped a pudgy hand over her mouth and her blue eyes registered genuine alarm.

'How did you discover that?' she demanded.

'The door was open and I saw his portrait downstairs.'

'Oh, Bobo said you were not to find out. He's going to be terribly, terribly angry with me.'

'I am sorry about that, *Baronin*, but I will not change my mind.'

'He was so set on it. . .so proud of the clever scheme he had devised. . .and now you say you won't accept. . .'

'No, *Baronin*.'

'I'll double your salary——'

'No, *Baronin*, not if you were to increase it tenfold.'

'Please. . .there must be something that will make you accept. Name it and it's yours. . .anything to stop Bobo being angry. He's so frightening when he's angry. . .'

Cassie had been making her way towards the door; now she came to an abrupt halt, not because of the Baroness's extravagant offer, but because of the woman's evident distress. She had collapsed back on to the sofa cushions, gasping for breath, her face an alarming crimson. Much as she wanted to get out of the house, Cassie could not leave the poor soul in such a state. She rang the bell, and the butler, who must have been hard on her heels, entered.

'The *Baronin*'s maid! Quickly!' she ordered, already on her knees beside the sick woman. Deftly she administered sal volatile, loosened the Baroness's gown and unlaced her stays. Then she opened the windows, to let a flow of air into the stuffy room. There was a bottle of cologne on a side table and, soaking her handkerchief in it, she dabbed at the Baroness's perspiring brow.

'There, take slow, deep breaths,' she said. 'Nice and slowly. Breathe in. . .breathe out. . .'

Gradually the terrible gasping eased and the hectic flush receded.

'Thank you, you're very kind.' The Baroness spoke faintly, her eyes still closed. 'Are—are you sure you won't come to me? I would like to have you as my companion, never mind Bobo's plans. You make me feel comfortable. It would be good to have you with me.'

'I'm quite sure,' said Cassie gently but firmly.

'But what shall I tell Bobo? What shall I tell him? He'll say it's all my fault!'

The Baroness had begun wringing her hands, and all at once Cassie felt very sorry for her. It could not be easy, being Pentransky's mother, and the unfortunate creature was clearly afraid of her son.

'I'll write him a letter, shall I? And you can give it to him,' she suggested. 'I won't mention anything about open doors or seeing his portrait. I'll say I guessed— that I saw the family resemblance—will that do?'

'It might! Oh, it just might!' The Baroness looked markedly more cheerful. 'There's pen, ink and paper on the little bureau by the window.'

Belatedly an elderly maid arrived, and tended most ineffectually to her mistress. Cassie wondered at the Baroness's continuing to employ someone so obviously incapable of performing her duties, then she had second thoughts. With a son like Bobo Pentransky, no doubt the Baroness was wise to employ only the old and the very plain.

The letter completed, she handed it to the Baroness von Hackenberg.

'Don't worry, *Baronin*,' she said. 'After reading this, Count Pentransky can't possibly blame you for my refusal.' She hoped she was right.

The Baroness grasped the letter as a drowning man might clutch at a lifeline.

'Thank you, *fräulein*,' she said. 'I do wish you would come and be my companion. You're clever and you make me feel so much better. . . But I understand why you refuse. Yes, I understand.' She spoke with sadness and a hint of shame.

Cassie felt very sorry for her. Yes, being Count Pentransky's mother could only be a trial and a sorrow. In addition the woman was clearly in ill health and without any competent nurse, despite all her money. Cassie wondered if the nuns at the convent might help. Visiting the sick was part of their religious duties. Could that include the rich as well as the poor?

For herself, she could not leave the Haus Hackenberg fast enough. She almost ran down the long drive, not caring if her departure lacked decorum or dignity. She emerged from the huge gates with such speed that she almost fell under the wheels of a passing chaise. Recovering herself, she filled her lungs with pine-scented air, then breathed out again in one long, long sigh of relief. Once more she had come close to falling victim to Pentransky. It had been a close-run thing. She set off along the road to Bad Adler at a brisk pace. As far as she was concerned, the greater distance she put between herself and the Haus Hackenberg, the happier she would be.

It was too much to hope that no one at the Kurhaus had noted her absence. She had barely reached her desk the next morning when Frau Arlberg came sweeping towards her like a ship under full sail.

'Fräulein Haydon, you were absent from your post

for the whole of yesterday afternoon! An explanation, if you please!' the Ice Dragon's voice boomed. Her classical features were set in lines of disapproval that might have been fearsome to anyone else, but Cassie had never been in awe of her, and she certainly was not going to start now.

'I had an appointment,' she said.

'An appointment? In working hours?' Frau Arlberg sounded as though she had never heard of such a thing.

'It was a very important appointment.'

'Then why did you not behave properly and ask for time off?'

'Because it would have been a waste of effort. You would never have granted it,' said Cassie coolly.

Frau Arlberg opened her mouth, then closed it again with a snap. Being unable to argue with Cassie's logic, she could only reply, 'Such behaviour is intolerable. It must not happen again!' Then she stalked off.

'And where were you yesterday afternoon, young lady?' demanded Sir George later. 'I missed you. Were you playing hookey?'

'Something of the sort,' admitted Cassie, and she told him of her adventures.

Sir George gave a low whistle.

'That was close! Too close for comfort, my dear,' he said. 'What a pity you did not mention Baroness von Hackenberg's name to me before you set out. I could have warned you about her.'

'It was foolish of me,' Cassie agreed. 'I simply didn't think of it.'

'In future I want you to promise that if something similar occurs, or you are asked to call upon someone you don't know, please consult me first, just in case Pentransky coerces any more of his relations into his nasty schemes. I know a deuced lot of folk in this town, and those I don't know I can soon find out about.'

'Surely Count Pentransky won't try the same trick twice?'

'He just might. It's just the sort of double bluff the

devious wretch might try. After all, who would have expected him to use his unfortunate mother as a bait to lure you?'

'That's true. Very well, I give you my word. If I get any more mysterious offers of employment, I will let you scrutinise the details first.'

'Good girl. Not that I like this idea of your leaving. A load of nonsense, and quite unnecessary, if you ask me. But then, nobody did ask me!' Sir George gave a sigh. 'Come on, Markham. Trundle me into the smoking-room and let's see what Hampshire are doing against Middlesex. Maybe we'll find some cheering news there!'

After he had gone, seeing that there was an unexpected lull in the number of visitors, Cassie retired to the back office, to catch up on some paperwork. She was engrossed in her typing when she heard someone enter. She turned round, expecting to see Frau Willendorf. Instead, there stood Anton. He looked grim and very, very angry. Cassie steeled herself for another rebuke.

'I trust you enjoyed yourself yesterday afternoon,' Anton snapped.

'Yes, thank you,' said Cassie, refusing to be cowed.

'I suppose it would have been asking too much for you to have had the courtesy to mention you would be absent? Just so that we could have had someone else take over your duties?'

'I didn't ask because I knew you would have said no.'

'Said no? How would I have dared? How would I have presumed to say no, when you had a rendezvous at the Haus Hackenberg?'

'Who told you where I had gone?' Cassie demanded.

'I didn't need to be told. I saw you leaving there with my own eyes. In fact, you almost threw yourself under the wheels of my chaise. Now you see why I am surprised that you went off without a word. Surely you must have known I am not so indifferent to my own career, to my future, that I would have prevented you from taking tea with the Pentransky family.' The sarcasm in his voice was growing heavier and heavier.

'I wasn't taking tea!' cried Cassie.

'Then for pity's sake don't tell me what you were really doing there! I would sooner not know!' The sarcasm faded and he spoke softly, his words full of pain. 'And to think that I believed you when you said there was nothing between you and Pentransky! Yes, I actually believed you. You must consider me to be the biggest fool in this world.'

'No!' Cassie protested. 'No, you don't understand. It wasn't like that at all. It was an interview. I'd been offered a situation. I didn't know who Baroness von Hackenberg was.'

'A situation, eh? But I thought you already had employment for when you leave here. I'm afraid you've lied once too often, and now your lies are finding you out. I, for one, will never believe another word you say. As far as I'm concerned the end of the month can't come too quickly. The sooner you leave here the better.'

'You don't understand,' protested Cassie again. 'Just listen to me——'

'No!' He held up his hand as if to fend her off. 'I know better than to believe anything you say. I'll never be taken in by you again.'

'It's not how you think!' cried Cassie in anguish. 'Please listen. . .' But she was too late. Anton had gone, closing the door firmly behind him.

Cassie was too dead inside even to feel miserable. All she was conscious of was a terrible numbness where her heart should have been, and a great longing to get away from the Kurhaus. Thank goodness she only had one more day to go. If her finances had not been in such a precarious state she would have left there and then, but such impetuosity was the prerogative of the wealthy, not the potentially unemployed.

Somehow she got through her work and, when evening came, made her dispirited way back to

Elizabethplatz. One thing she did not want was time on her hands. To fill in the empty hours until bedtime she wrote to the Reverend Mother at the convent, explaining the plight of the Baroness von Hackenberg, and asking if the sisters could help in some way. The letter finished, she took it to the post—anything to keep busy and to stop herself from thinking.

As she entered the apartment she heard the hum of voices—Trudi's and the deeper tones of a man. She stepped into the living-room, expecting to see Franz, and saw instead—Anton! He rose as she entered, and for a moment they stood staring at each other, speechless. Trudi gazed at them sympathetically then, murmuring something about needing to have a word with Frau Schroeder next door while the children were asleep, slipped diplomatically from the room.

Still neither of them spoke, Cassie because she was stunned at seeing him so unexpectedly, and Anton because he seemed to be struggling with his emotions. He looked white and haggard, far more so than during their short and distressing interview that morning. It was as if the intervening hours had taken a terrible toll on him.

'It's no use!' he said explosively. 'I've got to say it. I've fought against it, but it's no use! Cassie, I love you. I don't know if Pentransky is your lover or not! I don't care! I don't care how many lovers you've got or how many you've had in the past. I love you to desperation. I can't help myself. . .' He stepped forward and swept her into his arms, his mouth claiming hers passionately.

Cassie, taken totally unawares by this ardent onslaught, let herself be gathered up in his embrace, allowed her arms to cling to him, turned her face upwards the better to return his kisses with a fervour which matched his as hunger met hunger. All thoughts of turning her heart against him were completely forgotten in the joy of his presence and the heady sensuousness of his need for her.

Eventually they parted. Dazed and disconcerted,

they gazed at one another, then with a laugh Anton pulled her to him again, more gently this time but with no less warmth.

'Oh, Cassie, Cassie. . .' he said, his lips against her hair. 'You'll be leaving the Kurhaus tomorrow to go goodness knows where. I may never see you again, and that's why I have to speak out. Loving you is such a torment, yet I can't stop. I've tried! Oh, if you knew how hard I've tried not to care for you. And it's been totally useless. I've just grown to love you more and more, and my life has grown into a greater and greater turmoil. I never know what you feel for me. One minute I'm convinced that you care, another that you are merely amusing yourself until Pentransky or some other wealthy protector comes along. And then there are your views, this New Woman thing! I've never met a female who was so independent and forthright, and that's only added to my confusion. I'll admit to you, I'm not used to being in such a state of uncertainty. Being put through this agony has really shaken me. You've shattered my confidence and addled my brain. You've taken a terrible toll on me.'

Cassie listened to his every word, her face pressed blissfully against his chest. Could she really be hearing him say these things? Had she truly caused him to be so unsure, so confused?

'I didn't mean to,' she said. Such an understatement.

'What did you mean, then?'

'I'm not sure,' she admitted. 'I think I was as confused and mixed up as you.'

'Was? You use the past tense. Does that mean you've stopped being confused, and know what you're doing?'

'Yes,' she said.

'And what are you doing?'

'Loving you! I think I've been loving you ever since we first met.'

Anton held her suddenly at arm's length.

'Then why did you never say so?' he demanded,

shaking her gently. 'Why have you been torturing me all these weeks?'

'*I* torturing *you*?' retorted Cassie. 'What about the way you've been behaving with Anna Arlberg? Can you wonder that I had my doubts about you. . .? Yes, what about you and Frau Arlberg?'

'Ah, yes, Anna.' Anton spoke with resignation. 'Surely you didn't believe all those rumours, did you? Me, marry Anna Arlberg? Do you take me for a complete fool?'

'But you as good as told me you were going to marry her,' Cassie cried.

'I did? When?'

'At St Leopold! You'd invited her specially, she was your guest, she went to your home. You admitted you'd met every steamer, hoping she would be on it. And when I offered you my felicitations on your coming engagement you didn't deny it.'

'Your felicitations? My coming engagement? Is that what you were on about?' He stared at her, then let out a shout of laughter, only to smother it quickly, remembering the sleeping children in the next room. 'My sweet, adorable darling,' he said, gathering her to him again and kissing her brow. 'We were talking at cross purposes. Yes, I was eager for Anna to come, but I wouldn't exactly call her a guest. She was bringing me an urgent message, you see. One of the most important members of the Bavarian royal family had expressed a wish to come to Bad Adler to take the waters, but he wanted to be incognito. He was most emphatic about that. Of course, it is a great honour for the town, but quite a headache for me. The trouble with these illustrious folk is that they want their anonymity, but at the same time expect the deference and privilege usual with their rank. I had to make all the arrangements. No easy task, I assure you. The message was from the Bavarian court, informing me of times of arrival. I suppose I should really have stayed at Bad Adler and waited for it there, instead of going to St Leopold, but my father is getting old, and he does like to me to get back for the celebrations.'

'I suppose Frau Arlberg volunteered to bring the message to you?'

'Yes, she did, as a matter of fact.' Anton looked at the expression on Cassie's face and gave a chuckle. 'There's no need to look like that. I'm perfectly aware that she's been pursuing me ever since she came to Bad Adler, though I'm afraid it's control of the spa that she wants sooner than the joy of my company to the end of her days. However, since she did come all the way to St Leopold with the message, the least I could do was invite her to dine.'

'Frau Arlberg implied that it was a much more personal affair. Everyone thinks it's only a matter of time before your betrothal is announced.'

'Everyone except me!'

'But she was even flaunting the necklace you gave her.'

'I never gave her any necklace.' Anton looked puzzled. 'I'd never be rash enough to give her anything, I know exactly how much capital she would make out of it.'

'Yet she said you had! A present from Dr Sommer! It was all round the Kurhaus.'

In the midst of her new-found happiness, Cassie had to resolve this one trivial doubt.

'A present from. . .' Slowly enlightenment spread across his face. 'Ah, I see now. Yes, it was a present from Dr Sommer. Dr Anton Sommer senior, my father. Making jewellery is a hobby he has taken up since his retirement, and very skilled he has become. Most of his work he donates towards the upkeep of the Weissenbach baths, but he gives a lot away. I should think half the women and girls in the village have a necklace or bracelet that he's made. It gives him a lot of pleasure.'

'Oh. . .' said Cassie, not knowing what else to say. Such an explanation had never occurred to her.

'You thought I was going to marry Anna,' said Anton. 'Is that why your manner towards me changed so swiftly that day?'

She nodded.

'You thought that? After the time we spent together in the summer-house? You believed I could behave in such a way towards you, show you such love, then turn round and announce my engagement to someone else?' He sounded hurt.

She nodded again.

'You could have been amusing yourself with me,' she said. 'I didn't know I'd got everything wrong.'

'Do you know something?' said Anton gravely. 'I think that is one of the few times I've heard you admit to being wrong.'

'Well, it doesn't happen very often,' said Cassie to his shirt-front.

She felt as well as heard the chuckle rise within him. She reached up and, pulling his face down towards her, quelled his laughter with her lips. There was no laughter in his response, just love and tenderness and a growing passion that shot through them both like fire.

'Marry me,' he said urgently. 'Please marry me. And soon! I can't bear to be away from you any longer. End my agony for ever. Say you'll marry me!'

'Yes,' she said. 'Oh, yes!' Only when she had said the words, with her acceptance still ringing in her head, did she realise what had happened. She was going to be Anton's wife! Anton loved her and they were going to be married!

No more words were needed. They clung to one another, letting their closeness set the seal on their promises. Being together was all they wanted, a private world in which no one else intruded.

'Oh, to think of it!' breathed Anton later. 'All of our days will be spent together, from now until the end of our lives. Years of loving and caring—and quarrelling. Do you realise we can't even make love without quarrelling?'

'Arguing,' Cassie corrected him happily. 'It's not quite the same thing. Are you having any regrets? Wouldn't you sooner marry some nice, quiet local girl who will cook you superb dinners and keep your house immaculate?'

'And bore me to death within the first year? No thank you. Since I can afford to employ a good cook and a housemaid or two I think I prefer to marry a New Woman. At least life will never be dull.'

'No,' agreed Cassie. 'I don't think it will.' She stayed contentedly in his arms, trying not to let one small cloud blight her happiness. It was no use. She had to speak. 'There is one thing,' she said. 'I must tell you. I haven't been quite honest with you.'

'Oh?' She felt him grow tense.

'Yes, I did tell you one small untruth.'

'You did? And are you going to say what it was?'

'Yes, because I can't bear there to be anything wrong between us, no matter how trivial. When I gave in my resignation and you questioned me, I said that I had received a better offer. It wasn't true. You see, I didn't want you to know the real reason why I was leaving, which was because I loved you too much to stay. I pretended I had another job to go to, but I haven't.'

'And this is the enormous lie you told me?'

'Yes.'

'And is this the only one?'

Cassie considered carefully.

'I think so,' she said. 'Except that of course I kept declaring that I had no interest in you whatsoever, which wasn't true, either—I think I said that to fool myself rather than you.'

'And all the rest of the time you told me the truth. Cassie, will you ever forgive me?' He rocked her in his arms, his face pressed against her hair. 'The times I've doubted you, and the awful accusations I've made. . .'

'I've forgotten them all,' she whispered softly. 'I only remember you saying you love me, and asking me to be your wife. I don't remember anything else, because nothing else is important.'

How long they would have stayed like that, wrapped in each other's arms, talking of love, there was no knowing, if the town hall clock had not chimed.

'What time is that?' wondered Anton, taking out his watch, then his chin dropped in dismay. 'It can't be that late!' he protested. 'It really can't! I must go. Poor Trudi will be wondering if she'll ever get back in her own home again.'

'Do you have to leave?' Cassie clung to his coat. 'Can't you stay just a little longer?'

He disentangled her fingers and kissed them.

'Yes, I do have to leave,' he said. 'But we won't be apart for long. Don't forget, we've got the rest of our lives together. Isn't that a marvellous thought?'

Cassie had to agree that it was.

Anton gave her one more kiss that lingered on her lips.

'There,' he said. 'That's to last until tomorrow. What a day that will be! First I must inform my father that he's to have a daughter-in-law at last. I think he was beginning to despair of me.'

'I hope he'll like me,' said Cassie uncertainly.

'No, he won't like you, he'll love you. We're very much alike, you see. And besides, he's been terrified I might weaken and marry Anna Arlberg. She frightens the life out of him.' Anton scrutinised her critically.

'What's the matter?' asked Cassie. 'Have I a smut on my nose or something?'

'No, I was looking at your mouth and wondering if that kiss really would last you until tomorrow.'

'No, it won't! It was a pretty feeble effort. You can do much better if you try.' And she lifted her face to him.

'In that case I had better try,' said Anton.

The town hall clock had chimed the quarter-hour before they tore themselves away from one another and a reluctant Anton was obliged to leave. Cassie went with him to the top of the stairs, blowing kisses to him whenever he turned to give a backward glance, until finally he was completely out of sight.

'No need to ask if everything is all right,' said Trudi, from behind her. 'One look at your expression says more than words.'

'Everything is more than all right, it's absolutely marvellous. Oh, Trudi, we are to be married! Isn't it wonderful?' And she flung her arms about her friend.

'That really is wonderful!' cried Trudi, hugging her. 'I'm so glad for you both. And relieved too, for I wondered if I had been interfering in what was none of my business, letting him into the apartment to wait for you like that. But it would have taken a harder heart than mine to have turned him away—he looked so unhappy, poor man. Thank goodness I did the right thing!'

'You did exactly the right thing! I'll never stop being grateful to you.' Cassie was in such high spirits that she waltzed Trudi back into the apartment.

'Grateful enough to let me go to bed and get some sleep?' Trudi grinned. 'And to do the same would do you no harm. It's very late, and you have to get up early in the morning.'

'I'm far too happy to go to bed. In fact, I don't think I'll ever sleep agai-ai-ain.' Cassie ended her statement with an enormous yawn.

Trudi laughed. 'Being happy can be quite exhausting, can't it?' she said. 'Come on! Bed! For the pair of us!'

In spite of her yawn Cassie was convinced she would never sleep, but long before she had her fill of rosy, idyllic thoughts of Anton she had drifted into oblivion.

Next morning she was late getting up and breakfast was a very scrambled affair. Not that she cared. Life was too golden to be spoiled by anything just then.

'Is this to be your last day at the Kurhaus or isn't it?' asked Trudi, hurrying in with the coffee.

Cassie paused, a piece of roll, well buttered and spread with apricot jam, halfway to her lips.

'I don't know!' she said. 'We never even mentioned it.'

'You had more important things to talk about, I dare say.' Trudi beamed fondly. 'All the same, you'd better be on your way within the next five minutes if you want to get there before the doors open.'

Taking her advice, Cassie emerged into a brighter, sunnier world in exactly four minutes. As she sped on her way she decided that the sky was infinitely bluer than anything she had ever seen, and that the flowers were certainly more colourful. As for the birds. . . She came to a halt, not to consider the bird song but because the clop of hoofs and the rumble of wheels warned her of an approaching carriage—a rare event so early in the morning, when the streets were usually deserted.

Poised at the edge of the kerb, she waited for it to pass, but unexpectedly the carriage halted right in front of her. The next thing she knew, a blanket was thrown over her from behind, and none too gentle hands had bustled her in throught the open door. Immediately a powerful scent of funeral lilies overwhelmed her, pervading even the stifling thickness of the blanket.

'Now then, little English bird, I've got you well and truly netted this time,' said the regrettably familiar voice of Pentransky. 'I've been very patient with you, but my patience is at an end. Now it's time for me to have some real fun.'

CHAPTER ELEVEN

CASSIE'S automatic reaction to being seized was to kick and to lash out with her fists, but the force with which she was thrown into the carriage caused her to lie immobile, the breath driven from her body. That and the chilling sound of Pentransky's voice.

Oh, no, she groaned to herself, not him! Not now!

She had been so happy, the world had seemed so perfect, and now this had happened!

Gathering her befuddled wits together, she struggled harder, shouting at Pentransky to let her go. It was no easy task, trying to kick her way free from the all-enveloping blanket; they were moving at a great pace and the carriage was swaying violently from side to side. Slumped as she was, half on the seat, half on the floor, she could get little purchase with her feet. The best she could manage was a violent contact with someone's leg. The Count's, judging by the yell. The result was a blow to the ribs which robbed her of breath once more.

As she lay gasping she heard Pentransky say petulantly, 'The little vixen! She's bruised my shin, it's agony! Tie her up. That should keep her out of mischief until we arrive.'

Arrive where? She did not wait to find out, but struck out blindly again, in a flurry of hands and feet. It was an unequal contest. Hampered as she was by the folds of the blanket, she had no chance. The fingers which eventually captured her hands held them in an iron grip, then there was the rough chafing of rope being tied tightly round her wrists. The same treatment was meted out to her ankles, though she had the satisfaction of extracting at least one grunt of pain from her captor.

'That's better. I've got you exactly where I want you

212

now, haven't I, my little bird?' Pentransky's voice sent a shiver of fear through her. 'You won't be hiding from me any more, nor playing silly tricks on me.'

Cassie said nothing. She was reluctant to speak in case her voice shook and betrayed how frightened she was feeling. She had had to stop struggling, and not just because of her restraints; the blanket was a very thick one, and in the fracas it had become wrapped more tightly round her, to the point of suffocation. Already she was beginning to gasp for breath in its hot dark folds and her head was starting to spin. Although she was close to panic, her common sense told her to remain still and conserve both energy and air. Her struggles lessened to fidgeting, more to ensure that her skirts were not up round her knees than anything else. Once she was satisfied that she was decent she lay still.

It was no easy matter, lying there while the carriage hurtled her through the Austrian countryside to good-ness knew where. In an effort to keep her nerves steady she tried to remember points of note on the journey. At first it was easy—the hollow echoing of hoofs and wheels told her they were going north, crossing the bridge at the edge of town. The road was level and fairly straight, she could memorise the few bends, but once they began to climb it grew much more difficult. Their road was such a tortuous one that before long she was completely confused.

Fortunately Pentransky was content to ignore her while they were travelling. She heard him talking to whoever was also riding in the carriage. His servant, probably, and no doubt he had a couple more riding outside. The Count was not one to do his own dirty work.

The road was growing worse; their pace had slowed but the jolting and swaying had not. To Cassie, stiff and uncomfortable on the floor, the journey seemed to be going on for ever. Not that she wanted it to end! She knew all too well that once they reached their desti-nation her problems would really begin.

Quite unexpectedly they swung sharply off the road—the wheels ran smoothly, suggesting some sort of a drive—then they came to an abrupt halt. Cassie's mouth went dry with terror. The carriage rocked briefly on its springs as Pentransky climbed down, then she was hauled out and slung unceremoniously over someone's shoulder and carried indoors.

'Upstairs!' ordered Pentransky's voice. 'I've a nice little room prepared, complete with a good lock and key.'

Up the stairs they went. Cassie could hear a heavy tread as someone—Pentransky?—followed them. A door creaked open, and she felt herself being carried into a room. Then she was dropped on to a bed like so much laundry. To her intense relief the blanket was removed, leaving her blinking at the unaccustomed brightness and gasping in lungfuls of air. The Count leaned nonchalantly against the doorpost, leering at her triumphantly.

There was another man in the room, a servant. She recognised him at once, although he wore hunting dress instead of the green and gold Pentransky livery. He was the one who had reserved the luxurious suite for her at the Hotel zur Post. Now he stood respectfully to attention at the foot of the bed, awaiting his master's further orders. His action, so incongruous under the circumstances, caused laughter to rise in Cassie. She bit it back quickly, recognising how close to hysteria she was. With difficulty she struggled to a sitting position.

'What stupid game do you think you're playing?' she demanded angrily of Pentransky.

'I've abducted you,' he replied.

'Abducted me? I've never heard anything so ridiculous! It's exactly the silly sort of thing you would do!'

'That's what I like about you,' he said. 'There's no weeping and wailing and begging for mercy. You come out fighting. I like that. It'll make moulding you to my will much more interesting.'

'Moulding me to your will? What sort of phrase is that?' asked Cassie mockingly.

'A very apt phrase, because it is what I intend to do. I have you completely in my power, you see.'

'Really! Moulding me to your will! Having me in your power! You're talking like a cheap novella. In fact, this whole farce is like something out of a penny-dreadful. Really, a man of your background should have a better taste in reading.'

Anger flickered briefly across his face, then the leer reasserted itself.

'You should save your breath, little bird,' he said. 'I know what you're up to. You are wasting your time. You won't talk your way out of this. That glib tongue of yours will be no use to you here. No use at all.'

'What else should I use my breath for except to persuade you that this whole episode is nothing more than foolishness?'

He considered for a moment.

'You might use it for screaming,' he replied, then noticing Cassie's increased pallor he gave a sinister chuckle. 'Don't you wish you hadn't asked?' he said.

'Oh, honestly!' She gave a snort of derision. 'This is ridiculous! You've missed your vocation. You could have earned a fortune, acting in melodrama. I only wonder you haven't rigged yourself out in a black moustache and a flowing black cape.'

'I quite like that idea; I am very fond of dressing up, you know. But all that can wait until later.' He turned to the servant. 'Give me your knife and be quick about it.'

The man produced a hunting-knife from a sheath on his belt. The Count took it without thanks, and flourished its long gleaming blade so close to Cassie's face she could not help flinching.

'This is a good knife,' said the Count, the menace in his voice increasing. 'And a sharp one. Sharp enough to skin a deer or slit a throat, or ruin a pretty face.

Would you like a demonstration?' And he made a swift, vicious cutting gesture.

Certain he meant to wound her, Cassie closed her eyes instinctively, and fell back against the bedhead, steeling herself for pain. None came.

The Count began to chuckle, and she opened her eyes. The only casualty was her blouse. The fine cambric had been slashed right through to her camisole.

'You thought I meant to hurt you, didn't you?' he grinned. There was a wolfish quality in that grin.

'Certainly not!' she retorted.

He shook his head in disbelief. 'Perhaps later. Not yet, though,' he said, in a way that caused ice to settle in her veins. 'I must admit I like women to be unwilling, but not helpless. That's no fun.'

He darted forward with a suddenness that made Cassie gasp, and cut through the cords that bound her. Any doubts she might have had about the sharpness of the knife were immediately dispelled as the metal blade sliced effortlessly through the rope. She began massaging her wrists and ankles to ease the pain as blood flowed back into numbed limbs.

'What do you expect me to do now?' she demanded. 'Go down on my knees and beg you to let me go?'

'Oh, no. It's far too soon for that. I'm sure you'll be much more amusing. No, I think we'll dine.'

'Dine? But it's only halfway through the morning.'

'I dine whenever I choose. I am master here and don't you forget it.' His voice was harsh and pitiless. Then suddenly he returned to the sinister playfulness he had been employing. 'You can't come to table looking like that, I'm afraid. Your blouse is quite ruined, did you know? Never mind, don't let it distress you. I'll find you something suitable.'

He went to a large cupboard and flung open the door. It was packed with gowns, all hung on a rail as if in a dressmaker's shop. He began rummaging among them, discarding one then another. Any hope that he might provide something quiet and tasteful was rapidly dispelled by the dresses he flung on the floor. Without exception they were vulgar in style and garish in colour.

'Ah, this is an elegant one. You shall wear this.'

The count handed her a gown of black lace which at least seemed reasonable until Cassie held it up and saw it properly. Pentransky's idea of elegance had a loud bodice widely striped in black and gold sequins, remarkably little skirt and even less covering the bosom.

'Haven't you something quieter?' she asked.

'What's the matter? Don't you like it? I bought it in Paris.'

'At the back of the Place Pigalle?' she suggested. From the annoyed look in his protruding eyes, she guessed she had struck near the mark.

'Put it on,' he snapped.

She made no move.

'Come on. I want to see what you look like in it. Put it on!'

She looked markedly firstly at him, then at the manservant who still stood there.

'When you both leave,' she said.

'He can leave.' The Count gave the man a slap over the head and shouted, 'Get out!' Then he sat down on a chair. 'But I'm going to stay to watch.'

In this game of cat and mouse he was playing with her, he wanted her to object. She sensed he was settling himself to enjoy her protests, knowing there was nothing she could do to get him to go.

'Please yourself,' she said calmly, determined to thwart him.

Pulling the black and gold creation over her head, she turned her back on him, then deftly and modestly divested herself of her torn blouse and linen skirt beneath the folds of the 'Paris' gown. If the count wanted something salacious to look at while she was dressing, he was doomed to disappointment. She began rummaging in the pots on the dressing-table.

'What are you looking for?' he demanded.

'Hairpins. Thanks to your crazy antics I've lost all of mine, not to mention my hat. Surely you've got some here somewhere?' She made it sound as if not to have such an essential commodity was a slur on his manhood.

'I don't know. Try the drawer. Are you going to be much longer doing your hair?' Was Pentransky beginning to look disgruntled?

'Yes, it always takes me ages. Of course, if you want me to sit down to dine looking like the witch of Endor. . .'

'No, do the job properly. I hate untidy women.'

Painstakingly Cassie combed and secured each strand of hair, taking three times as long as she normally did. Pentransky began to sigh with impatience. Then, to her relief, he got to his feet.

'I'm not going to waste time waiting,' he said. 'I'll be back in five minutes. Be ready for when I return.'

Cassie watched him close the door behind him with considerable relief. She had been hoping against hope that he would leave her alone, if only for a brief time, so that she could try to get her bearings. She had to escape, and it would be so much easier if she had some idea of where she was.

The view from the window, where she dashed the moment after Pentransky's departure, was not helpful. She found herself overlooking a small valley, the only distinctive feature in a landscape of trees, steep mountain slopes, and more trees. The house was perched on a promontory. The Count had obviously chosen the room in which to imprison her with care, for immediately below the window was a sheer drop of at least fifty metres. If she were going to escape, it would have to be from elsewhere.

To this end Cassie hurriedly returned to her toilette. At least the Count's bizarre notion to dine would give her a chance to see more of the house. When she had finished she looked at herself in the mirror and, in spite of her predicament, had to chuckle. Pentransky was going to be disappointed again. On anyone else the

dress would have been low in the bosom and high on
the leg. But not when she was wearing it! With her
diminutive height the hem-line came nearly to her
ankles and, as for the décolletage, thanks to her slight
figure and a bit of judicious pinning the result would
not have been out of place at a vicarage dinner-party.

The unmistakable sound of Pentransky's feet coming
up the stairs made her start, and she put out a hand
against the bed to steady herself. In doing so, she
touched something still entangled in the heavy blanket
in which she had been wrapped. Her hat! And in her
hat would be her hat-pin! Frantically she retrieved it
and stuck it in the bodice of her dress, masked by lace
ruffles and whalebone. When the Count entered the
room he found her calmly dabbing cologne on her
wrists, betraying no sign of the terror she was feeling.

'Ah, you are ready?' he said, then regarded her
critically, shaking his head. 'That doesn't look right on
you. How disappointing! Never mind, I'll find you
something else. Something floating and diaphanous. Fit
for a sultan's harem, eh? Yes, I like that idea. I can
dress up too, in all silks and golds, and be the sultan,
and you can be my slave girl. What fun!'

Cassie felt her stomach contract with fear. How a
man could be so childish and so menacing at the same
time she did not know, but the combination was one
which filled her with dread.

'We'll dine first though,' he said. 'Come!'

He took her hand to lead her downstairs. Outwardly
they must have looked like any other prosperous couple
preparing to dine, but Pentransky's grip on her hand
was far tighter than etiquette demanded. He was deliberately crushing the bones of her fingers. Cassie refused
to wince; she concentrated upon her surroundings.

They were in a hunting-lodge; the rows of dead
animal heads glaring balefully from the walls was proof
of that. The lodge was far from being a rough hut in
the forest, though. The wooden staircase swept down
to a sizeable hall which, although gloomy, was well

furnished, with polished oak and fine leather much in evidence. As they passed, Cassie counted the doors leading off to other rooms, and tried to establish where, in relation to the bedroom and the precipitous slope, she was. She came to the conclusion that any attempt to escape to her right would not be practical, not with the prospect of a fifty-metre drop. Her escape would have to be made in some other direction.

The door to the dining-room was held open by the manservant whom she already knew. That would be another valuable exercise, she decided—to discover how many men Pentransky had with him. By the time they had sat down at table she had established there were at least three. There could have been more outside, but unfortunately the curtains of the dining-room were drawn, in spite of it still being short of noon, a fact which Cassie found disquieting.

Candles illuminated the room, and huge arrangements of hothouse flowers added their overpowering scents to an atmosphere which was already growing stuffy. The table was laid with the finest porcelain, silver and Bohemian glass, all embellished with the Pentransky coat of arms. But it was only set for two. Such magnificence did not look right paired with such intimacy.

'Now we will eat,' said Pentransky, flicking his fingers to command the serving to begin.

'I'm not very hungry,' said Cassie.

'Ah, yes, fear takes away the appetite, doesn't it?' He peered at her, searching her face for some sign of nerves.

'Does it?' she replied calmly. 'In my case I happen to have had a very substantial breakfast.'

He gave an irritable snort and applied himself to the soup in front of him. In turn Cassie made a show of eating, but in fact consumed very little. All the time she kept a watchful eye on the food being served and the wine being poured, for she would not have put it past the Count to try to drug her. Course after course was brought in, each with its accompanying wine and, although the thought of so much food and drink made her already nervous stomach turn, she was glad to see Pentransky tucking in well. Anything which slowed him down was welcome in her eyes.

She brushed a casual hand across the bodice of her dress, thankful for the comforting rigidity of the hat-pin. She knew she would have to fight Pentransky off soon. It would not be long before he got tired of tormenting her, and when he did she would have to defend herself to the utmost. No sharp stab in the arm or leg with a hat-pin point was going to deter him. She would have to aim for somewhere vital, and the thought caused her overwrought stomach more distress. Unless she managed to escape first, of course. Perhaps he would fall into a drunken stupor.

The Count had stamina, she had to give him that! He ate enthusiastically of every course, drank deeply of every wine, and still he was conscious at the end of the meal. Crimson of face, and glassy of eye, but conscious! With a dismissive wave of a hand he sent the servants away. Cassie watched them go with misgiving. He lumbered to his feet and staggered round the table to her.

'Thish. . .ish where the fun. . .beginsh,' he slurred. 'In a minute we'll go. . .we'll go upstairs and play at shultans and shlaves, but I want a little amusement. . . right now.'

He lurched forward and grabbed at her. Cassie promptly leapt up, dodging round the chair to evade him. Wine bottles still stood in the cooler on the sideboard and she grabbed one as a weapon, bringing it down on him as he made a lunge for her. In the candlelit gloom and the urgency of the moment her aim was not too good. The bottle hit his shoulder and smashed ineffectually, shattered by the gilded epaulette of his uniform. She dodged back, reaching for a second bottle, but at that moment there was a crash somewhere behind one of the heavy velvet drapes. Light flooded in as the curtain was wrenched back, and a figure leapt at Pentransky.

It was Anton! How he had got there she had no idea, but at the sight of him she felt quite dizzy with relief.

As he fell beneath the onslaught of Anton's attack, the Count clutched at Cassie's skirt, pulling her down into the mêlée of struggling bodies and crashing china. On hands and knees she crawled out of the fracas. Still on her knees, she grasped a heavy candlestick, and would have brought it down on Pentransky's head, but it was not so easy. The fight between Anton and the Count was so frantic, with first one gaining the upper hand, then the other, that she could not get a chance to aim.

There was another hefty crash as the two men collided with a side table, bringing down with it a large vase of flowers. The noise brought Cassie to her senses. The servants! They would hear the row. She tried to scramble to her feet, no easy matter among the slippery stalks and wet leaves of the floral arrangement. Somehow she reached the door, all too aware of running feet approaching. She slammed it shut, her hand was on the key, but she got no chance to turn it. The door burst open, and her light frame, no match for the two hefty men who rushed in, was slammed against the wall.

'Cassie! My darling, are you hurt?'

She was vaguely aware of Anton's anxious voice calling to her. Dazed and winded, she forced her eyes open. Pentransky was a groaning heap on the floor. But it was Anton who held her attention. Ducking and weaving to avoid the pursuing servants, he was making his way to her, his arms outstretched to snatch her up.

'Watch out!' she cried. 'There's another——' She got no further. Even as Anton's hands closed over hers, a third servant sprang in through the doorway and felled him with one blow of the wooden club he wielded. Anton crumpled up and lay ominously still.

'Oh, no!' Cassie cried. 'Anton! Anton!'

She crawled to him, and gently smoothed the hair

back from his brow. On his temple a livid bruise was already beginning to swell, and a gash on his forehead oozed blood. He looked so white, and not even his eyelids flickered.

'You've killed him!' she shrieked at the servant, who now towered over her.

'Not him!' The servant grinned maliciously. 'Just given him a nasty headache. What shall we do with him, Excellency?' He addressed his remark to Pentransky, who had been hauled back into his chair by the other two, and was being administered first aid in the form of a very large brandy.

'Anything! Get rid of him over the cliff, I don't care,' the Count retorted pettishly. The shock of Anton's onslaught had certainly sobered him up.

Cassie gave a gasp. 'That would be murder!' she cried in anguish. 'Not even you can get away with murder!'

Fortunately her cry stopped the servant in his tracks.

'Perhaps it wouldn't be a good thing to act hastily, Excellency,' he said nervously. 'Not when you're still shaken up. I'll put him in the cellar, shall I? Then you can make your mind up what to do with him at your leisure.'

'I've given you an order!' roared Pentransky. 'Obey it, if you know what's good for you.' Then, as the man lifted up the still unconscious Anton and slung him roughly over his shoulder, the fury died from the Count's expression. Instead a look of mean cunning lit his protruding eyes. 'On second thoughts, put him in the cellar after all. I think I may have plans for the saintly Dr Sommer, plans he won't like.'

Upon hearing that Anton was not to be killed, relief had swept over Cassie. Now that relief was dimmed, lessened by the triumphant malice on the face of Pentransky.

She rounded on the Count. 'You're not to hurt him, do you hear?' she declared.

'Such ferocity! Quite the little tigress!' he smirked. 'First dear Dr Sommer comes dashing to your rescue like a hero in a fairy-tale, and now you leap to defend him! This gets better and better.'

'You are planning something, I can tell. What are you going to do?' demanded Cassie.

'Nothing, for the moment! I want time to think things out,' retorted the Count, then he winced and folded his arms protectively against his chest. 'I'm sure the devil's cracked one of my ribs. Well, he's going to pay for it. I'm going to make sure he rues the day he ever interfered with my plans. He'll wish he had never heard the name Pentransky! Take her away! Lock her up!'

Cassie began kicking and protesting as one of the servants picked her up and carried her from the room.

'Don't be so reluctant to leave,' Pentransky's voice called after her. 'You'll be back soon enough. My plans involve you, too.'

She was taken to the same room she had occupied before, flung on the bed, and the door locked. When she had first been abducted she felt she had never been so frightened in her life; now that fear had increased twofold. The fate of Anton occupied her so much that for a while she could not think straight. She paced restlessly up and down.

It took some time for her to marshal her thoughts and try to think of some positive way to help both Anton and herself. Her hat-pin was still secure in her bodice; it proved to be her only consolation. Though she peered from the window for an age, she could find no way down the sheer precipice.

The door proved equally useless. She had hoped the key might be in the other side of the lock and that she might be able to retrieve it in some way, but when she peered through the keyhole she could see right through to the landing. Worse still, the servant who had carried her up was lounging against the wall a bare two metres away. Any attempt by her to pick the lock, even if she knew how to go about it, would have been immediately heard by him. Eventually, she curled up on the bed, and lay there, worrying about Anton and dreading the moment when Pentransky would summon her again.

All too soon the door was flung open and the manservant stood there.

'His Excellency wants you downstairs,' he said.

He looked so menacing, filling the doorway, that Cassie sank back against the bed.

'Come on,' he snapped impatiently. 'You can walk or I can carry you. The choice is yours.'

'I'll walk,' she said.

She was taken not to the dining-room but to the drawing-room next door, although it was like no other drawing-room she had ever seen. Its furnishings were hardly appropriate for a hunting-lodge—exotic brocaded sofas, nude statuary, mirrored walls, and above the mantelpiece was a huge, lurid painting of nymphs and satyrs disporting themselves in such a way that Cassie's cheeks went hot. Averting her eyes, she turned her attention to the waiting Pentransky.

In any other situation she would have burst out laughing, for he was reclining on one of the sofas, dressed in voluminous crimson silk trousers bound with a multicoloured cummerbund round his ample waist, a gold brocade coat, and an enormous turban of white silk on his head. There was even a hookah-pipe at his side. He reminded her of the comic caliph she had once seen in the pantomime *Aladdin*. There was nothing funny about Pentransky, though, not when he held both her and Anton prisoner.

'Where is Anton? What have you done with him?' she demanded.

'Such concern. It does you credit.' He took an unsuccessful swig at his hookah-pipe. 'I promise you, your sweetheart is resting in the cellar. I've done nothing to him. . .yet.'

It was that one word 'yet' and the way he said it that filled her with terrible foreboding.

'Let him go,' she pleaded. 'I'll stay and do anything you like, only let him go unharmed.'

'This really is most touching. I'd not expected this.' He leaned back on the cushions and sucked contemplatively on the pipe. 'You know, for the last two years Dr Sommer has been a terrible thorn in my flesh. I've spent many hours thinking how I could punish him. And then along you come and give me the perfect solution, something I had never even dreamed of. Dr Nuisance Sommer is in love! And in love with my little English bird, who just happens to be in my power at this moment. Isn't that perfect? It's given me all sorts of interesting ideas, so many I've had a hard time choosing, but now I am sure I've devised the worst possible torment for him.'

'You're not to hurt him?' cried Cassie.

'Of course not. I'm going to leave that to you!'

She swallowed hard.

'What do you mean by that?' she asked.

'Let me explain. In a few minutes I'm going to have your beloved Anton brought here, and you are going to send him away. More than that, you are going to mock him, ridicule him, laugh in his face for being such a fool. How could he possibly imagine you loved him in preference to me?'

She stared at him in disbelief.

'You're mad,' she said flatly. 'Anton will never be taken in by such nonsense.'

'Then it is up to you, little bird, to make sure that he is. You are to convince him that he has made a complete and utter fool of himself. When he leaves here I want him to be totally humiliated.'

'I won't do it!'

Pentransky sighed.

'In that case I will have to take other more physical measures. You noticed Stefan and Werner, my two servants? Very strong fellows, they are. In fact, they just don't know their own strength. I'm afraid that by the time they have finished with your doctor he will be quite unrecognisable. Such a pity, that strong profile beaten to a pulp. And he is so athletic too. I fear all

that will change. The last person to whom Stefan and
Werner dealt out a punishment is still in a wheelchair,
I understand, and that was. . .oh, a good eighteen
months ago.'

'You wouldn't do such a thing!' Cassie's voice was
low with terror.

'Oh, but I would! Though reluctantly. I much prefer
to pin my hopes on you.'

A vision of a bleeding, crippled Anton filled her
brain like a nightmare. Not for one moment did she
doubt that Pentransky would do what he said. A
broken, helpless Anton! She could not let that happen
to him, not when it was her fault that he was in this
predicament.

'What do you want me to do?' she asked through stiff
lips.

'I knew you would see sense! Come and sit here by
me.'

Gingerly she perched herself on the edge of the sofa,
but the Count dragged her back, forcing her to recline
alongside him.

'Now we must set the scene properly,' he said with
glee. He tugged at the neckline of her dress, causing it
to slip off her shoulders and exposing an indecent
amount of breast, then he hitched her skirt so that her
slender legs were displayed. He leered, his eyes devour-
ing her, then sliding one arm about her waist he began
to fondle her. 'This is better,' he said. 'I want Sommer
to be in no doubt that I mean to have the pleasure of
his beloved after he has gone. . .just to complete his
humiliation. No, don't flinch, little English bird. You
must relax, otherwise our doctor friend won't be convinced, will he? Here, have some wine. That should do
the trick.'

With his free hand he poured some wine and thrust
the glass at her, spilling some over both of them in the
process. Cassie drank deeply, needing the alcohol to
steady her nerves. She no longer worried that it might
be drugged. She was past caring.

'There, I think we are quite ready for our impetuous friend now. Shall we request his presence?' He rang the bell, and when a servant entered—Stefan or Werner, Cassie did not know which—he ordered, 'Fetch the prisoner.'

While they waited his hand stopped its fondling and his fingers dug deep into her soft flesh. Putting his lips close to her ear he whispered, 'Be convincing, my dear, otherwise it will be your darling Anton who suffers.'

Filled with fear and pain, Cassie choked back a sob. She dared not break down now. She dared not.

The door opened, and in came the two servants with Anton between them. He looked very white, blood from his wound stained one side of his face, and he was still unsteady on his legs. Then he saw Cassie reclining in Pentransky's arms. The sight would have made him halt in his tracks if the servants had not dragged him forward. With puzzled eyes he took in every detail.

Cassie could not blame him for his reaction. She knew just what sort of a picture she and the Count painted, lying on the sofa like that. The painful grip of Pentransky's fingers spurred her into action.

'Ah, darling Anton!' she cried mockingly, unconsciously using the Count's own phrase. 'Darling Anton, do come in.' She waved her wine glass in his direction. 'Have a drink. Pour darling Anton a drink, someone, he looks as though he needs one.' And she buried her face against Pentransky's chest and giggled.

'Cassie! What has he done to you?' Anton ignored the proffered wine and staggered towards her.

'That's close enough, Sommer,' Pentransky said. 'You've caused enough damage for one day.'

'I'll—I'll cause a great deal more. . .if you don't free Fräulein Haydon and myself immediately,' Anton stated, swaying precariously.

'Free you? What can you mean? Of course I had to restrain you after you broke into my house in such a violent manner, though you are welcome to leave if you wish. My lawyer will be contacting you for reparation for the damage, of course, but there is certainly no need for you to stay.'

'I won't go without Fräulein Haydon,' declared Anton.

'Off you go with the doctor, Cassie, my pet. I won't stop you.' Pentransky held his arms wide. 'Stefan, the door, if you please. The *Herr Doktor* and the English *fräulein* are leaving.'

'Do I have to go, Bobo?' pouted Cassie.

'Certainly not, my sweet. You can stay here with me if you prefer it.'

'Oh, I do! I do! I don't want to go off with that stuffy doctor.'

Anton closed his eyes for a moment as if struggling to maintain consciousness.

'C-Cassie, what has happened?' he faltered. 'What—what has he done to you to make you like this?'

'Done to me? You mean Bobo?' Cassie managed to sound surprised. 'Now let me see. He has given me this lovely dress—it's from Paris, you know. Then we had an absolutely gorgeous dinner, and after that. . . Why, after that you came. It was awfully tiresome of you, bursting in in such a way. The dining-room is in a frightful mess. What were you thinking of?'

'Thinking of?' Anton said, bewildered. 'Why you, of course. I came to rescue you.'

'Rescue me? From whom?'

'From. . .from that devil.'

'From Bobo?' She gave a peal of laughter and, turning to Pentransky, who was beginning to smirk triumphantly, she said, 'Did you hear what a terrible thing the doctor called you? A devil! Not that you aren't a naughty boy at times. Yes, very, very naughty.' She put all sorts of innuendo into her voice, as she playfully walked her fingers up his arm. Pentransky seized her hand and began kissing it ardently.

Anton looked confused. 'I don't understand this!' He moved forward, brushing off the guards who would have stopped him, and collapsed on his knees in front of Cassie. 'I don't understand,' he repeated. 'You do hate Pentransky. I know you do.'

'And I know I don't! I love him!'

'Love him. . .?' Anton rocked back on his heels. 'Now I really don't believe you.'

'Well, I can't help that. You are being a terrible bore! I wish you would go away and leave Bobo and me in peace.'

'Cassie, why are you behaving like this? What has happened to make you behave so strangely? For goodness' sake tell me!'

'Tell you what? I keep telling you to go away, but you don't take any notice.'

'Do you think I would do that and leave you here? Do you imagine I'd abandon the woman I love?'

'The woman you love? Is that what I am?'

'How can you question it? I love you and you love me. We are to be married. Surely you can't have forgotten?'

Confusion and pain were etched on his face in a way that cut her to the heart. But she dared not falter now.

'Married? Oh, dear!' She gave a giggle that was half apologetic, half mocking. 'You didn't take all that seriously, did you? I mean, you couldn't. . . Oh, it's just too funny for words!' And she went off into peals of derisive mirth that even to her own ears sounded horribly convincing. 'If that isn't the silliest thing. . . Me, in love with you. . . You were actually taken in by all that charming idyll stuff in the summer-house!' And she collapsed against Pentransky, apparently sobbing with laughter, though, in truth, the sobbing was perilously close to being real.

'You do love me! You do!' Anton spoke forcefully, his lips two white lines.

'I do! I do!' Cassie mocked him. 'Do you hear that, Bobo? I love Dr Sommer. He's just told me so.'

'Oh, dear! I don't think I can stand the competition.' Pentransky's laughter shook the sofa. 'I can offer you a title, wealth, property, a place among the greatest in the land, whereas Dr Sommer can only offer you. . . treatment for rheumatism!'

Anton recoiled from their glee as if he had been struck. He rose unsteadily to his feet.

'Cassie!' he said. 'Cassie!'

'Anton!' she mimicked. 'Anton!' Then she let her laughter fade and said, 'Oh, do go away, you tiresome man.'

'Cassie!' he said again, stunned.

'Go away!' she snapped, her voice petulant. 'Honestly, I wish I had never gone to that wretched festival at St Leopold. It was the beginning of this nonsense. I did nothing more than have fun. I sought a little amusement because I hadn't seen Bobo in ages and I was bored, that was all, but if I had realised it would lead to all this I wouldn't have bothered. Bobo, can't you get rid of this wretched fellow? I'm sick of him pestering me.'

'If that is what you want, my pet. You know your wish is my command.' The Count gestured to the two servants, fairly purring with triumph.

'There's no need. . .to throw me out.' Anton's face was a numb mask of anguish. 'I'll leave by myself.'

He turned slowly round and began to leave the room. At the door he staggered slightly and had to clutch the doorpost in support. Taking a deep breath, he looked back at Cassie, his eyes so tormented they seemed to burn right through her.

'I loved you—I trusted you,' he said in a barely audible voice. 'Never in my life have I so misjudged anyone. Believe me, I will never make the same mistake again.'

As he went, Cassie watched every step he took. She watched him leave the room, cross the hall, then walk unsteadily out through the front door. She rushed to the window in time to see him stumble along the path and away from the house. The further he went, the greater was her relief. Only when his beloved figure was lost among the trees did she dare to believe he had

truly escaped. He was free from Pentransky, because
of her. She hoped he would never know the terrible
price she must pay for his safety. Though he was only
half conscious from his injuries, he was free. He was
safe, and that was all she cared about. It mattered more
to her than still being in the Count's power. It mattered
more even than the certainty that she had now lost
Anton forever.

CHAPTER TWELVE

ANTON had gone and now Cassie was alone with the Count. Delighted at the success of his scheming, Pentransky was braying with laughter. The raucous sound filled the room and beat against her ears, accentuating her misery until it was beyond bearing. Suddenly all her unhappiness and fear crystallised into a burning rage. Storming across the floor, she slapped him hard across the face.

'Stop that stupid noise!' she yelled. 'And listen to me!'

Pentransky was so shaken by her fury that he stopped at once.

Cassie pushed her face close to his, speaking with angry emphasis. 'I did what you wanted, and Anton is out of your clutches for the moment,' she said. 'I say "for the moment" because I don't trust you any further than I could throw your fat carcass. Therefore I am going to make you a promise. When I leave here—for leave I must, not even you dare to keep me here indefinitely—when I am free, if I hear that any harm has befallen Anton, that he has been hurt or his career damaged in any way, then I will retaliate. I will let the whole of Bad Adler know that you abducted me, then tried to rape me but were not man enough to manage it!'

It was a terrible risk she was taking, but it was the only weapon she had. Pentransky's great weakness was his vanity about his sexual prowess. The threat struck home.

'You wouldn't!' he gasped. 'You wouldn't dare. . .! Your reputation. . .!'

'I would chance that. I don't want to do it. What

woman wants to have her name bandied about town?
But I would do it unhesitatingly if Anton were hurt.'

'No. . .no one would believe you. . .'

'Don't fool yourself! The whole town despises you.
Do you imagine the local gossips would care whether
such a rumour about you was true or not? They'd be
too busy whispering it into every ear they could find. It
would go through Bad Adler faster than an autumn
wind. And not just Bad Adler! I can think of several
people who would be only too delighted to spread such
a juicy morsel the length and breadth of the country.'

'You wouldn't dare!' he repeated.

'I dare! Never doubt that for a moment!' She fairly
spat the words at him. 'You would be a laughing-stock
throughout Austria, an object of ridicule. I can imagine
the reaction of the officers in your regiment; I do not
suppose you are any more popular among them than
you are here. They would laugh themselves silly. And
it is certain to reach the court. I could name at least
three habitués of the Kurhaus who would waste no time
making sure it reached there.'

Seemingly Pentranksy could think of a few names of
his own.

'Do—do such a thing and I'll make you regret it for
the rest of your life,' he blustered.

Cassie gave a bitter smile.

'Somehow, at this moment the prospect of the rest of
my life is not a happy one,' she said. 'You couldn't
make it much worse. But no matter what nasty little
scheme you think up, harm Anton and I'll make sure
you are ruined. By the time I'd finished there would
not be a corner of the Austrian Empire where you
would dare to show your face.'

'Brave words! Yes, very brave words!' Pentransky
was beginning to rally. 'But while you have been
leaping to the defence of your beloved doctor, I rather
fancy you've forgotten your own predicament. No one
knows you are here, do you realise that? Only Sommer,
and I don't for one moment think he will tell anyone.

As far as everyone else is concerned you have disappeared off the face of the earth.'

Cassie had not forgotten. She was only too aware of her perilous situation.

'They will notice at the Kurhaus when I don't turn up for work,' she said.

'No doubt, but I can't see anyone there raising a hue and cry simply because an employee had taken an illicit day off.'

'My landlady will raise the alarm when I don't return home.'

'Ah, yes, and when will that be? Not until this evening? No one will even miss you for hours and hours yet.'

The Count was rapidly recovering his confidence. Without warning his hand shot out and grasped Cassie's wrist. He would have pulled her back on to the sofa if she had not snatched out her hat-pin from its hiding-place among her lace ruffles, and stabbed him sharply in the arm. He gave a squeal of pain and released her. Immediately Cassie leapt to her feet, knowing the wound was trivial and would not hinder him for long. But which way to go? The door presented no escape; one of the servants was certain to be hovering close by. It would have to be the window.

By now Pentransky was on his feet too. He could be surprisingly nimble when he wanted to, and he wanted to now. She could see the lecherous gleam lighting up his face as they dodged round the room. First one way then another, she darted and weaved through the exotic furniture, using all her strength to hurl small side tables at him or to pull down marble statues in his path. The noise was tremendous, and she wondered that the servants did not come running to investigate. Then she stopped wondering. Clearly happenings like this were not unusual at the hunting-lodge; the servants knew better than to interfere unless called. Nevertheless, she feared Pentransky would summon them eventually,

once he tired of his sinister game of chase, and she
knew she stood no chance of evading four of them.

As she hurried to elude him round the back of a sofa,
she thought she heard a noise outside. Fearful that it
might be the servants coming, her attention was
diverted, she failed to see a footstool right in her path
and fell headlong.

'I've got you now!' puffed Pentransky. 'I'll teach you
to lead me such a dance.'

She was trapped in a corner, her way out blocked by
his body. From her position on the floor his legs seemed
the best target. Slowly she got to her knees, as if
defeated, then promptly sprang at him, sinking her
teeth into one plump calf while her hat-pin jabbed into
the other. The Count let out a roar, and clasped at his
legs in anguish, throwing himself enough off balance
for Cassie to charge past him. He almost caught her.
His fingers grasped her skirt. Fortunately the fabric of
the dress was as cheap as the style, and the material
gave way.

Cassie was close to sobbing now, from breathlessness
and desperation. She had to get to the window and
somehow open it and make her escape. It seemed
impossible, but it was her only chance. Her way was
blocked by one of the brocade-covered sofas, so she
tried to climb over it, but Pentransky reached it as she
was scrambling over the back. Seizing the edge of the
piece of furniture, he tipped it up, sending Cassie
sprawling to the floor. The bang on the head she
received partly stunned her; worse still, her precious
hat-pin shot out of her grasp and went skidding across
the polished floor. Before she could even think of
recovering it Pentransky was upon her, his heavy body
pinning her down.

'The games are over now,' he said, in a voice which
sent terror shooting throught her. 'Now I'm going to
make you pay for all the trouble you have caused me
and when I've finished no one, not even the biggest

simpleton, will believe any stupid rumour you care to
spread about me.'

Cassie gave a scream as his mouth settled on her
neck. His lips, warm and moist, made their importunate
way to her breasts, and she kicked and fought with all
of her failing strength. Frantically she struggled, yelling
and biting, trying to throw him off. Somewhere in the
distance she thought she heard a horse whinny and
voices raised in anger, but her head was still singing
from its hard contact with the floor, and she could not
tell the real from the imagined. Then one of her flailing
fists caught the Count in the eye. He winced and hit her
hard on the side of the head. The world spun round in
a burst of crimson, and she strove to prevent herself
from sinking into the black abyss that was trying to
claim her. She must stay conscious! She must. . .!

A great eruption of noise—shouts, cries, blows,
running feet—roused her drifting senses. All at once
the door burst open and the room was filled with men.
Someone hauled Pentransky off her, and she heard him
gasp as knuckles hit flesh. The instinct for self-preser-
vation caused her to roll into a corner away from the
flailing fists and lashing feet. As her senses cleared she
recognised Franz and Sir George's man, Markham,
among the mêlée, and two or three other faces that
were familiar. They were pitching into the Count's
servants in a battle royal.

Then, as suddenly as it began, it was all over, and
Franz was standing over her, his face full of concern.

'Are you hurt?' he asked. 'That devil, did he. . .?'

Cassie was still too exhausted to do more than shake
her head.

'Good.' He grinned with relief. 'You're safe now.
Trudi's outside. We've come to take you home.' Looking about him, he found a chenille table-cloth on the
floor amid the debris of the fight. This he wrapped
round Cassie, and would have carried her out if she had
not protested.

'I. . .can. . .walk. . .thanks,' she puffed.

'Are you sure?' Franz looked at her anxiously, then grinned. 'All right. I know better than to argue with you. But you must take my arm, do you hear?'

Cassie nodded, thankful for his support. The fact of her rescue had not sunk in. It had been so sudden, and absolutely in the nick of time. The drawing-room looked what it was—the scene of a hectic battle. The Count's servants lay prostrate and groaning on the floor, guarded by a handful of middle-aged Englishmen. To a man they were panting from their exertions and nursing bruises and cut lips, yet they looked extraordinarily pleased with themselves. She knew them all from the Kurhaus.

'I don't know how to thank you, gentlemen,' she said unsteadily.

'There's no need to thank us, dear young lady,' replied one of them sincerely, a retired colonel who often frequented the queue in front of her desk in the pump-room. 'This is the best fun most of us have had since we got to Bad Adler. My only regret is that I didn't get a chance to give that Pentransky the hiding he deserves.'

'He made off, the cur,' said another, a normally mild-mannered banker, who was now proudly dabbing at a rapidly closing eye. 'Sir George's man has gone after him. He won't trouble you again, Miss Haydon, never fear.'

'Thank you,' said Cassie, then because those two words sounded so inadequate, she said, 'Thank you. Thank you. Thank you!'

'Come on. We've a carriage waiting.' Franz gently propelled her out of the front door.

In fact there were two carriages standing outside. Peering anxiously through the windows of the first were Trudi and Sir George.

'You're safe! Thank goodness!' cried Trudi, as Franz lifted Cassie in beside her. 'I've been out of my head with worry.'

'Trudi! Sir George!' Cassie was still having trouble collecting her thoughts. 'It is so good to see you both!'

'Not half as good as it is to see you, my dear,' said Sir George. 'We were all most concerned for you. Most concerned. Now, let us get you away from this place as quickly as possible. We're only waiting for Markham. Where is the fellow? Ah, here he comes at last.'

The tall, spare figure of the manservant came hurrying up.

'The Count had too good a head start. I lost him in the trees, Sir George,' he reported.

'That can't be helped. Pity! I'd have liked to have been sure Pentransky got a sound beating.' He turned to Cassie. 'You'd never think Markham was a very useful light heavyweight when he was young, would you? Not surprising. To look at him you'd never imagine he was ever young!'

At this comment Markham did the unthinkable and actually grinned, despite having a split lip and a multi-coloured bruise on his cheek.

'You're safe, miss, that's all that matters,' he said.

'Very well put!' agreed Sir George. 'Now, get yourself up on to the box and let's be going.' He gave a wry grin. 'What wouldn't I have given to have joined in the scrap instead of only being fit to hold the horses.'

'Don't say such a thing, Sir George!' Trudi scolded him, as the carriage began to move. 'If it hadn't been for you we wouldn't be here. We would never have realised that poor Cassie was in trouble.'

'How did you know?' Cassie asked.

'Well, when you were not at your post this morning I thought you must be ill so, knowing it was your last day at the Kurhaus and not wishing you to go without saying goodbye, I called at your lodgings. When Frau Meyer here said that you had left for work as usual, then we knew something must be wrong. And something wrong, where you are concerned, usually has Pentransky involved somewhere.'

'It was my Franz who suggested that we should come

looking for you up here at the Count's hunting-lodge,'
said Trudi proudly.

'Yes, an excellent fellow, that Franz. One of the
best!' agreed Sir George. 'We stopped off at the
Kurhaus to collect reinforcements—fortunately I knew
where I could find some sound chaps. In the smoking-
room! It was time for the cricket results to be put up,
you see. Then off we went at the gallop. We stopped
the carriages a little way off from the lodge while Franz
and Markham did a bit of scouting. They came back to
say they had spotted you, and as soon as they had given
a report on the lie of the land we were in! A regular
cavalry charge! A very successful manoeuvre.'

'Yes, very successful,' said Cassie. 'You don't know
how glad I was to be rescued. . . If you hadn't
come. . .' her voice faltered '. . .if you hadn't come. . .
just when you did. . .' It was no use. A nightmare
vision of her narrow escape swept over her, as all of her
dreads and fears took hold. She could not bear it any
longer. She collapsed on to Trudi's comfortable bosom,
sobbing   uncontrollably,   until   they   reached
Elizabethplatz, and Franz carried her up to the security
of the Meyers' apartment. Once there, she unburdened
herself to her kind friend, telling of all that had happened, and the terrible hurt she had been obliged to
inflict upon Anton. Then she fell to sobbing again, her
misery only ending in an exhausted sleep.

Cassie's first instinct next morning was to go to the
Kurhaus in search of Anton. She had to explain to him,
to try to undo some of the pain she had given him.

But Trudi would have none of it. 'You are not setting
foot out of that bed today, never mind going to the
Kurhaus!' she said with unaccustomed sternness.

'But Anton. . .!' protested Cassie.

'You can write him a letter for now. I'll take it
myself. Don't be in too much distress. You haven't lost
him, I'm sure you haven't.'

Cassie was not so sure, but she found some comfort
in writing a long, loving letter of explanation to Anton.

Trudi's reassuring smile was a little less certain when she returned.

'He wasn't there,' she said. 'No one's seen him since yesterday. Seemingly he sent a telegram to Anna Arlberg saying he had been called away for a few days.'

'She was lying!' said Cassie. 'He wouldn't leave the Kurhaus unexpectedly. She's trying to keep us apart.'

'That's what I thought. I went to his house.' Trudi looked at her sympathetically. 'His housekeeper told the same story, so it must be true. She offered to take the letter and give it to him when he returned, but I reckoned you'd prefer to hold on to it yourself.' She put the letter on the quilt.

'Yes. Thank you.' Cassie fingered the white envelope that had held so many of her hopes and dreams. 'How—how long before he gets back?'

'No one seems to know. "A few days" was what he said in both telegrams.'

'Then I will just have to be patient.' She spoke with an optimism she was far from feeling.

Next day she went to the Kurhaus herself, but Anton was not there, nor had anyone news of him. Day after day she returned, repeatedly braving the malicious scorn of Frau Arlberg.

'Dr Sommer does not accept personal messages at the Kurhaus,' she stated.

'I am not sending him any, I am merely asking if he is here.'

'It is no use asking. The *Herr Doktor*'s appointment book is full for today. If you wish to make a proper appointment he is free. . .let me see. . .next Friday week?'

'Never mind, thank you!' Cassie was not prepared to put up with the Ice Dragon's prevarication. Anton was not at the Kurhaus, that much was obvious, and no one knew where he had gone. She had her own theory about his disappearance.

'It's because of me,' she said to Trudi. 'I made him so unhappy he just had to go away. Oh, if you had seen

the misery on his face. He believed every word
Pentransky made me say, you see, and I hurt him
terribly. He's gone away because he doesn't want to
risk seeing me or being reminded of me. Why else
would he have disappeared so completely?'

'Disappeared? Who says he has disappeared?' said
Trudi, determined to be reassuring. 'Didn't he send
telegrams saying he'd return in a few days? Then he'll
be back, you mark my words.'

But even her optimism began to look strained when
the days passed and there was no sign of Anton.

At the Kurhaus Frau Arlberg responded irritably to
Cassie's persistent enquiries. Cassie did not mind the
anger; she was more bothered by the underlying disquiet that she detected in the other woman. The Ice
Dragon was concerned, though she was trying not to
show it.

'Dr Sommer is away on business,' was her stock
reply. 'When he returns I will tell him you called.' But
her cold grey eyes looked troubled.

Anton's housekeeper was more open in her anxiety.

'I'm really worried, *fräulein*, and I don't care who
knows it,' she admitted. 'Yes, I know the *Herr Doktor*
sent me a telegram, and said he would be back soon,
but when's soon? That's what I'd like to know. Two
whole weeks he's been away without sending another
word. Usually he's so precise about such things. It's not
like the *Herr Doktor*! It's not like him at all, and I'm
really bothered about what's happened to him.'

Cassie could have told her Anton's reasons for going
away. She did not say anything, of course, but merely
apologised to the housekeeper for troubling her further.

There was one more person to whom she could apply
for news of Anton. His father! At first she felt awkward
about approaching him. Would he not think the worst,
finding a strange female on his doorstep, demanding
news of his missing son?

'Not him,' Trudi assured her. 'He's a lovely old
gentleman. Besides, you would not be completely

strange to him. I'd be most surprised if young Dr Sommer hasn't told him all about you long since.'

'I doubt it,' said Cassie, unable to throw off her gloomy mood, 'because, until recently, there was very little to tell.'

'So you say,' commented Trudi, unconvinced. 'Nevertheless, it would do no harm to take yourself off to St Leopold and find out. Only for pity's sake keep your eyes open for signs of that Pentransky! I know Franz and the English gentlemen drove him off with his tail between his legs, but with him that doesn't signify. He's quite likely to turn up again.'

The thought made Cassie shudder and caused the colour to ebb from her cheeks, but she knew her dread of the Count would not keep her at home. She was too determined to find Anton and explain things to him.

As she approached St Leopold next day, a thousand bitter-sweet memories assailed her. This time she walked from the station, instead of indulging in the extravagance of a steamer trip; the air was clear and sunny, holding a crisp hint of autumn, instead of being hot and sultry, and the village had a busy work-a-day atmosphere about it instead of being *en fête*. Despite this, every step she took seemed to present her with some landmark that reminded her of Anton, until she feared she could bear it no longer. Only the knowledge that she was drawing close to the Sommers' family home drove her on.

Thanks to Trudi's detailed directions she soon found the house, a large, comfortable villa built in traditional style, and with a superb view of the lake. Buoyed up by her hopes of being able to contact Anton at last, she chose to ignore the closed windows and the drawn curtains. When she had hammered persistently on the door without success, she was forced to admit that there was no one at home. In her desperation she would have been quite prepared to sit on the doorstep until Anton's father returned if a middle-aged woman carrying a basket had not arrived. She looked surprised to see Cassie.

'I hope you aren't wanting to see Dr Sommer' *fräulein*,' she said. 'Because he's away.'

'Away?' The dismay must have been evident in Cassie's voice.

'Yes, *fräulein*. He's gone to Innsbruck to visit his sister. He goes every year at this time.'

'When will he be back?'

'Not for a good three weeks, at least. I come up while he's away just to give the place an airing.'

Cassie could have wept with frustration. He was her last hope. Then in desperation she asked, 'I suppose you don't know where I could contact his son, do you?'

'Yes, I do, *fräulein*,' replied the woman, sending her spirits soaring. 'He lives in Bad Adler. He's the director of the Kurhaus, for all he's no age, and doing tremendously well for himself. Of course, no one here was surprised, we all knew he had it in him——'

Clearly the woman would have been content to carry on singing Anton's praises if Cassie had not cut in.

'Thank you,' she said, trying to swallow her disappointment. 'I am sorry to have taken up your time.'

Trudi was all kindess and consideration when she returned to Elizabethplatz.

'He'll be back eventually, you'll see,' she said consolingly. 'Then everything will be fine again.'

But Cassie would not be convinced. She knew she was the reason for Anton's staying away so long; it was she whom he wanted to avoid. Inadvertently she had been the cause of so much trouble to him, when all she had wanted was to make him happy. The best thing she could do would be to get out of his life forever. She would go back to England.

'When will you go?' asked a dismayed Trudi.

'As soon as possible,' Cassie replied. 'I'll go tomorrow.' Then she had second thoughts. 'Oh, no, I can't. The banks are closed. Very well, I will leave first thing on Monday.'

Having made her mind up, there was nothing left for her to do but start packing.

The next day being Sunday, after church she set about the dismal duty of saying her farewells. That was to say she tried, but where Sir George was concerned she found him far too excited to listen to her.

'You can have your turn and talk all you want presently, my dear,' he said. 'First, though, there is something you must hear. Come, let's take a turn along the esplanade; it seems to be the done thing this morning, judging by the crowds, and I will tell you my news. It will gladden your heart, I am sure of it.'

'Anton? You have news of Anton?'

'Our absent doctor friend? I fear not.' Sir George looked crestfallen, but only for a moment. 'No, what I have to tell you concerns that unsavoury character, Pentransky.'

'Pentransky? Oh. . .'

'You'll say "Oh" with a deal more cheer when you've heard this. Last evening I met an old friend of mine at the Café Tauber, the Baroness von Zirl. She has just returned from visiting her daughter in Vienna and she had such a tale to tell that she could scarcely speak for laughing. Seemingly someone has at last caught up with Pentransky and given him the thrashing he deserves. The unlovely Count is even less beautiful now, having two of the finest black eyes ever seen and being minus a fair number of teeth, not to mention assorted blemishes and bruises.'

'But who did such a thing?'

'No one seems to know. Some say one person, others another, but there is no doubt about his plight, for the Baroness's son-in-law, who is an aide-de-camp to the Emperor Franz Josef, actually saw Pentransky in all his glory—or should I say gory?' Sir George chuckled at his own joke. 'You see, I haven't got to the best bit yet. Apparently Pentransky should have been waiting upon His Imperial Majesty, and when he failed to turn up the Baroness's son-in-law was sent to investigate. Now if there is one thing the Emperor is set against, it's having his courtiers involved in brawling. When he heard of Pentransky's state he lost his temper and said a few pertinent things about officers who behave like street fighters. . .and the upshot is. . .' by now Sir George, too, was having difficulty in recounting the story for laughing '. . . upshot. . .the upshot is that, by Royal Command, Pentransky has been sent to a post in the Montenegro Mountains. . .which is infamous. . .as the worst posting in the entire Austro-Hungarian Empire. . . It is cold, wet, isolated. . .for excitement the locals have to rely upon the occasional. . .earthquake!' At this point Sir George collapsed with glee. Even Markham joined in.

Cassie also began to smile. Her smile grew the more she thought of Pentransky's predicament. Her pleasure held a large measure of relief, for with him so far away he would have less chance to cause trouble for Anton, and she would not need to sacrifice her reputation in order to carry out her threat.

'That is the best news I've heard in ages!' she said.

'Yes, isn't it splendid? As you may imagine, the whole of Viennese society is having a field-day—not a popular fellow, is the Count—and I fancy it will be some time before the Emperor will allow him to come down from those very uncomfortable mountains.' The old gentleman mopped his streaming eyes and pocketed his handkerchief. 'Now, my dear, I think you had something to tell me. What is it?'

'Yes, Sir George.' She grew instantly serious. 'I am about——' She got no further, for hurrying towards her through the fashionable throng was a tall, athletic figure she knew all too well.

At the same moment Anton recognised her and stopped abruptly in his tracks. He looked pale and tired; his face still bore the vestige of a bruise.

The pair of them stood there, staring at one another transfixed.

Cassie was so relieved to see him that she was struck

dumb. There was so much she wanted to say. She had to explain, to try and smooth away the terrible hurt she had dealt him, yet somehow the right words would not come. She stared up at him, hoping to find love in his expression, but dreading lest she saw repugnance. In fact she saw neither. The emotion which burned briefly in Anton's eyes at their meeting was one she could not identify. Was it pleasure? Relief? Or was it pain? Whatever his true feelings he suppressed them rapidly, giving Cassie no clue as to his real reaction. She found herself confronting a mask of polite inscrutability.

'*Gruss Gott*,' he said, his eyes never leaving hers. 'A pleasant morning for a stroll.'

'Yes, it is, isn't it?' she replied automatically.

'We must make the most of this weather; the long summer days won't last much longer.'

'No, they won't,' she agreed, not sure she could believe her ears. 'Already we need the lamps lit quite early in the evenings.'

After all that had happened between them they were exchanging pleasantries like mere acquaintances.

This subject of conversation exhausted, they remained standing there, as immobile as rocks in the river, letting the surge of elegant strollers sweep past them unheeded. Neither seemed to know what to do or say next. Cassie was convinced she knew the reason for the extreme formality of Anton's behaviour. He was remembering only too clearly the scenes he had been obliged to witness at the hunting-lodge and was having to struggle to control his disgust of her. She had to do something or say something to put matters right, but what? One glance at his beloved face, set now in such rigid unapproachable lines, and she did not know where to begin.

Somewhere in the background she was vaguely aware of Sir George's voice, addressing his servant.

'This is no place for these youngsters to be reunited,' he was saying. 'Far too public. See what you can do to rectify matters, Markham, there's a good fellow.'

She was not conscious of any activity near them. The fiaker that pulled up must have been drawn by some winged horse, for she heard neither the clatter of hoofs nor the rumble of wheels as it approached. The first she knew was the homely scent of leather and stables as someone, presumably Markham, handed her into the carriage. The next thing she knew, Anton was there beside her, and they were being driven at a sedate pace through the streets. Side by side they sat, only inches away from one another on the well-worn seat. To Cassie, however, those inches seemed an impenetrable barrier.

They had driven for some distance before Anton referred to their last meeting.

'You managed to get away from Pentransky, I see,' he said, so impersonally that he might have been discussing the activities of a total stranger.

'Yes.'

'Did he let you go?'

'No, Sir George came to my rescue.'

'It was Sir George, was it? A resourceful gentleman. And what do you intend to do now?'

'I shall go home to England. I leave tomorrow.'

'Ah, yes, to your brother with the exploding electric light bulbs.'

'After the events I have experienced here, life with my brother is going to seem blissfully peaceful, despite the explosions!' she exclaimed, unable to bear the frigid politeness between them any longer.

'That is understandable. I am sure you are only too eager to get home.'

Was that concern she detected in his voice?

Before she could decide he suddenly exclaimed, 'You've no idea how glad I am that you are safe! When I went back and found you had gone I nearly went mad with worry.'

'You went back?' She stared at him.

'Yes, of course. Did you think I was totally taken in by your performance? If it had not been for that blow on the head which muddled my senses, I would not have been taken in for one moment. He threatened you, didn't he? I should have seen what was happening at once and not left you there in his clutches. I quite understand how you must despise me.'

'Despise you?' repeated Cassie in astonishment.

'I expect that is only mildly expressing the way you must feel about me. You have no idea how much I have regretted it since. I have been in torment, worrying about you. I was convinced Pentransky had fled, taking you with him. I have been looking for you ever since.'

'You were looking for me?' She knew she was repeating everything as inanely as a parrot, but she could not help herself. She was stunned by what she was hearing.

'Certainly I was! There can't be a corner of the Austrian Empire I haven't scoured in these last few weeks. And all the time I was calling myself every sort of a fool for being taken in by Pentransky's charade.'

'Thank goodness you were taken in!' cried Cassie, appalled by the thought of what might have happened.

In her anguish she reached out and grasped his hands tightly. At once he winced, and she let go again immediately, fearing that, despite his reassuring words, some part of him still did not trust her. Then she realised her mistake. That wince had been one of physical pain. Looking down, she saw that his knuckles were badly cut and distorted with bruises. Normally so fine and well cared for, they now looked as though they belonged to a prize-fighter.

'Your poor hands!' she exclaimed in horror. 'What happened?'

'I did not find you. I *did* find Pentransky,' he said simply.

'It was you!' She gazed at him incredulously. 'It was you who gave Pentransky the good hiding! The whole country is talking about it, and it was you!'

'Yes, it was me.' Anton flexed one injured hand and gave a bitter grimace. 'Giving him such a thrashing goes against everything I stand for as a doctor, I know. But I couldn't help myself. I was in such a rage with him because of the suffering he had caused you. . . I was in a rage with myself too.'

'You were angry with yourself? Why?'

'For being such a fool. How could I have been taken in for a second? A blow on the head is no excuse for such stupidity. I have paid for it, though. Not knowing where you were or if you were safe has caused me the worst torture of my entire life. I didn't dare believe Pentransky when he said you were free. Not until my housekeeper told me she had seen you with her own eyes did I begin to hope——'

'You knew I was here, yet you didn't come near me!' exclaimed Cassie.

'I've only been back here in Bad Adler a couple of hours. . . But, yes, that was ample time. . . To tell the truth, I thought you wouldn't want to see me.'

'Why ever not?'

'Because I failed you so miserably. I didn't rescue you. I let myself be beaten. I fell for Pentransky's scheming——'

'Only at first. You'd been badly injured. You weren't thinking clearly.'

'It makes no difference. Under the circumstances, I thought you would never want to see me again.'

'Never see you again?' Cassie was amazed at the idea. 'Because you didn't succeed against four vicious men? You were alone! What chance had you against Pentransky and his servants? You fought bravely, but you were outnumbered and overpowered. Sir George had reinforcements! And thank goodness you did believe my play-acting, otherwise you would have been in the most terrible danger.'

'Nevertheless, Sir George succeeded where I failed. A man twice my age, who is crippled with rheumatism. . .' He stopped and turned towards her. 'Did you say that *I* would have been in terrible danger?'

'Why, yes.'

'Do you mean that Pentranksy threatened me? That you took those terrible risks to protect me?'

'Yes,' said Cassie in a small voice.

'I thought he had threatened *you*! That you were protecting yourself. . .' Again his voice faded away, and he seemed to be grappling with a momentous problem.

When he spoke again it was with suppressed emotion. 'Cassie Haydon, I love you,' he said. 'Do you love me?'

'Yes.' Cassie's voice was even smaller.

'Then why the devil are we sitting so far apart?' he roared.

'I don't know,' she replied, not certain whether to laugh or cry. Then she held her arms out to him, and in an instant the vast gulf that had been separating them disappeared as she was swept into his embrace.

Where the fiaker driver took them they never knew. The carriage eventually came to a halt somewhere in the open countryside, and the horse grazed happily while his master enjoyed a leisurely pipe, without either Cassie or Anton being aware that they had stopped. They were in each other's arms, that was all they cared about.

'One thing puzzles me: how did you know I was a prisoner at the hunting-lodge?' Cassie asked, her head comfortably against Anton's chest.

'Of all people, it was Sister Kathleen who raised the alarm. Reverend Mother had sent her to Baroness von Hackenberg, in reponse to your letter. When she got there she found the *Baronin* in a terrible state. The poor woman knew what her son planned to do and was desperately worried about you. Sister Kathleen got a message to me at once.'

'Good old Sister Kathleen,' murmured Cassie drowsily. 'I shall miss her when I go.'

'Go where?'

'Back to England. Have you forgotten? I leave tomorrow.'

'No, you do not,' said Anton firmly. 'You must let

your brother know as soon as possible that you are going to marry me immediately.'

'Immediately? Then since there is such urgency, have I your permission to use the telegraph?'

'Just this once!' said Anton with mock severity. 'But don't let it become a habit.'

'No, *Herr Doktor*,' said Cassie meekly, and she gave a happy sigh.

'Am I to understand that you agree to marry me immediately, without any arguments?'

'I do.'

Anton eased her away from him, the better to look her full in the face.

'I hope this no-argument business does not become a habit,' he said, half joking. 'I'm looking forward to some good verbal battles during our marriage.'

'I do not promise never to argue,' Cassie pointed out. 'But just at this moment I can't think of any reason for disagreement.'

'What, not even any of your New Woman principles? Doesn't the prospect of losing your independence and all those things you hold dear cause you any regrets?'

'Certainly not,' she said, a little too quickly. Then she added more honestly, 'That is to say I know I must choose. I can't have everything I want, no one can. And my choice is to be your wife.'

For a moment Anton was too moved to speak. He took her face between his hands and kissed her with infinite tenderness.

'That is a choice you will never regret, not if I have my way,' he said gently.

'I won't regret it, I know I won't, only. . .only. . .'

'Something is troubling you?' He looked anxious.

'Just that. . . You did mean it when you said we could afford a cook and a housemaid, didn't you? You see, I know I am perfectly capable of running an efficient household if I have the staff, but to be honest I can't cook. I doubt if I would ever have the patience to do things like starch doylies or fold dinner napkins into the shape of water-lilies.'

Anton gave a shout of laughter, and enfolded her in his arms again.

'I would never ask you to do such things, never fear, and yes, we will have enough servants to run the house properly.' His hold tightened about her and he became serious. 'Nor would I ask you to give up your principles to become my wife. I have given your ideas a lot of thought recently, and I have come to see your viewpoint. That is why I want our marriage to be a partnership. Instead of one making all the sacrifices, we should be working side by side.'

'At the spa?' asked Cassie breathlessly.

'If that is what you want.'

'I do, very much so. I would love to continue with my schemes to attract English visitors; I have lots more ideas we could implement. . .'

'I am sure you have,' chuckled Anton. 'Never fear, the spa at Bad Adler will be run jointly by Doctor and Frau Sommer.'

Cassie gave a grin. 'That was what Anna Arlberg wanted, only she planned to be Frau Sommer.'

'Not quite. She wanted to be Frau Sommer right enough, but it was her intention to be in complete charge. I would have been severely henpecked, never doubt it.'

The thought of a henpecked Anton made Cassie chuckle.

'That is one thing I promise never to do,' she stated.

'What, not even the slightest peck?' He pretended to be so crestfallen that, laughing, she was obliged to kiss him. Then kiss him again, and again. . .

'And the baths at Weissenbach, can't I help there?' she asked, when breathlessness eventually drove them apart.

'The Weissenbach baths?' Anton was having difficulty in marshalling his thoughts away from her lips. 'Yes, there is plenty you can do there. We desperately need someone to organise the fund-raising, for example. Someone like you—responsible, imaginative, hard-working.'

'Responsible, imaginative, hard-working. They sound very sterling qualities. Are they what you were looking for in a wife?'

'They are the qualities I would look for in a partner,' said Anton seriously, all the laughter and joking over. 'But from my wife I look for something infinitely more wonderful and precious.'

'And what would that be?' asked Cassie, her voice barely steady.

'Love,' he said. 'The love I feel for you is so very great, far more intense than anything I ever imagined I would experience for anyone. I ask only that you try to love me in return.'

'Try? Try?' For a moment Cassie was quite indignant. Then her indignation faded into tenderness. 'I have no need to try,' she said softly, 'because already I return your love in full, and will do for all eternity.'

'Eternity? That's not nearly long enough,' said Anton. And he took her in his arms.

The other exciting

MASQUERADE
Historical

available this month is:

REBEL HARVEST
Pauline Bentley

The Jacobite uprising of 1715 had engendered suspicion
everywhere, even in Sussex, and Katherine Winters was
sure her younger brother Paul had been lured into
planning insurgence by Viscount St Clere.

When Luke Ryder brought his dragoons into the area,
concealing Paul's idiocy was Katherine's abiding
concern, despite the fact that she and Luke struck sparks
whenever they met. With the cards stacked against
them, could she keep her brother safe, yet still have the
man she knew she loved?